Additional Acclai

"*He Sleeps* is both haunted and haunting, a veritably spellbound book. A sensitive and accurate portrayal of the uneasy interface between Black Americans and African culture, this novel follows the tangled roots of racism back to the germinal point, but leaves with a sense of common humanity, shared beneath the skin."

—Madison Smartt Bell, author of *Master of the Crossroads*

"A fecund little novel . . . McKnight writes wonderful prose, and he is a master of his material, of the slow enlightenment of his character. There are moments of very hard beauty in this book. . . . Exceptional."

—*American Way* magazine

"An ambitious inquiry into the nature of self: identity at risk. *He Sleeps* walks the tightrope—between first and third person, black and white, growth and dissolution—with great skill. In the process of delineating this no-man's land between America and Africa, Reginald McKnight again claims territory all his own: that place where daydream and nightmare conjoin." —Nicholas Delbanco, author of *What Remains*

"McKnight examines Bertrand from every angle, gracefully switching between first-, third-, and even second-person narration, creating a complex portrait of a deeply conflicted man." —*Booklist*

"*He Sleeps* is a love story in letters and an anthropologist's report. Its subjects are language, sexuality, and race. Although it is set in Africa and its protagonist tells us thrilling dreams, the revelations of this tough, taut novel are about the waking realities of how we live right here." —Frederick Busch, author of *Don't Tell Anyone*

"A compact, multi-voiced novel . . . ambitious." —*Kirkus Reviews*

HE SLEEPS

HE SLEEPS

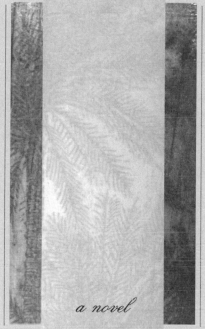

a novel

Reginald McKnight

PICADOR USA

HENRY HOLT AND COMPANY

New York

www.picadorusa.com

Picador® is a U.S. registered trademark and is used by Henry Holt and Company under license from Pan Books Limited.

For information on Picador USA Reading Group Guides, as well as ordering, please contact the Trade Marketing department at St. Martin's Press.
Phone: 1-800-221-7945 extension 763
Fax: 212-677-7456
E-mail: trademarketing@stmartins.com

Library of Congress Cataloging-in-Publication Data

McKnight, Reginald, 1956-
    He sleeps : a novel / Reginald McKnight.—1st Picador USA ed.
       p. cm.
    ISBN 0-312-42104-4
    1. African American anthropologists—Fiction. 2. African American men—Fiction. 3. Americans—Senegal—Fiction. 4. Married people—Fiction. 5. Senegal—Fiction. I. Title.

PS3563.C3833 H4 2002
813'.54—dc21   2002067326

First published by Henry Holt and Company

First Picador USA Edition: September 2002

10 9 8 7 6 5 4 3 2 1

FOR JULIE

HE SLEEPS

chapter 1

He Sleeps

N'Gor village
June 19, '85

Dear Rita,

Looks like your birthday wish that I not be alone came true, but in the most bizarre way. Get this. I come home from working all morning in a nasty rainy Dakar on the 17th and find a family I've never seen before having lunch in the foyer of my house. There they are—mother, father, daughter—hunkered down on the floor in the customary Senegalese style, eating fish and rice from the customary big enamel-covered bowl. The father, a guy named Alaine Kourman, rises from the floor smooth like a gymnast, his oily skin and his glasses shining under the yellow light. He forks over his hand, says, "Hey, welcome home," and invites me to dine. "I show you my family," he says, "and then, you eating."

I can't tell you how disconcerting it all was, Sis. Actually, I should say, How it's been, 'cause they're still here. Here to stay, apparently. I mean, one day I'm walking around this place in my ass-eaten underwear, my tapes and papers and clothes strewn all over the house, and next day there's a family living here—

completely moved in—and all my stuff placed neatly, lovingly, in my bedroom. Everything's as orderly as a post office now, a credenza in the common room, a big potted rubber tree between the common room windows, loud African prints, matted, framed, and hung on the walls, and three comely strangers named Kourman using and having access to parts of the house that I either had no use for (the kitchen) or was told were off limits (the big, well-lighted bedroom just off the foyer).

Monsieur N'Doye, my landlord, is down in M'Bour this week, so I can't ask him who these folks are and why they're here, and it wouldn't be right to give the Kourmans the third degree. But I have learned a few things about them in the first 36 hours of their residency.

Kene, the wife, teaches math, French, and earth science at the village school. She's gorgeous and tall, broad shouldered, graceful, toothy, buxom, and an amazingly good cook. The tjebudjin lunch I sat down to the first afternoon was as good as I've had in my three months here: the grouper was tender, the rice perfectly sweet, tomato-y, onion-y, firm, oily, the vegetables as savory as Ma's gumbo. Kene tried to make sure I got plenty of everything, telling her husband to slow down so I could catch up to him. She even smacked his spoon hand. At dinner she served this dish I've never had here before, these small fish about the size of bluegill, which she sliced width-wise, three deep cuts right down to the spine. She dipped them in flour, salt, and pepper and fried them. They reminded me of Ma's Friday fish fries, only none of the Hail-Mary-Full-of-Grease indigestion afterward. Ol' Kene has a very light touch with the grease. She met her lucky bastard at the Sorbonne, where she studied chemistry (and he studied government), so maybe she knows some kind of scientific maneuver to siphon off all the oil.

Alaine, the lucky bastard, is, in his own words, a "pure Marxist." And he appears to be, right down to the Leninish Vandyke and round spectacles, just that. He's a little shorter than his wife, a shmendrick, as Rose would say, but he's very good looking, has a big presence; he's muscular and lithe, kind of an African Bruce Lee. He apparently doesn't mess around when it comes to how-do-you-dos. He asked me before I'd had my second spoonful of fish, that first afternoon, "Do you like Reagan?"

I told him I hated Ray-gun as passionately as I love my wife.

He asked me how the American people could have voted into office—not once, but twice—a man who made movies with a monkey. I told him I had no idea. "Let him eat, Alaine," said Kene, but, without missing a beat, said, "Why didn't you bring your wife here to live with you?" And before I could answer (thank God), Alaine said, "Kene, it's all right for you to talk and not me?"

"Politics!" she spat.

And then they left French behind, going into a language I don't know. I'm guessing it was either Pular or Bambara. If it was Wolof, they had an angle on it I've never heard. Whatever it was, you wouldn't have needed no stinkin Ph.D. in anthropology to get the gist. The skirmish lasted only a couple seconds, though, and apparently lucky boy won. He said, kind of abruptly to me, "If he don't have so many bombs, no one could ever take him serious." My answer was that he didn't need to speak English, but, like I told you last time I wrote, if a person speaks only two words of English, I'm gonna hear 'em. "No, no, I need to practice," Alaine said. Then he asked me about "cowsboy" Reagan again.

I did go ahead and talk politics with him, in English, but I felt funny about it. Kene was clearly steamed. She fussed over the little girl, Mammi (pronounced Mommy), as though she were six months old rather than six years old, and it was easy to tell she was doing it to annoy Alaine, who kept flicking glances at wife and child. Finally, Alaine said something rather tart in the mystery lingo, and Kene stood up, took Mammi by the hand, and went into the big bedroom off the foyer. Then Alaine excused himself and went in after them. Then I heard Kene tell the lucky bastard to go fuck himself, and I think she threw something at him, 'cause the door thumped and rattled.

Well, I said to myself, this is going nicely, and I laid down my spoon, walked out into the rain and to my assistant Idrissa's place, which is on the west side of the village.

I tapped on Idrissa's door, and the first thing I said to him was "Idi, there're people in my house." He looked at me like I was crazy, and I suppose it must've sounded kind of crazy, the way I said it, or maybe it was the look on my face. He looked at me as though there were indeed people in my house, that I'd invited them but had forgotten I'd invited them. He has these big thick eyebrows that he expertly arches whenever he's annoyed or confused. He arched the left one and pursed his lips. So I said, "I mean they're living there. A family. In my house." He didn't say anything at first, and I was silent too. After a second or two, he said, "Have you eaten yet?" and I said I'd had a bite or two with the people living in my house and then told him about the fight. He tossed the book he'd been reading onto his bed, said, "Let's go chop," and we walked in the rain to the bus stop without a word, and when we got there, he still said nothing, but I could see his brain working. So I watched Idrissa's face, his alert, fox face, as a metallic green van carrying tourists from the airport to the Meridien Hotel glided past us with hardly a sound. The air momentarily filled with the smell of its exhaust, and I wrinkled my nose, squinted a little.

It was in such a van that I met Idrissa my first day here, and his last day as an airport shuttle driver. He's a good guy, Idrissa.

I'm surprised I haven't said much about him to you before, but I clearly haven't, since you said, "Who's this Idi-guy?" in your letter. It's just that I've said so much about him in my letters to Rose and Ma, and mention him so often in my journal and my daily notes, that I feel as though everyone I know already knows him.

Before I came here to collect data for my silly little ethnographic survey, Jewel Hefler, a colleague of mine from the University of Denver, told me it would be unwise to befriend anyone I met at the airport. She aimed her sharp nose at me and said, "They're vultures (she pronounces it 'vulchaz'), the whole airport crowd. God, they even stoop like vulchaz. Wear vulcha haircuts." She told me to ride with the shuttle drivers from the airport to the village, speak little, pay them no more than fifteen hundred francs, plus a small tip, say merci, au revoir, and keep going. But Idrissa has charmed me, it seems. His English is good, he's extremely well read, he's droll, and I was intrigued by the fact that he wouldn't take a tip (the stuff of monstrous scams, Jewel would say). But if we anthropologists are supposed to be serious about studying other cultures, we should investigate the real as well as the ideal. We should, from time to time, study trouble. But so far, the dude's gotten me out of trouble and never got me in it.

When he delivered me to the Masatta Samb Hotel that day, he merely helped me with my bags, shook my hand, and wished me a good afternoon. When I held out the one hundred CFA coin, he folded his hands behind his back, nodded his head a shade, and said, "It's OK, man." He turned and left. But I saw him later that day, just after he delivered a tourist couple to the hotel, and when they offered him a tip he took it. I approached him, asked him why he'd accepted their tip and not mine, and he replied, "You came to work; they came to play. People like to pay for play, not work." I liked that, added it to my compilation of West African proverbs, in fact, and invited him to have a drink with me in the hotel bar, the Blue Marlin.

We sat at a table near the center. The place was virtually empty, save for two tomato-skinned "white" men at the bar. Their utterances were furtive—gripes about Africa, no doubt— and their voices were more like the grunts of apes than the whispers of men. Idrissa looked at the men and arched his brows, but I think it was amusement that shaped his face rather than contempt. "Are you still at work?" I said. "Yes," he said, "I'm still on the clock." Then he smiled when I evinced surprise at the level of his idiom. "I take a lickin' and keep on tickin'," he said, then laughed, held out his palm so I could slap it. "How'd you know I came here to work?" I said.

"I've done this job a long time," he said. "I'm older than I look. I'm about thirty." He looks nineteen or twenty, and I told him so. He nodded and said, "You got a tape recorder and a serious camera. You got a pen in your pocket and a valise full of writing paper. You don't wear sunglasses or got on a flowered shirt or shorts. You don't smile so much. You look sad. You look tired."

"You're good," I said.

"You're on the clock," said Idrissa.

We sat quietly for several minutes. I ripped at the label of my beer. Idrissa folded his arms and gazed at the table. Finally he said, "We used to get a lot of anthropologist here in the seventies, but they tell me your Mr. Reagan doesn't care for that sort of thing and won't pay for it."

"Well, that's not exactly right, but I, for one, am glad the old bastard can't run for a third term. But how do you know I'm not a journalist?"

"Same reason I know you're not CIA. Journalist act like he know everything; CIA act like he know nothing."

"You mind if I write that down?"

"No charge."

I write everything down, eventually. That's my problem. Rose would tell you it's one of many. Have you heard from her lately, by the way? I haven't. Not a single goddamn word, though I've written her two letters a week since my arrival.

He finally asked me what I was dying to tell him—what's my project—and I told him that aside from collecting contemporary proverbs, I was looking for urban legends, but he didn't know the term, so I told him that they are the only folktales around any-more that most people believe. Still he didn't get me. I said, "Stories that are passed by word of mouth, but that can't always be found in newspapers and books. I told a few from Brunvand and Dorson, a few from high school and college, the Decapitated Biker, the Death Car, the Sewer Gators, the Gerbil story, etc. I'm not entirely sure he understood that these things aren't necessar-ily true, but this was no big deal at the time, since he wasn't my assistant. He said, "You have heard about disappearing pick-pocket?" and I asked him what he meant, so he told me:

"As far as I know, this story is true. My cousin, who live in Saint-Louis, told me that, one day, a friend of her mother was shopping in the grande marché. It was in January, so the harmat-tan winds were making a lot of dust in the air. People were in a bad mood, as they are this time of year. There was a lot of push-ing and shoving at the market, and Mrs. Wade, is her name, I think—"

"Spell it?"

"W, A, D, E."

"Wah-day?"

"Close enough. Anyway, she was being pushed aside to side. But she had her money in her hand, and not in her clothing or bag, so no one could take it from her. She had five thousand

CFA—back then, maybe twenty American, now, maybe seven-teen. OK?

"Yeah, so her husband, this guy who did electrical work, was on strike, so he told her that the money was little, so they had to buy only what was necessary. But she was tired and in a bad mood. She was angry about the crowds pushing her aside to side, and about the dust on everything, her *eyes* and everything, you see?

"She said the winds were making her mad, and angry, and she thought all the meat bad, and the fish too soft. She bought only three vegetables and a small, small piece of fish to go with the rice she was going to cook that day. She had almost all her money left over. Four, four and a half thousand. And at the leather stand she saw a pair of sandals that she loved, so she asked to see them. They were her size and very beautiful. Just as she was handing over the money, a strong hot wind blew, and for a second, dust was in the air very heavy. When it settled, a man in a brown khaftan was standing so close to her that she almost fell over. But in a sudden, the wind blew again. When it settled again, the man was gone. And so was her money. It was gone, completely gone from her hands." Idrissa held out his hands, palms up, and shook them a little. Then he lit a cigarette and sat back. That's my boy Idrissa. A natural anthropolo-gist, a born raconteur, a sharp research assistant.

The thing I liked about the dude was when I showed him two other versions of that story in my notes, he didn't get defensive and tell me how his was true, etc., etc., as other folks do. He seemed delighted. To do what I do for a living, you've got to let go of the usual tendency people have for believing good stories. You've got to have a full-tilt bullshit detector. Idrissa seems to have the right stuff.

Anyhow, the village grapevine led him to the place I'm now living—a tidy, ranch-style house with flower gardens, lots of space, but only a fair amount of light—not five minutes, by foot, from the beach and an equal number of minutes to Idrissa's room. He helped me negotiate the rent I pay to Monsieur N'Doye, and I was so pleased with the price, one hundred dollars a month, that I decided I'd better keep Idrissa close to me, and hired him as my administrative assistant. Idrissa has shown me good and inexpensive places to eat and helped me get a box at the airport post office, something that foreigners can't easily do. Or so he tells me. The most important thing is that he's introduced me to practically all my informants, the older folk in the village who are full to the brim with the proverbs, the traditional and urban folktales, and sacred stories I've been trying to collect since my arrival. I'm not ashamed to say that without him I'd be quite lost here in Senegal. Anyway, that's Idrissa.

So we take a table at the airport café that rainy afternoon, and the guy, the born raconteur, says, "I knew about these people in the house." I asked him why the fuck he didn't mention them to me, and he told me he'd meant to but that he'd been so busy doing library research for me that it just slipped his mind. What could I say? I *have* been pounding him pretty hard lately. I got wind of this story about peanut skins causing liver cancer that sounded like a classic urban legend, and had him burning oil into the wee hours for five straight days, digging up every article he could find, while I conducted interviews with medical and lay people. I'm pretty certain it's a UL. Not as fantastic as the Penis Thief and the Vanishing Thief and some of the older tales, but ULs is ULs. I'm not picky.

Idrissa said to me: "I have told you, have I not, that the first grapevine ever planted was planted in N'Gor village. People talk about everything all the time, even while they sleep. But you? You don't listen."

I told him my job is to listen. That's all I do.

"You tape," he said, "and you write down, but you don't listen in your ears." And he pointed at my left ear with his fork. God-damn Africans. Always got to be a step ahead.

So lunch, late as it was, and hungry as I was, wasn't so great. Nothing like Kene's chop. Nothing. The rain let up, though, and the ride from the airport café was pleasant, what with the sweet-ened air, and the uncrowded bus, and Idrissa's customary chatti-ness. The sun broke out, and everything glittered golden pink—the ocean, people, the skins of baobab trees, the road. I watched a bunch of fishermen spreading out their nets on the beach, hoping, I guess, to catch the last couple hours of sun. And I saw a half dozen stick-legged boys chasing a stray cat with toy spears, and an old woman pounding millet with a pestle the size of a baseball bat as I listened (with my ears) to Idrissa talk about the Kourmans—people he swore he didn't know—as if he knew them. He told me Alaine worked for one of the government agencies not far from the American embassy (though he didn't know which) and that he had grand political aspirations. Idrissa said Kourman believes that the watery socialism of the current regime is insulting, and seems obsessed with revolution. I could tell that Idrissa isn't fond of the man, but can't tell exactly how I could tell.

He described Kene as "more brillianter" than her husband but added that she wasn't at all interested in politics, excepting feminism. I told Idrissa there wasn't anything more political than feminism, and he smirked and said, "What I mean is that she does not dream as her husband does. If you look at her close, you can see that she is no talk but action." I told him that I didn't mind looking at her in the least, and he gave me the strangest look, pregnant pause and all, then said, "You're married, man." I would have said something like "I'm married, not dead," but I'm sure that retort is just as stale here as it is back in the United States.

"The village women don't like her," Idi told me, and I asked him why. He said he heard some of the village women gossiping about her this morning on the bus while he was on his way to the university library. "They said she was holding Alaine's hand while they were walking to the market."

"And?"

"This is something only Frenchwomen do around here."

"So it's OK for guys to hold hands—"

"And women, too, but not men and women. I thought you knew that. They think she should have left her French habits back in France."

I told him I did know it but didn't think it was such a big deal, and Idrissa said that they weren't especially fond of foreigners here. Seems that Kene is from some southern ethnic group, but Idrissa didn't know which. And it seems I'm so wildly foreign to the folks here that, like a white man, I don't really count. Alaine, he tells me, is originally from Yoff village, meaning, like the people here in N'Gor, he's a full-blooded Lebou, and while they might have preferred that he marry a homegirl, they're all right with him.

So I was feeling pretty educated about the Kourmans, but the thing that really bothered me was the deal with their room. See, the room off the foyer was the one I'd initially wanted. It's twice the size of the room I'm in. It gets more sun than any of the other rooms in the house, and it's got more windows, meaning that when it gets hot, the place gets nice cross breezes. "What about the room, Idi?" I said. "Didn't Monsieur N'Doye tell you to tell me it belonged to some itinerant German artist who was away for a couple months?"

All Idrissa said was "Apparently it wasn't true."

So that's basically all I know, which isn't much. I've got room-mates now, so be careful what wishes you make for baby brother from now on, OK? If I can't live with my own wife, I can't see, right now, how I'm going to live with these folks.

Thanks for the beautiful card, the compass, and the (ha ha) toilet paper. You're quite the comedienne, Rita. But maybe you thought *I* was joking. I wasn't. I really and truly don't use it any-more. (Except maybe if I catch cold. I can certainly use it for blowing my nose.) Anyway, no one uses TP, except, I'm pretty sure, the Westerners and Westerniks who live in Dakar.

Using the can is a whole different trip here. It's hard to describe, but I'm told this type of toilet can be found in Europe, too. Imagine a toilet bowl that is countersunk at floor level. Somewhere nearby is a kettle or a can filled with clean water. On either side of the bowl, east and west, you've got footrests. You put your feet on these and hunker down into a full squat. You do your thing, and when your thing is done, you use the water from the kettle and wash your flue with your left hand only. People shake hands all the time here and would probably kill you if it somehow became known that you washed down with your right. But anyhow, I swear it's a great deal cleaner than toilet paper, though I don't imagine there will be any practical way to carry the custom back home with me when my year is up, or my proj-ect finished, whichever comes first.

The thing that bugs me, though, about the plumbing is that now and then I'll see the occasional crab scuttling out of the bowl, which suggests that our waste is being flushed directly into the Atlantic. Can't say I like that, but I'm not about to squat in the long grasses outside the village. But still . . .

Good God, am I tired. Long, strange couple days here. Tell Ma I love her and I'll write her soon. Tell the Dad I'm well and the fishing is pretty good, but I haven't had much time for it. And kiss baby Syria for me. And even though she hates me, tell Chloe I said hello. Write when you find the time.

I Love You,
Bird

P.S. One more thing, Sis. The happy couple made up that very night. I got home about 8pm, after hanging out for a couple hours at Idrissa's crib. Kene offered me the delicious fried fish, and I chatted with Alaine and ate. Alaine and I talked for a while. He wants English lessons (of course), and I want to improve my Wolof. We agreed to meet after dinner twice a week for the exchange. They all went to bed at about ten, and I read for about an hour then went to sleep myself. Woke up to the sound of them shrieking the springs at maybe about one in the morn. It seems they make up a lot. They made up twice more that very night. More than Rose and I ever did or probably ever will. Alaine really is a lucky bastard. And Kene is very noisy.

———

Thought you were dead.

As you can hear, I'm not.

What's wrong?

Just writing. Living. Nothing's wrong. I've just been really busy.

Well, you're not writing *me*.

I've been busy. My thesis was due in April, you know.

Yeah, I know, Rose, but I manage to—

I did write you. Did you get my card?

That was a month ago. I've written you. . . . Are you getting my letters?

About twenty cards and letters, yes.

You sound annoyed.

I'm a little overwhelmed right now. I've been eating, sleeping, and thinking Paulo Freire for six months now and—

Have you bought your ticket yet?

Excuse me?

Are you still coming out?

I'm kind of broke.

Rose, I left you—

I know you did, but after I paid your storage fee and your—

I gave you the money for the ticket. I told you I'd take care of all my own stuff.

Then why didn't you? You know how many times those people have called here?

They should be calling my folks.

Well, they're not. They call here. So I just sent them the money.

I'll send you more money, then.

No, that's OK.

You need money, I'll send it. I told you that. Don't give me crap about money. It's cheap here. I can get by on almost nothing. It wouldn't cost—

Bert, I don't think I should come.

What? What did you say?

I'm too busy, I'm not ready, and I don't have the money.

Don't insult me. Don't insult me. This isn't about money. What's going on? . . . Rose, I said, what's going on? . . . Are you still there? . . . Hello?

I'm still here, Bird. I called Kevin today.

Oh, God, Kevin. I haven't even written him yet. Jesus, he must think I don't give a damn about him. How's his boy? How's Cha?

The chemo seems to be working, but Cha doesn't think a baby should be subjected to radiation—

Isn't that unusual? Radiation for an infant?

I don't know. It depends on the doctor, I suppose. You should ask Kevin.

I feel so ashamed I never returned his call. Haven't written. You know? It's just all these weeks have gone by, and you start thinking that no letter would be adequate. You'd have to write a whole book to make up for the silence.

I think anything you have to say, at any time, would be all right, Bird.

Is that how you're feeling?

I don't follow you.

I mean about your not writing me. If it is, I just want you to know you don't have to match me letter for letter. . . . Rose? You still there?

Yes.

Why haven't you written me? Are you feeling overwhelmed? Is that it?

My thesis has just been so—

Fuck!

If you're going to curse at me, I'll hang up.

I wasn't . . . I miss you, Rose, but you know . . . what's going on? Why don't you write? You say you're not coming. You don't seem the least bit happy to hear my voice. You send me a birthday card with five words written on it. Five fucking words, when I've told you all about this place, and what I'm doing, and the people I've met. You . . . I know I just said money's no thing out here, but you know how much this call is costing me? I didn't call you to give you grief, but you're my wife, Rose, my best friend. What's going on? . . . Rose? . . . Rose, you still there? . . . I didn't mean to make you cry, Babe. I just . . . you know, I just miss you, Baby, and I can't understand what's going on. I mean, have you met someone or something?

No!

All right, all right.

I'll write you.

Promise?

I'll write.

Note #53

July 17

3pm

Mrs. A. Fall (check spell.) made a reference to some locoweed that grows around here that some of the older men smoke. She says it has powerful hallucinogenic properties. According to Mrs. F., the users develop an immediate aversion to clothing and to most foods. She spoke of an addict who lives near Yoff village (her former home) whom some of the women feed. Says he used to be some sort of minister in the federal gov. Since he only comes around at night, and since no one knows him by name, I'll treat this as a probable UL. Idi feels less certain, says the place is lousy with these addicts, but since he can't identify the weed, and doesn't know the name of it, will keep designation till I find otherwise.

July 22

Note #55

4pm

No confirmation whatsoever on trip to Yoff Island. The story of the island spirits is so deeply imbedded in social mind that not even Westerners will go. Can't even persuade colleague, Prof. Doucet from U. Dakar, to take me there. I'll leave it be for now.

July 24
Note #57
Afternoon
No new version of Disappearing Pickpocket as Idrissa suggested. Story by M. N'daiye (check sp.) is, note for note, like last two. No new version of story of Disappearing Wife, either.

July 25
Note #58
Late
I stayed in the village all day and slept. Slept like a cadaver. Idi came by with mail, but it was all bills. Got the storage bill, too, and I found that Rose didn't give them a nickel. $182.55. Not one goddamn nickel.

July 26
I helped Kene with the plumbing in the kitchen after twelve, count 'em, twelve hours of sleep. I was angry with the Kourmans at first because they were so loud last night. Don't think I drifted off till about three. Even after I fell asleep, I could still sense them. It was as though they'd moved their ruckus right into my room. When I awoke, Kene fed me and told me Idrissa had come by to drop off the liver cancer notes. All four of us took the bus into town this afternoon to get the J-pipe and the gaskets, but Alaine stayed in town to meet someone. Mammi sat on my lap the whole way back, and I could see that Kene liked that very much. I played the good uncle and teased and tickled the whole way back. Despite my antics, it felt like my brain had been replaced with clay, I was so tired, but Kene's so goddamn funny, my spirits soon lifted. Brain came back, but I still haven't done a lick of work today.

While I worked on the pipe, Kene told me about this French dude she met in Paris who wanted to marry her. "Ugliest snake I ever met," she said. "Covered from head to toe with freckles, and he used to say that if I'd only sleep with him he'd get more and more freckles until all the white would go away. But I couldn't stand him. He spat when he talked, and his teeth were green.

"He'd grown up here, and spoke pretty good Wolof, and even a little Bambara, my language."

I asked her if she found white men attractive, and she said something I've been pondering all day. "Sure, sure," she said, "though if you ever tell Alaine, I'll deny it. When you meet a person you find attractive, the last thing you look at is the color. People think they love the eyes and the hair and the face, and all that, but we see everything with the spirit eyes first. We see the soul first."

July 31
Liar. She said she'd write. She said she paid that bill. Fuck this noise.

August 4
Note #59
9:15 pm
Idrissa was able to find several references to slave trading in Mauritania in the local news going back to the 40's, so it seems pretty solid. Talked to Profs. Doucet and Koumba, and they confirm that it's all fully documented and I'd be foolish to go north, myself, and start digging around. So I'll leave it be. I'll just follow up the more fantastic local tales. Maybe.

#60

~~She clearly has something to tell me. Why doesn't she just get it over with?~~

Spent the afternoon with Kene and Mammi, fixing up Mammi's room. Had no idea that what lay behind the doors down the hall were bedrooms. I thought they were closets. Evidently, M. N'Doye has given all the keys to the place to the Kourmans. I have to admit I'm offended, though I haven't said a word to anyone, not even Idrissa. N'Doye seems to have restricted me to my room, the common room, and the bathroom.

I know I'm just one guy, and a family of three needs more space, but I'm feeling more and more like I don't really count here.

Aug 21
Early Morn.
Woke up with a mouth full of blood and Kene and Alaine in my room. My head was on Kene's lap, and she was wiping my face with a cold cloth. Alaine was sitting in the chair in the corner smoking, looking worried. He said, "Kene heard you talking in a loud voice. She walk in here and then call to me. How you feel, sick?"

It was bizarre. My gums were bleeding, so I'm assuming I'd been gnashing my teeth. Kene said I must have been having a nightmare. I told her I'm not prone to them. I felt fine, except for the shock of waking to find Kene so close and my mouth so red and coppery.

Alaine left to find someone with some medical knowledge, and I was alone with Kene for twenty minutes or so. I really felt fine, but I didn't act as though I was because I didn't want her to leave. Her thighs were soft and warm, and she smelled like incense, mint, olive oil, seawater, warm cotton. After a while she put down the cloth and stroked my face with her hands. She leaned so close to me that her breasts were flush against my forehead. I could feel my cock filling with blood, and I guess I began to feel embarrassed and weird because I sat up, told her I was fine. She said, "Yes, you are, aren't you?" but her tone wasn't coy, and she gave me nothing like a meaningful look. In fact, she looked as though she pitied me.

Alaine returned with Madame N'Doye, my landlord's wife, who is said to know everything about healing "that the white men wish they knew." She felt my head, looked into my eyes, ran a sandalwood-scented finger along my gums. She asked me what I'd been smoking, drinking, eating, and I answered. She asked me if I drank kinkiliba (sp?) tea, and I told her no, but that I'd heard it was good for you. She laughed and said, "This one is like a baby. Make sure he gets plenty of the tea." She told me I was fine, but that I should be careful of where I take my meals. I distinctly saw Kene stiffen when she said that. "Bad food," said Madame N'Doye, "can give you bad dreams." They apparently really don't like Kene, these women.

Alaine told me that he ran into Idrissa this morning, and that Idrissa was going to pick up my mail.

Cataplexy

Bertrand *knows* he isn't God. Not to himself, not even to the insects he obliterates in his hot little room, though they may rapturously jitter at his feet as he sprays them dead. He *knows* he isn't God. He can't amend the actions of others by telepathy, if that's what God does. He cannot apport himself to other worlds or hours. He won't rise from death. He knows no thoughts but his own. He can't do magic, or walk through walls, or talk to the dead, or fire bolts from his fingertips.

He is here, in the flesh, minutes after rising, writing in his journal his first remembered dream. But as he writes, the dream fades. This troubles him. All he can summon is the image of his face against the copper-brown breasts with the nipples like swollen raisins. He's lost her face, her name, her arms, everything but her breasts warming his face and her voice saying to him, "You know, you're not God." He writes, "Freud lives!" then slashes through the remark because it strikes him as mock levity. He admits to himself how stirred up he feels. And how could he deny it? He's breathing hard, and his heart's tumbling. He scribbles: "I think her breath was very hot. It warmed my whole body. I think I liked the smell, too. Was it like wood? Bread? Something dry. Something everydaylike."

He's lost everything else, though, what must have been an entire story.

He wants the dream back, but he's hungry, and a rooster crows outside in the white-hot afternoon sun. Birds sing, a chicken clucks from close by, a bus purrs in the distance. The dream won't come back, except for the brown breasts, the curious words. He wonders how or if the image and words are meaningfully connected. "They have to be, what with Rose's letter," he writes. The letter got to him just four days ago, and it consisted of just nine words: "Go ahead. Find your black girls. Fuck them all." He writes, "I don't understand the God part, but I sure know where I got the breasts."

Voices of children and mothers outside in the white air. Voices of car rapide boys, chanting names of destinations, "Yoff-Yoff-Yoff!" and "Dakar-Dakar-Dakar!" "Ouaccam! Ouaccam!" Engines send their vibes through the air, and it makes his windows hum. He closes his eyes to recapture the dream, but nothing comes. He smells his underarms. His clock ticks. He thinks of his best friend Kevin's boy, eight thousand miles away, and dying. Kevin told him this by phone two days before Bertrand's departure. He had called at the worst possible time: Bertrand and Rose had been fighting. She kept yelling from the bedroom, "Why did you pack rubbers, Bertrand? Can you tell me that, huh? Can you tell me?" while Kevin kept repeating, "He's fuckin' dyin'. Dylan Edward is dyin', man." He told Kevin he'd call back, but he never did. He has yet to write or call.

A bird flies by his window, which again sets in flight his wife's image through his head. How she was at breakfast three days before his flight to Dakar. Baggy white jeans and her blue Windcheater. She's laughing. The next day she's distant and avoids sex, and then they fight. On departure day she's kind. A saint. A few days ago, after four months, she writes words he couldn't have ever imagined her writing.

"The breasts I understand," he writes, then slashes the words away. "I don't understand squat," he scribbles, "since I'm not God, and everything."

He feels momentary anger, momentary shame, then sudden as an itch he thinks of the mutton and potatoes at the airport diner. "So I'm not God," he writes. "Tell me something I don't know."

For two weeks now, Bertrand's head had been buzzing with strange voices, flickering images, and, most discomfiting of all, a rigid breathlessness, a great black hand squeezing heart and lungs, invisible ropes and bands restraining arms and legs, everything in him ossifying, toughening, tightening. These things alone were enough to enthrall him, but not until this morning did the strangeness coalesce into scene and story, dialogue and action. He had never imagined the feeling of dreaming, how the thing lingers like yesterday's drunkenness—somewhere deep in the body where the mind can't see it. He writes, "It's like being in a movie." He clicks the nib of his pen several times, stares into space for a moment, then writes, "I had always suspected that people were talking about something they'd invented, imagined. I always believed dreams took one's will. But this thing *happened to* me."

The microphone at the mosque screeches, and the muezzin utters the Wolof equivalent of "Testing. Testing." Bertrand tenses in anticipation of the prayers. He can't bear the noise, and so he pricks his ears more squarely toward the sounds that soothe him, the goats, the chickens. The dream won't come back. He thinks about lunch and lights a cigarette, thinks about writing Rose for the pointless hell of it, or his parents for money, or Kevin, but what could he say to Kevin? It seems so late now. He closes his eyes to recall the entire dream but summons nothing but the breasts, the voice, the pointless message, which is so true it means nothing. But there was more, much more, and he hopes it comes to him. He has read in popular psychology maga-zines, and the like, that if you write your dreams down upon wak-ing, you'll be able to dredge up every detail, but his stomach knots up. He must eat something.

He opens his eyes in time to see two birds, large as hawks, fly into view at his southern window, and the microphone screeches again. He scribbles in his journal the words "Wish I could write faster." Cigarette smoke twists upward in blue and gold plumes, and for the briefest time they carry the whole of his awareness. He writes: "If I can dream now, if that was a dream, then perhaps it'll reveal the source of all folktales—talking animals, thumb babies, flying Africans, ghosts, soul eaters, animal/human hybrids, multi-armed, -eyed, and -headed gods, sewer gators, water-walking demigods. Maybe I can sleep my way through the dissertation rather than pulling all this research together. Maybe I can sleep for the next nine, ten months and go home.

"As for the urban folktales I'm after, the Disappearing Pick-pocket, the Penis Thief, and the like, well, who can say, but they sound like nightmares to me. Perhaps I'll interview a few infor-mants about their dream life." He puts down his pen, decides to leave for his meal before the prayers begin. But he must shower before going out.

He collects his towel and kit and slips into his flip-flops. Just before he closes the door, he takes up the bug spray, which sits on the shelf next to the light switch. He mists his tiny room. A habit, something he does every afternoon or morning or night he rises from sleep. And as he mists the room, it occurs to him that four months of bug spray permeating walls, floor, bed, clothing may account for this dream. He imagines himself a tumor and headaches, blindness, madness, a futile sortie from Dakar to New York, and New York to Denver—Swedish Hospital—where neither CAT scans, nor chemo, nor surgery can save him. By the time he has returned the can to the shelf, he has embalmed, manicured, coifed, suited, buried, and eulogized himself. He's rotted in his grave, which Rose has spat and Kevin pissed on.

Flies fall from walls and ceiling, twirl in downward spirals to the floor, gyrate like dervishes on their winged backs. A roach races from underneath his bed, so he takes up the can again, bends at the waist, and blasts the creature point-blank. Sprays until the roach is white with poison. It stops running, and its antennae fold like long eyelashes over its back. A red millipede wriggles from a crevice between floor and wall. He steps on it and closes the door.

He hears clucking from inside the house as he makes his way through the common room. He stops, turns around, scans the furniture he's just passed. The bamboo coffee table, the leatherette-and-bamboo chairs and sofa. The rubber plant in the corner. Nothing. Nothing more. He kneels and looks beneath the furniture, even under the credenza against the wall opposite the furniture. More nothing. He shakes his head and under his breath says, "This place is too fucking weird," thinks, Roaches in the bed, the occasional lizard clinging to the walls, flies and mosquitoes chanting high-pitched Gregorians as they zoom by my head. Goats wander in to keep cool. Turkeys drop by for leftover rice, and today . . . goddamn chicken in the house. Well, all right.

He returns to his room, takes up pen and paper, writes, in his shaky French, "Alaine, Kene. There's a living chicken somewhere in the house, but I don't have time to look for her. Is he yours? I think she is somewhere near my room." He leaves the note on the coffee table, goes through the common room again, but hears the bird once more. He puts down his kit and moves toward the sound. At first he thinks he hears it coming from his room and moves haltingly toward it. Suddenly, he realizes it is coming from beneath the couch, and though he already checked, he checks again. He pulls the couch from the wall, and it's as though the couch itself has clucked. His towel slips from his waist, and he pauses to fix it. Then he sees the two-foot slit in the black leatherette couch back. The bird clucks, and Bertrand parts the slit and peers at the bird, reaches into the slit and picks it up. It's small, the size of a large mourning dove, and its wings and legs are bound with coarse twine.

Though the look of it disturbs him—the small, white thing with the cocoa speckles, trussed tight, its red eyes straining with empty, reflexive alarm—he figures that it must be either a gift hidden away or a good luck charm. He places the bird back where he found it, leaves the note too, because he's curious, and goes outdoors to the shower. The heat screws into his back, the crown of his head, and he squints into the brittle white light. Now, he remembers the whole of the dream. It falls on him like a sandbag of image and sound so heavy and fast there's room for no other kind of awareness. The dream swallows him whole. He's not even aware that his physical eyes are locked on the white dot of the sun, and when the memory is finished with him, he finds himself flat on his back, staring up at the clouds, and bleeding from his tongue.

chapter 2

Ocularium

The muezzin's midday call floated overhead as Idrissa and I waited along the roadside for the number 7 bus which we'd take to Dakar. I wanted to be away from the village, alone with Idrissa so I could tell him about this weirdness I've been having since the Kourmans moved into my place. I've been in Senegal 134 days, and it's clear to me there are things in this country I may never get used to: the cold showers, my perpetual nausea, mosquitoes and flies, the taste of the food, the insects scuttling my sleeping legs at night, the heat—we'd been outdoors less than five minutes and already my clothes were rubbery with dampness, my socks gummy.

Today the sky was so piercing a blue it hummed like wind on wire, so blue that Idrissa's pupils contracted to nothing. The road was all the blacker in his irises. The sunlight shimmered on every surface—road, stone, the wind-bent back of the tall grasses behind us, Idrissa's coffee-black brow. The sea was a rim of yellow-white foil in the distance, its brightness so intense I shut my eyes for a moment and sighed for relief. The air smelled of hot grass and tar, Idrissa's limy aftershave.

All of it, the air and sun, should have been bracing, even stimulating, but I couldn't wake up. I was still in the feeling of the dream, which I described to Idrissa in this way: "I was somewhere in southern Colorado, about thirty or forty miles from where my folks live, you know, driving my '67 Volkswagen Beetle—when all of a sudden the car died. I got out and pushed it to the side of the road. I walked for miles until I came to an old garage my sister's ex-husband owned. But he was different from what he is in real life. In the dream he was as tall as you and built like a weight lifter—thighs like bows, arms like American footballs. You ever seen American football?"

Idrissa gave me one of those looks that says, "You think we Africans live in trees?" Mouth crumpled into a smirk, eyebrow arched. "All right," I said, "don't get huffy. I'm just asking.

"So anyway," I said, "in real life Bradley, my first brother-in-law, is a bit of a pud—a weakling, you see?—beer gut and everything, but here he is huge and handsome and, of all things, a mechanic. So I told him about my car troubles, and he nodded and nodded, folded his arms, and nodded some more, but he asked me no questions. Then, before I even finished telling him what I thought was wrong with the car, he turned from me and went into the garage. Then out he came with a box full of hardware junk—you know, wires, screws, tools, brackets, etcetera, and walking out with him was my second brother-in-law, Barry Mack, who looked exactly as he does in real life: glasses, ochre skin, pointy ears." I think I've told Idrissa my sister's been married twice. Hope I didn't confuse him. Maybe he thinks I have two sisters.

I paused for a spell and studied Idrissa's two-tone shoes, a creamy eggshell, a caramel tan. He shifted his weight from foot to foot. Am I boring him? I said to myself. Does he have to piss? I pretty much hate it when people tell _me_ their dreams. Idrissa slipped his long fingers into his pockets, jingled his change, and removed a pack of Lucky Strikes. He's been smoking Luckies from about the time he started working for me. He says it's easier to smoke what I smoke. He lighted two cigarettes and squinted at me as he passed me one. "Good idea," I said. "Hey, Idi, is this boring?"

"Go on," he said, all sphinxlike, as some of my students might say.

I did.

"We piled the junk and ourselves into an old Ford pickup and drove down the road, but the road got more and more rugged, full of deep pits and huge stones. It wasn't at all the same road I'd walked, and the distance seemed a great deal farther—and I said so, but Bradley kept insisting that he knew where the place was. But the road got worse—so bad, in fact, that we decided it would be better to leave the truck and travel on foot. Bradley pointed and said, 'It's just over them hills.' But I looked ahead, and there was this enormous mountain range of blue-green glass that looked absolutely unassailable. I told my brothers-in-law no way should we even think about it, but they both laughed and Barry Mack said it wasn't nearly as tough as it looked.

"OK, so we hiked, and at first it wasn't that bad. The elevation rose so gradually that it seemed almost level more than halfway up. The weather was clear, temperate. But little by little, the land grew strange. There'd been trees before—lodgepoles, firs, ponderosas, aspen—but they gave way to twisted, stumpy things with hardly any needles and exposed roots that looked wet and purple, like veins. The air began to feel humid, the trail steeper, and alarmingly narrow until it was barely three feet across and one side of it plunged into a deep rocky ravine, and on the other side a gorge, hundreds of feet deep, where a great huge waterfall churned. It got so that even Barry Mack and Bradley were scared, and Bradley decided it was too dangerous to carry the box of junk and he tossed it into the gorge. The box shrunk to the size of a mustard seed, then vanished.

"So later the path broadened a bit and the gorge and the ravine receded into the distance, but suddenly we came upon this swamp that was filled, as far as the senses could go, with decay, garbage, rot, trash, stuff piled up over years and years. And the farther we traveled, the worse it became, and God, did it stink. Swill so deep, so vile, that I could barely think, let alone breathe. Filth upon muck upon waste. Plastic bags full of shit, broken toys, rotting animal carcasses, human skulls. There was nowhere you could place your feet with any certainty that you wouldn't plunge hip deep, then neck deep, into all this decay. The swill sucked my shoes clean off my feet, and I felt a horrible sensation all the way up to my mouth. My brothers-in-law were up to their chins in the muck, and I could feel what they felt, taste what they tasted, smell what they smelled.

"Finally, just when it looked like things were hopeless, I spotted solid ground. I pulled myself onto the bank, and found a freshwater stream running alongside it just a few yards away. I rolled into the stream, washed myself, and then followed the stream until it led—check this out, man—until it led me to my father's garden. It was my father's garden, man, now that's got to mean something, right?"

Idrissa hucked on his cigarette and shrugged. "Means what you decide it means," he said.

"Anyway, I called to Bradley and Barry Mack, told them to wade to where I was. I planted my bare feet in the soil of my father's garden and gazed at all those fruits he grows—reds and purples, yellows and greens, shapes like breasts and penises, elbows, brains, faces, all of it bordered by marigolds and lilacs. It smelled sweet, a sweet pink smell you could say [Idi smiled at that], and the clear stream ran through its center, between the collards and the yellow squash.

"I looked for Barry Mack and Bradley, but they were gone. I washed myself in the stream one more time, then walked to my parents' house . . . and, well, that's about it. I think I woke up before I actually saw my folks."

I folded my arms and looked at Idrissa's two-tone shoes, cream and tan, and said, "Weird, huh?" I didn't mention the other parts, the stuff about the woman telling me I'm not God. She was in my folks' house, and I wanted her, but she laughed at me and told me I wasn't God. Why didn't I tell him? Because maybe it's none of his damned bidness.

Idrissa has been my guide in both the inner and outer worlds of my life here in Senegal, but he made no other reply to what I'd just told him. I hadn't expected him to. I've been here 134 days, and he has explicated at least a quarter of these days for me, but we've never talked about dreams. I'm sure his surprise had much to do with his silence. He stood there smoking, squinting down the road. He'd hooked an arm behind his back like a sergeant major, said absolutely nothing. But that was all right, for what I hadn't told him is that until the Kourmans moved into my place, I have never, ever, ever dreamed. Not ever.

The one constant, the one thing I have always depended on, until the Kourmans moved in, was my dreamless sleep. Never in all my thirty-four years have I ever dreamed. At least I've never remembered doing so. My sleep has always been black, empty, colorless, silent—no impressions or thoughts of any kind. But from the very day that Alaine, Kene, and Mammi moved in, I began dreaming those proto-dreams, I guess you could call them—weird sounds, whirling colors. I guess I will tell Idrissa all this, sooner or later, but it has to be worked up to, perhaps even worked for. This is the African way, Idrissa tells me. It's rude to begin with the point.

"Idi, explain something to me," I said to him while we were waiting for the bus, and then I paused, as if for effect, but to be honest, I didn't know where to begin. My head was a logjam of synaptic misfirings and false starts. How to go at this, this thing with the Kourmans? They are good to me; yet it often seems they mean me no good. Since they moved in, don't I have a family now? Kene cooks my meals, cleans my room, does my laundry, ignores me, talks about me behind my back. But I don't mind the contempt. She's so beautiful, I can barely stand to be in the same room with her. And Mammi, their little girl, don't I draw pictures for her? Don't I bounce her on my knee? Don't I listen to her screams as Alaine whips her for, say, wasting food? And what _about_ Alaine? Aren't I thankful for someone to tutor me in Wolof and French? And we have some good times together, he and I. I remember the first time we went fishing off the jetty, how we laughed like brothers, like fools when the first breaker washed our bucket of fish away, and the second one dumped a wall of water on our heads. I remember every franc he's robbed me of, how frequently he's lied to me: There <u>was</u> coffee in the house last Monday. He <u>did</u> have the money for the water bill. He <u>did</u> forget my quinine tabs, and he does owe me the eleven thousand CFA. But do I stand up to him? I do not. How can I even <u>imagine</u> seducing his wife (which I do) when he has my balls in his back pocket?

And these dreams. Why these dreams? The Ila of northern Zimbabwe are fond of saying, "Buttocks rubbing together do not lack sweat," and I suppose that's true. Cohabitation does often make for conflict, but I can't tell my buttocks from a bundt cake with the Kourmans. Do people cause dreams? Is dreaming like a contagious illness? It's not that I don't know people. I have family. Both parents and a sister, my sometime wife, Rose, too, but since we've never lived together, since I've lived alone all my adult life, always had my own room, kept my own counsel in my journals, do what I can to secure my own dark privacy, I take it I've never had the illness. I certainly know I've never dreamed.

The best thing, I suppose, is to ease into it with Idrissa, tell him only a little at first, so finally, I said to him: ". . . like, the other day, last Wednesday, I was in my room, you know, doing what I always do—transcribing material, studying Wolof, writing Rose, and so forth, when suddenly I heard this yelling. Just screeching. It was coming from our front yard. It got more and more intense, and it started freaking me out. Thought someone was busy getting murdered. I mean literally, man. Head lopping, limb hacking. I left my room and slinked to the foyer, and I saw Kene out front, wielding a broom and hollering at three other women who were all hollering back. Idi, I tell you, man, them girls was smokin'." Idrissa grinned. He loves it when I "speak Americain noire."

"Of course, you know me, man, I don't know enough Wolof to fill a babe's mouth, but you don't have to know the language to know hot, so I just stood where it was cool and watched, you know, hoping that no one would get violent. Didn't wanna go out there.

"No violence, though. Things petered out after about four or five minutes, and when Kene turned back to the house, I slipped back into my room. Another five minutes went by, and then there was a knock at my door. It was Kene. You know the woman—to me she's about the second most beautiful woman I know, but she was packing ugly Wednesday. She stood there and cussed me out for a good two minutes. Finger wagging, head jerking. I didn't catch many of the specifics, but I got the point. Then she slammed the door in my face and didn't talk to me for two days.

"Well, when Alaine came home from work that evening he chewed me out . . . sweetly, nicely, understand, as though he was my grandfather giving me guidance or some shit, but I could see how pissed off he was. He told me that we're a household, they and I, that we're a family. He told me I should have defended Kene.

"Defended Kene! Like how? I mean, I ask you, how . . . I mean the language thing and the—"

"Bertrand," Idrissa said, holding up a hand. He was clearly exasperated, impatient. Maybe I was being _too_ roundabout. I'm a lousy African. "Bertrand, you must know that it was impossible for you, but perhaps if you had just left the house and stood in front of everyone to let them know you are there, it would have been enough. The women would have gone away. Remember what old Madame Gueye taught you? She say that the tree which is not taller than you cannot shade you. I think you very much disappointed Kene that day. The women who fought with her are to respect you, you see, but they can't do it if you don't stand. When Alaine is gone, he expect you to head the household."

"I see."

"You are second because he is older by five years."

"OK."

"But it will be well for you. Don't worry."

The bus rolled up, we boarded. It shook and churned and hummed until Dakar appeared outside the windows. All along the way there,

I screamed in my head, But I didn't ask to be part of anyone's family! Which is true. They moved into what was my place, not I theirs.
What's all this You-are-second-because-he-is-older-by-five-years
jism? Should I have reminded Idrissa of the evening I came home and
found strangers having dinner in the foyer of my house? Should I have
reminded Idrissa of my resentment when I discovered that Kene and
Alaine were renting that large, airy, sunny bedroom I'd originally wanted,
the room the landlord told us belonged to the itinerant "German artist"?
I thought about reminding my friend, but he knows these things. Maybe
I'm being too territorial, suffering some "American illness," as Idrissa
would put it. I guess I'm not being particularly African, because I want
solitude. I'm used to it. And I want dreamless sleep. I'm used to that, too.

As we disembarked, I said to Idrissa, "So what do you think the
dream means?"

Idrissa frowned. He cocked his head. "Dreams always mean the
same thing," he said. "Means you're asleep."

Still on our way to lunch—on foot now—we saw a woman begging on
the corner of Lamine Gueye and a street I don't know. I started at the
appearance of her skin. It was like a freckled apricot, sun dried, sour,
bruised. I thought vitiligo, age, and sunburn. My friend said leper. Her fingers splayed, then cupped, reached out as we made our way to her. A
thousand rags walked by, but she wanted me. She was hungry.

I reached into my pocket and took one hundred francs, breathed heat
and motor oil, noon warm goat leather, brine, the smell inside my own
nose. I felt the white walls of the city settle on my shoulders. The city
flitted through my peripheral vision in bursts of color. "This enough, Idi?" I
said, and he said, "Up to you." I bent down low to drop the coin. I studied
every fissure, line, and curve of her oak palm. The coin burned yellow-
green there in her hand, then boom! it was gone, her hand snapped
closed, and we moved on. A taxicab swooped around the corner we
were headed for; it tumbled on and vanished.

Abruptly, four boys, looking like a thousand, accosted me, encircled me like satellites, hands upthrust like sun-shrunk leaves on branches worried by wind. "'Mericain brudah, you godt mawney? You godt mawney, toubobie?" They weren't poor; even I could see that. Western clothed and Bata shod, they dripped oil milk fat honey. They saw me coming before I even heard of Dakar. And they wanted me, being hungry. "Idi," I said, "how do I lose these guys?" Up to me, he said. Let's go eat, he said.

––––––––

He stops his writing for a moment. Looks over what he's written. He realizes that he really ought to have mentioned the copper woman to Idrissa, but tells himself he didn't because he could find no way to fit it with what he would call the main narrative, and to a degree this is true. What had breasts to do with the mountain of glass, the hellish pit, the stream in his father's garden? What had God to do with anything? He had never thought much about God. But the woman? He knows, but he can't tell anyone for now.

There is a gentle tap at his door. It's Alaine, who says to him, "Ready?"

"Ready for what?"

Alaine lets himself in and offers his hand, so Bertrand shakes it.

"Today we go to the dimanche marché. What you call it?"

"That flea market thing? I forgot."

"You promise today. It is late already."

"I slept late. It's so hot, I can't sleep till four or five in the morning. Is your friend with the truck here?"

"He have someplace else to go but will come back soon. I knock on your door when he came. You weren't here."

"Went to lunch. Now I'm working. I'm really sorry, but we'll have to pick up the fridge tomorrow. Besides, you said you didn't have the money."

Alaine inhales deeply and blows. "We do it tomorrow then." He clutches the doorknob, and just as he is about to exit, pauses, slowly shakes his head, and says, "No, no, tomorrow's no good." He pats his chest with the palm of his hand. "I'm too busy tomorrow. Kene teach all day."

"Do you have your half?"

He strokes his beard. "Of the money? No, but I pay you back. Sure I do, but you must pay two times for the truck. Six thousand."

Bertrand notices he's not breathing, and when he exhales his heart thuds. "Hand me my bag there." And as he takes the bag, his hands are trembling, and a thin glaze of tears blurs his eyes. His neck is hot. He hands over two bills and croaks the words "I need the change."

"Sure, sure," says Alaine, and he closes the door, and Bertrand returns to his journal, but before he truly settles in again, he rises from his chair and walks into the common room. He finds the entire Kourman family sitting with their friend Allasambe. Kene is plaiting Mammi's hair, and mother and daughter are speaking in Wolof. Alaine and Allasambe are smoking, talking politics in French. Bertrand observes that his presence doesn't make a ripple in their activities. Though he listens to the men (for he understands French much better than conversational Wolof), his eyes are on Kene. In the afternoon light, he can see where he must have acquired the skin color for the dreamwoman. He looks at her, and his heart slows down; everything in him eases. Her skin shimmers where the bars of sunlight lie against it—her right foot and leg, her right arm and collarbones. After a moment, he realizes that the men are no longer speaking; they are, in fact, watching him. His face flushes. Six male eyes shift from man to man for the briefest moment, say, the duration of breathing in then out. Allasambe's eyes smile, Alaine squints. Bertrand says, "I forgot to ask you about the chicken."

"Sit down, sit down," says Alaine.

Bertrand shakes Allasambe's hand and sits in the chair closest to his bedroom door. "Didn't know you were all out here. You were so quiet."

"The heat keeps things quiet," says Allasambe.

Bertrand hardly knows him but likes him, stops to speak to him whenever they meet. Allasambe's English is good, better than Idrissa's. He is a tall, thickset man, with large earlobes, slow-moving eyes. He shaves his head and is given to wearing long-sleeved Western shirts always untucked and the voluminous trousers called chayas. Genie pants, Bertrand calls them. He also knows that Allasambe sells boom boxes part-time and in summers takes care of an American diplomat's home on N'Gor Island.

All summer long, Allasambe has offered invitations to Bertrand to visit the house for a weekend, relax, socialize. He promises good French food, an island breeze or two. Bertrand always puts him off, for though he likes Allasambe, he feels what he would call an "agenda" lurking behind Allasambe's generosity, nothing sinister he imagines, but he feels that Allasambe looks at him the way a man would look at a friend who has come to a party with his zipper down and wishes to get him in private to point it out to him. But because Bertrand is ashamed of how little he, the anthropologist, knows of N'Gor village, of Senegal, of Africa, he'll accept counsel only from Idrissa. Bertrand doesn't want to be shown his open zipper by someone he hardly knows. But he does often consider asking Idrissa about Allasambe— since they are in the same social circle, being age mates—but doesn't know how to go about it. He can think of no way to make the question sound unparanoic.

"Ah, the chicken," says Allasambe, "we found it. We got rid of it."

"No worry about it, Bert," says Alaine. "It's a child's thing to do." His eyes are darker than usual, but Bertrand doesn't know whether it's because he caught him ogling Kene, or because he has something to hide. He wishes to say, "So it's Mammi's chicken? She should keep it outside," but he says, "You mean neighborhood kids?"

"He means childish," says Allasambe. "Alaine doesn't believe in those sort of things."

"Do *you*?" says Alaine.

"Me?" says Allasambe. "Depends."

Alaine says, "If we had Marxist revolution, this sort of thing would die. People would believe in science."

"We have our own science," says Allasambe.

Alaine waves those words away.

"What," says Kene, in French, "you think white people are so smart?"

"Kene, you understand us!" says Alaine, and she answers in English. "I know 'Marxist,' I know 'science,' I know you." Bertrand loves the way her gums show a little when she smiles. "You're teaching her English, too, Bertrand?" Alaine says.

"He speaking, I learning."

"Man smart, woman smarter," says Allasambe.

Everyone, except Mammi, laughs, but Bertrand sees Alaine's eyes, even behind the thick, smudged lenses, are unsmiling. Don't be ridiculous, he thinks, I'm not boning your wife. At least not while awake.

When the Africans begin speaking again, it's in Wolof. Kene is singing "Man Smart / Woman Smarter" in Wolof and holding an

index finger five inches from Alaine's nose. He grabs the finger
and pretends to bite it. He pulls her into his lap, kisses her shoulder and neck, but she leaps up and says, in Wolof, "None of that.
I'm still mad at you. I want my refrigerator, old man," but she is
looking at Bertrand. Winks at him. He looks away and says to
Allasambe, "Why was the chicken in the couch?"

"Yes, *inside* the couch. Can you believe it?"

"How—"

"Have you seen this sort of thing before?" says Allasambe.

"I don't follow you. You mean my research? This isn't exactly
my area. Not—"

"You and I must talk. Why don't you ever come to the island?"
Bertrand sees how hard Allasambe is gripping the armrests of
the chair, and he feels his brows involuntarily lift.

"Been meaning to."

"So," says Allasambe, "you don't know the chicken was bound
with cord? That it was being used for magic?"

Just then, the man with the truck calls from the foyer, and
Alaine says, "Come, Bert, we go get her fridge at the fleas market. You, too, Allasambe. We need your muscles."

"Only if you promise to come to the island for dinner."

"We come."

"Mister Bertrand Milworth, you'll come too?"

"I'm there."

"I'm shock," says Alaine. "You all the time say you are too
busy."

"Don't be. I think I—"

"Ah yes," says Alaine. "Don't forget the six thousand CFA
more for the driver. Remember you must pay twice."

"I just gave you ten thousand, man. You owe me. Sorry I can't
come with you."

"See?" says Alaine, "all the time, too, too busy. You work too hard. I bring back your change."

————————

So Idrissa and I got to lunch. We started the meal with braised whitefish, crisp fins, skins, and tails. There was crumbly rice as white as the teeth that glow from a black girl's mouth. I tipped my head and swallowed from my lemonade bottle. I squinted the fizz from my nose and said to Idrissa, "How's Colette?" But I was thinking of something altogether different. I was thinking about this silly nonsense with the chicken today. I was thinking of dreams. I was thinking of the slope that leads from Kene's throat to her collarbones. I was thinking of my wife and her pale hands, her broken heart. Mostly, I was thinking of the chicken.

"She is still in France," said Idrissa, "but when she get back I'm going to dress sharp, wear good cologne, sing pretty to her, like Marvin Gaye. She will fall down dead, I think." Idrissa is quite the killer, what with the mustachio brows, the square jaw, the long, long fingers. I see how women melt for him, but I cautioned him about the singing. "You couldn't carry a tune in a milk wagon," I said. I thought that sounded pretty good. I took another sip from the bottle, caressed it with my thumb.

Idrissa looked at me for at least fifteen seconds before he said, "How is your Rose?" I take it he didn't care for the jest. He glanced over my shoulder, then down at the table, flicked a fly off the salt cup.

"Didn't I tell you about the letter I got from her a few days ago?"

"Nope."

I told him, "She couldn't trust me anymore, said it was over. All the cologne and Marvin Gaye in the world won't save my ass . . . I guess." I couldn't tell him about the thing about the "black girls," but was I lying? Idrissa can't help me here, unless he's got a sister.

So Idrissa said something like, "Thought she was coming to see you."

"Not this lifetime. I should probably go back to the States for a few weeks, straighten things out, if I can, but . . ." I thought of all the money I've spent, the paucity of research I've done. Two thousand dollars left, nine months of work to go. I thought of the reason behind her letter, those ugly words I could never imagine her using. It was all too much to explain. I said, "Hey, let's get off this shit. Something I wanna ask you." But before I could, the waiter brought our salads in two Chinese bowls. Sharp green bed of lettuce, soil-sweetened carrots, the bloody beets, the radishes, the purple onions. My mouth watered, but suddenly the taste of my mouth turned bitter, oily, smoky, sour. My tongue still throbbed from where I'd bit it yesterday. Still does.

"Idi," I said, "why on earth would someone truss up a live chicken and leave it behind the couch?"

If my question took my friend by surprise, he didn't show it. I was expecting him to arch one of those Cro-Magnon eyebrows at me, but he didn't. He eased his fork into a beet round, raised the beet to throat level, and said, "It's a way of weaking the mind of someone so he will give you anything you ask him for." He paused to eat the root, then said, "Who do you think put it in there?"

"So you heard? Figures. Who put it there? Who the hell knows? The front door's never locked. I walk into that place, and God knows what I'll find. My landlord's kid brings his friends into our living room all the time to throw these friggin' dance parties when they think we're all out. Maybe they check with the Kourmans, but no one says jack to me—"

"'Jack' to you?"

"It means 'nothing,' sort of."

"Two negatives."

"Skip it. My point is I have no idea what to expect. Last Sunday I found one of Monsieur N'Doye's goats in the goddamn living room. The thing about the goat is I'm sure it wandered in by itself, but the chicken—"

"Berdt, whoever put that bird in that place lives in the house. I guarantee you." He poked his fork at me. "I guarantee you."

"Idi, I don't think so. Hey, you want the rest of my salad?"

"Quois? Doh lekk?"

"No, I don't think so—the chicken, I mean—because Alaine and I both heard the bird clucking at the same time." I have no idea why I lied to him, why I told him that Alaine and I searched for it together till we found it under the couch. "Under it or behind, I can't remember, but he seemed genuinely surprised to find it. He was pretty upset, seemed to me." I think I lied because I've always hated it when the people around me can't get along. I sense that Idrissa and Alaine despise each other, and this sort of trouble I don't need.

I remember the time, two, three weeks ago, when Alaine was in my room one evening, giving me a Wolof lesson. Idrissa popped in to receive his pay for the week. He had a date that night and looked sharp all the way from his cream-and-tan shoes to the pressed collar of his off-white shirt. I handed him his 10,100 CFA, roughly 33.50 American. He folded the money into his wallet, grabbed my hair oil off the bookshelf, greased his palms then his short Afro. "Jocma bene cigarette," he said, and when I gave it to him, he flamed it up, held out his hand for a slap, and when I fived him, he nodded to us and spun from the room in a smooth pirouette. Looked like a Temptation, he did. As soon as the door clicked shut, Alaine sprang to his feet and mimicked everything Idrissa had just done, the hair oil rub, the palm slap, the pirouette. "He's take advantage of you, Bertrand," he spat. "He has no respect for you or this house. What he does for you? Nothing. You pay him too much." He sat down hard on my bed and looked at the floor. My face felt hot, and I had no idea what to say. Maybe a full minute went by before Alaine lighted a cigarette, exhaled the smoke, and thumbed his glasses back into place. "He is not a good guy," he said. I cleared my throat, or something of that nature, and said, "Maybe he could do more. I don't know."

I plucked a radish from my bowl and popped it into my mouth. "I'm really not hungry, for some reason," I said. "I should have ordered chicken, huh?"

Idrissa didn't smile. He arched an eyebrow. "He was angry when he found the bird?"

"Alaine? Sure. Looked like it."

The waiter shuffled up and scooted a small plate of tjebudjin from the edge to the middle of our table. He smiled with all eighty-eight teeth. "You are Americain?" he said.

"Liberian," I said, and his smile shrank ever so slightly. He nodded a bit and slid away. Idrissa has taught me, and it makes me sad, that Africans have little interest in other Africans. But being an American in Africa, he tells me, "is like you are a movie star in a small, small town." Maybe I should get me some shades. Don't really need them, though. When I don't want to be bothered, I'm Liberian. "When did you order that?" I said.

"There's a lot you don't see, Berdt. Doh lekk?"

"Not hungry. And can the inscrutable crap, Idi, I'm not in the mood."

"Yam, man, yam! He's smiling up at you."

"If it was someone in the house, it would have to have been Mammi. I can't imagine folks as sophisticated as the Kourmans doing, you know, occult shit like that."

"Regard the oily red."

"No thanks. But where would a six-year-old get the money to buy a chicken? Do you think a kid that small could tie up a chicken? Or do you buy them like that?"

"Ah! Real tomat, deux carottes, and little purple eggplant. The smell, Bertrand, she rise up to the heaven in the center of your nose."

I laid both hands flat on the table, leaned forward, and said, "The joke's getting stale, Idi."

Idrissa leaned back in his seat and smiled. "OK, OK, calm down." He put down his fork, took up his spoon, and dug into the fish and rice. I looked out the window, could see nothing but the inside of my head. A field of dustballs, hairballs—gray, fuzzy. I wasn't hungry. No. "Idi," I said, "I can't say I actually know the Kourmans, but it doesn't seem to me that

people who were educated at the Sorbonne, that people who are Marx-
ists, that people who're atheists—hey, do you think a bound chicken can
make you dream?"

"Sleep makes you dream, Berdt. Sleep. A tied-up bird is one thing,
but you really need to do something about your wife. She's your wife,
man."

I rubbed the sweat off my lemon bottle, then traced my finger around
its mouth. "Hey, man," I said to Idrissa, "finish up so we can get the hell
out of here."

chapter 3

Night Side of Nature

"The wrongdoer forgets, but not the wronged."
"He who cultivates in secret is betrayed by the smoke."
"A crime eats his own child."
"Everything forbidden is sweet."
"The heart cannot hold two."

A Jewel is not a Rose, but he saw Jewel more often, since she was his office mate there in Denver, and Rose, an M.A. candidate at The Colorado College, lived sixty miles away in Colorado Springs. Rose and Bertrand married four years ago, and it was his desire to live separately, to maintain their current lives, which to him seemed perfectly coordinated.

She grappled with him, eventually gave in. "The thing will be based on trust," she said, "not . . . watchfulness, I guess you could say. Besides, you snore." She giggled. "And you have lousy taste in music." He never let himself perceive how dark her eyes were and how thin her laughter was when she said these things. He'd looked at her and saw what he always saw, her young-for-forty face. The short black hair and her eyes, large, sad, open, clear, cool, wry; the sharp-angled face that's somehow soft, perhaps because of its olive tone. He saw the small, slightly veiny hands she ran through the black ringlets of her hair as she said, "I mean your need for solitude, your strange hours, your clutter and smoke—sounds like a Bergman movie: 'He smokes. He burns candles on the hour. He watches TV, listens to the radio, and reads at the same time. And he wants to move in with her, Mitzi Cleaner, the sexy dustress of a white-carpeted flat on the West Side. See *Clutter and Smoke,* and you'll never see or hear again. Opens Friday at a theater near you.'" She was sitting lotus fashion on the dark green pillow on his bedroom floor, and when they both stopped laughing, she leaned forward and said, "It's not like we can have kids, so we can do what we want." She leaned back, and her smile faded. "But what happens when we've finished our degrees? I mean, what if we get jobs in another state? Are we supposed to go around getting two apartments wherever we go?"

He didn't know how to answer that, at first, then thought of his friend Jewel, who was married and whose husband was also an anthropologist. "We love each other," said Bertrand. "We'll always find a way to be with each other." That's what Jewel would say. That's what her husband wrote her, anyway, while he studied dance in India.

Jewel did live with her husband when he was around, but he was never around. And Bertrand couldn't tell what she really felt about the man. He knew what he felt about Jewel, though, and he often wished he could graft parts of Rose and Jewel together. Jewel loved the bruisingly loud rock music Bertrand listened to, and she tolerated his smoking, which Rose never could. And Jewel had a wide soft mouth, always wet, always red, that gushed obscenities, vitriol, wisecracks, gossip. She was stunningly neurotic, inexplicably angry, Rose's opposite in nearly every respect. Each morning she would stomp into the office with some new complaint about her husband's boorish manners, or how the stingy Denver air made her a living mummy, or how the chair had stolen her ideas about reorganizing the department; she complained about her salary, her hair, her digestion, her car, her freckles. It may have been the rage that shimmered from her that stirred him so. Her nipples were perpetually erect, her throat and chest remained perpetually flushed. Her eyes, the color of lime slices, always gazed at him with predacious intensity. She wasn't what he thought of as beautiful, but magnetic, galvanic.

When he was with her, he would somehow bend himself to the contours of her personality in the same way light bends to the contours of a celestial body of great mass. He joked more, swore with greater vigor, gossiped as though he'd been born to do so. There were times when he would even hear himself speak in her Queens accent: *vulcha, culcha, wattah, Denvah.* He loved how she could, in a single sentence, connect Asimov to Adrienne Rich, *Starsky and Hutch, Dr. Atomic,* Michelle Cliff, James Brown, and Barbie doll commercials. And she hated so many people, he felt honored to be her friend. Being in her presence, he often said to himself, was like being on speed. Rose knew nothing of speed.

In their one and only night in bed, Jewel bit, scratched, snorted, cursed, drooled, put her tongue and fingers anywhere she pleased, directed him as though he was an athlete or a slave. She even slugged him several times while in the throes of orgasm. When it was over, she cried as though it was he who had abused her, cried as though she'd spent the night under the torment of demons. Bertrand held her, tenderly stroked her freckled face, her auburn hair, as she convulsed and coughed and howled. He felt helpless, even alarmed, for he thought that maybe she was ill. His heart rocked so violently that his upper body spasmed as though he was moving to a bass beat. Finally, when she gained some measure of composure, Bertrand calmed himself enough to ask her what was the matter. She rolled to face him, kissed him on the lips, and said, "I think I'm in love with you."

"Truth is greater than ten goats."
"Lies, though many, will be caught by truth as soon as she rises up."
"Scandal is like eggs; when it is hatched it has wings."
"Shame has watchmen."
"The truth, even though it be bitter."

———————

I remember she said, "Would you have told me if I hadn't read it?"

And I said, "I guess."

"You guess."

"Well, I don't know. It was just that one time, but she acts as though we were betrothed or something. Goddamn, Rosiegirl, she's married, too! I just figured it was some little—"

". . . hate when you call me 'Rosie-anything.' Stop calling me—"

". . . dalliance for her. I never thought—"

". . . always used to call me that, and I always hated it, and you know it. So just don't, OK!"

Whenever she says this, I always half expect her to say, "Stop pretending I'm black," but she would never do that. Besides, she would probably say, "Stop pretending you're black." Anyway, there she sat—her arms were crossed; her legs were crossed there on my little blue couch—and there were no tears in her eyes, no blush behind the olive of her cheeks. She bobbed her leg up and down, glared at the cow skull on the end table, or at the lamp next to it, or at some place where people like her see visions of the future or see their own pain hovering like a hazy red globe somewhere in the air. I wanted to take her small hands in mine, press my nose against her throat, weep, beg for her forgiveness, but I couldn't. I didn't feel guilty, just exposed. She had no business reading my journal. "I'm sorry," I said.

"For what? Sleeping with Jewel or calling me Rosie."

"Both, I guess."

"Still you're guessing."

"Rose, it's my journal. It was private. I've asked you to never read my journal. You know? I mean, I'm sorry for what I did, but . . ." What could I say? This was impossible.

She closed her eyes for a moment and sighed. When she opened them again, she was staring right at me, looking at me as though she'd never seen me before, as though I were a creature she had never even imagined seeing. Her face seemed on the verge of something definable, but for me, it remained unreadable. There was nothing clear about it, neither anger, nor regret, nor disgust, nor blithe indifference. She stopped her leg pumping and looked so deeply into my eyes I blinked and looked at her sneakers. "Tell me something, Bert," she said. "Do you have even the vaguest idea of what I feel? Guess if you have to, but tell me, do you?"

I felt around in my head for anything that would come my way. Anything. I knew that if I answered what I usually answered whenever she tried to penetrate me so, namely, "You feel bad," she might have kicked me in the head. I thought and thought, but nothing would come. I felt as though I couldn't breathe, as though I would ossify in my uncertainty and break into a thousand pieces, but all that would come to my mind was, "You feel bad; you feel bad; you feel bad." What more was there? I felt bad, too. My journal, my private thoughts; from my pen to God's eye. This is bad, I was thinking, this is bad that she can't see. I wanted to say, "See? This is what you get when you violate someone's privacy. I thought we said we didn't believe that marriage makes one person from two, that we each must have our own lives. You once said, 'It's like we have one house with a sixty-mile hallway.' You said you felt as close as you could possibly feel, that if we lived in the same house, even in the same city, you'd 'explode from joy, wouldn't be able to stand it.'" I couldn't see that the hallway metaphor implied that the single home was what she really wanted. Is probably what everyone, but I, wants.

Finally, she sighed once more, unfolded her arms, and patted the cushion next to her. "Come sit by me," she said. And when I did, she rested her body against mine, laid her right hand on my chest, and it felt so good that I began to shiver. She said, "What is this? Is this a marriage?"

"I just thought that this would be better than what everybody . . . There are certain cultural—"

She sat up, ran her fingers through those black ringlets on her head. "I mean do you <u>feel</u> married?"

I remember how much I wanted to pull her back into the embrace, but her sudden anger made me cautious. Actually it made me angry. I said, "I don't know, Rose, I don't really know what marriage is. I mean, we can't have kids or anything."

She sat back, but a little away from me. Folded her arms again, too. "I don't know either . . . so I forgive you. I guess I have to forgive you is all. But don't do it again. Don't you dare do it again."

I believe she did forgive me, but it took all my strength to keep from saying, "And I forgive you, too." Yet I believed that biting the tongue made everything even. I'd committed the greater sin, so eating crow with shame was roughly equal to her painful humiliation. But I know how people think. Phil Donahue or Geraldo Rivera wouldn't do a show called <u>Wives Who Read Their Husbands' Journals</u>. They give us <u>Rat Bastard Husbands Who Cheat on Their Wives</u>. In fact, I imagine it's thought perfectly all right for a wife to rifle her husband's pockets and desk drawers, his tackle box, his briefcase. I think people believe that spouses have every right to hire private dicks and psychics, to interview neighbors, to surreptitiously follow hubby or wife-y, whether or not there are grounds for suspicion. Maybe you don't really feel married until you begin to feel watched.

———

"It is sleep that makes one like the wealthy."
"What gives pleasure when going to sleep is answered
   when waking."

He sleeps more often, now that he dreams, though he is unaware of this. He doesn't see that the time he spends in bed grows by half hours each day, partly because he has never been able to make rhyme of his sleep patterns. Since childhood, it had not been unusual for him to doze off at 3 P.M. or 5 A.M., and he seldom slept more than five hours or so, but within five days of the first dream, he is sleeping close to ten hours, night or day, and the dreams grow thicker, more real, and nearly every time he dreams of either Rose or Kene or both.

On the evening of August 16, he wakes to the words "Yes, I had sex many times when you were gone. I like older men, so hard and mean." As he writes the dream down, he ponders the odd, antique syntax she'd used. Had he heard it in some old movie? Read it somewhere? He might have disregarded the words if not for the odd cast of them. He believes the real Rose would say to him, "Sure. I slept with someone. Does it matter?"

Upon rising that night, he writes: "The thing I hate about dreaming is that you never dream about what you want to dream. I don't want to dream about Rose's bed. Actually, I'd rather dream about whether Alaine and Kene are ever going to pay me back, whether they've charmed me as Idrissa suggests. I want to dream about Kevin and how his boy, Dylan, is dealing with the leukemia, or whether I should spend some of my ill-used and rapidly vanishing grant money on French classes at the University of Dakar or fly back to see Rose.

"Another thing I don't like about dreaming is that it's more interesting than life. It shimmers with meaning, though God knows the meaning. But its grass is green as malachite, like Astroturf. Dreamwater is perfectly black, perfectly blue, perfectly gray or clear. Dreamsex is deeper, more engrossing, more intense than real sex.

"I often fall asleep to the sound of the Kourmans fucking. They were at it tonight, in fact. They fuck like newlyweds. Kene shrieks like nothing I've heard. She keens; she wails like violent weather. The first time I heard it, I thought I was hearing the yowl of a panther, and my blood tore through my body, my heart split like glass. There's terror in her voice, and love, too. In my head I see Alaine plow deep inside her, sparking an ancient ribbon of nerves that few men seek or even unwittingly find. Nerves that stretch from their bodies to mine to the world's navel. It arouses me, unstrings me. Perhaps it's what makes me dream. Tonight as my African brother and sister, my cousins, my parents, whatever, had sex, I plunged into sleep and rose from it, in this tiny dark room, with these images in my head:

"Invited Rose for dinner. Rose and her brother, Mike, actually. The two of them discovered my deepest, darkest secret: that I ate human flesh. I don't remember whose, how often, how much. But I do remember the sandwich, its meat sliced from the flank of some body on the kitchen table. I ate the hamlike flesh— fatty, meatpink, cold, as I crouched in the kitchen while my friends drank wine in the living room. When Mike and Rose found me, I slunk out the kitchen entrance and into the living room. Later, I went back to the kitchen, and my wife and brother-in-law were gone, but my sister, Rita, her lover, Chloe, and my niece, Syria, were there, gazing with disgust at the body.

Chloe berated me for being a cannibal. Or at least that seemed to be the reason for her criticism at first, but later it came out that she thought I was boring, and that I was creepy, that she had never liked me, nor could she imagine ever liking me, that she and Rita should keep Syria away from me. Rita defended me, but Chloe would not be moved. I hid in the bathroom until they left. And when they did, I stepped into the middle of the kitchen, which was now a pizza parlor.

"Approached a black man wearing a red beret and looking at me with sad bloodshot eyes. He sat at my table as if waiting to be served. 'You're in my way,' he said and pointed in the direction to which my back was turned. I spun around and saw there was a stage upon which Diana Ross and the Supremes were singing "Love Child." Diana danced lewdly. Even lay on the floor, opened her legs, and fingered herself. She moved across the floor, supine, knees drawn up to her shoulders, rolled as if on wheels. I stiffened like a bull. Suddenly I noticed that Ross was no longer wiry, brittle, bony, but took on the voluptuous hips, breasts, and lips, the broad shoulders, the almond eyes of Kene, and we made love right there on the floor. I lifted her blouse, kissed her stomach, brushed my fingers over her lips; I slowly unwrapped her blue pagne skirt, and she rolled once, twice, and again; so I kissed her across her waist, and down between her globes, and ran my cheeks across them. Three moles, faint hair just above her tailbone. She removed her blouse and her bra and rose up on hands and knees.

"When I was inside her and we'd built up the right heat, she began to make those god-awful noises. I tried to shush her because I knew the man at the table was Alaine, and I thought that if I could keep her silent he wouldn't notice us. But Alaine tapped me on the shoulder, and when I turned he was with Rose, who said that strange thing about sex with older men. I started so violently I awoke.

"Awoke frowsy, sweaty, hot, rank, bitter, horny, pissed off. It was as if I'd been washed upon the shore of someone else's consciousness. I was surprised to find myself still here. I dressed in my underwear and sandals, took cigarettes and matches, left my room. I stepped into the living room, crossed to the foyer. I stood outside Kene and Alaine's door, listened to the rattle of their sleep for a moment, then stepped outside. It was still as the moon outside, but not as quiet. My ears filled up with cricket trills, the whir of frogs, the hiss of cicadas, the heavy thrum of night, which rumbles just beneath hearing. I looked up at the stars and found Orion, gazed at him till my cigarette burned to the filter. I went back into the house and again stood in front of the Kourmans' bedroom door. It was still quiet in there, but this time, too quiet. I sensed they were awake. And sure enough, I heard Alaine mumble something, and his wife mumble something in reply. Her whisper was sharp as a stick in the eye. I heard her say, in French, 'I did not!' Then two beats later, 'I do not! I do not! He's ugly. He smells.'

"I went back to my room, dressed, and walked down to the Masatta Samb hotel. I went to call Rose. I believed I'd figured things out."

Hey.

Hi.

Reading? Sounds like your reading voice.

I was in the shower, actually.

I'm sorry, sweetheart. Should I call back?

I'm fine. Got my robe on, shades are down.

Get my letter?

I've gotten several. The last one came Tuesday. I haven't had time to read it, but—

Oh, thanks.

Well.

I know, I know, I write too fucking much.

Don't be angry.

I just wanna know what you mean by that, Rose.

Bird, I don't want to go into all this now. I'm in the middle of—

Reading for your thesis, I know, but I just feel sick inside. All the time. I can't explain any of the things I write in my journals. They're just thoughts. They come and go.

That one comes more often than it goes.

You had no business reading my stuff! Goddamnit. It's private. It's *private*. Do you know what that—

Don't make me hang up, Bertrand.

God, please don't hang up. I stayed up all night to talk to you.

You stay up anyway.

You're divorcing me, aren't you?

Are we married?

Look, I love you. The fact I could leave my journals and stuff just lying around the house means I trust you and love you.

I'm happy to hear you trust me, Bertrand.

Will you quit calling me "Bertrand."

You have an African name now?

So we're gonna be *that* way, huh?

I'm sorry. I'm sorry . . .

(Long, long silence)

Bird, I do love you, too, but I don't think this is working. I think we—

Aw, jeez, Rosie, no.

It just isn't. I think I made a mistake in marrying you.

Can't you see I'm changing? Read my letters. I'm working on my—

We've both got things to work out.

Two clichés for the price of one.

Pardon?

Jesus, Jesus, Jesus. Nothing. I didn't say anything. Do you have a lawyer, I mean, how far along are you with this thing?

All I'm saying is that I have some thinking to do. I'm in no hurry. Listen, I've got some bad news for you . . .

———

N'Gor village
Aug 17, 1985

Dear Kevin (and Dear Cha),

I called Rose today, and she barely talked to me. She did tell me about Dylan, though. I am sorry. I don't know what to say. Almost everything I could say you already know: He was just a baby. It isn't fair. Just barely old enough to say, "I love you, Daddy; love you, Mommy." Just started walking. The pictures Rose sent me break my heart so much I couldn't look at them today. Everything I write seems so obvious, and I figure you're sitting there with your right hand upthrust and your left scratching your beard in the usual way, and you're saying, "And? And?"

I'm sorry. I'm just sorry. I'm sad.

I know you can't write. How could you? I can't afford to call you. I've already blown my budget, and this morning I called Rose and it cost me a hundred dollars. I shouldn't have called Rose, but my letters don't seem to be getting through to her. I'll write two or three a week, and she answers a couple times a month or less. I guess you'll be hurt to know that while I've found the time to write Rose three or four letters a week, I haven't sent you so much as a postcard, but I don't want to lie to you. I haven't been a good friend at all, Kevin. Maybe Rose has told you, maybe not, but she's been seriously contemplating divorce, and that's got most of my attention. So just as you can't write right now, I can't get any work done. I was going great guns for the first three months, like I told you, but since I got this brutally short, angry letter from Rose I can't do anything but write her letters, smoke cigarettes, stare at the ocean. I still keep a journal, of course, write down all my hopes and worries and hide from the world, like that guy in *Sherman's March to the Sea,* who could never come out from behind his camera. I see myself in every flawed character I've seen in the movies or read of in books. You can't imagine how shitty I feel about myself.

I know you're in pain, man, but I miss you. I need you. Am I being selfish? I mean, clearly you're carrying the greater pain, ~~but~~ See, Kevin, I've been afraid that part of the reason I haven't heard from you directly, that I only hear from you through Rose, is that you no longer respect me because I pissed on family, while you've been going through the fight of your life to keep your own family whole.

You're a good man, a faithful husband, and maybe you'll never understand why I did what I did. All I really want to do is try to explain what your absence in my life feels like. It's like food without salt, rhythm without melody, like waking up and finding someone has painlessly, bloodlessly removed a leg. With your absence has come the excision of twenty years of my life. Full-blown stories are shrunk to anecdotes.

Since you and Cha share everything, I know, Cha, that Kevin'll be reading this letter to you, or that he'll hand it over when he's done with it. Far cry from the mystery man here, who won't live with his own wife, keeps boxes within boxes, struggles for secrecy as billions struggle for closeness. So anyway, the "story" I'm about to tell, your husband can certainly corroborate. But I tell it, mainly for you. Cha, I mean. It's the Red Barn story, Kev. I know you remember it, but since you don't even like to discuss it with me, I'm betting you haven't told Cha about it.

But before I tell it, I want you to know that I see it differently since a peculiar thing began to happen to me a month ago. Lately I've begun to have dreams, and as Kevin knows, I've made my dreamless life the basis of nearly all my beliefs or disbelief. I've never believed in God or put much stock in the subconscious, or metaphysical pseudoscience. I've always disparaged my fellow black Americans who come to Africa seeking some spiritual whatever. I'm certainly not saying I believe in these things now. But I can say that these dreams now give me a new understanding of my relationship with your husband, with Rose, with my own work, and give me a kind of pause I've never before had.

This was about three years before you two met, two years before Kev and I graduated from Colorado College. It was October, a cold clear evening, and Kev and I had been studying for "midterms," which at C.C. meant two weeks into the term, with about a week and a half to go. I was in my own apartment studying American religions, Kevin in his, studying Spinoza's ethics. It was getting on toward 10 P.M., and I hadn't eaten anything since noon. I dog-eared the Michael Novak I'd been poring over, walked up the hall to Kev's joint, and asked him whether he'd like to join me for some fast food. Our intention was to ride to McDonald's, have a couple of their large sleeping pills between buns, and return to our respective flats to snooze. It was fairly chilly. I was dressed in clogs, olive-green military trousers made of wool, and a rather funky, fuzzy short-waisted sweater. Kevin wore some kind of car coat, hard brown shoes, a plaid shirt, and jeans.

I'm not sure Kevin's clothing is important to this story, Cha, but mine is, for I assumed for quite some time that my dress might have accounted for the strange thing that happened that night. Kevin looked like Kevin, a really normal guy: thick, auburn beard, shaggy 70's hair—blondish, middle-parted, thinning. A handsome, roundish Irish face, large and rounded shoulders. Glittery hazel eyes. You've seen the pictures, I'm sure. You know he wasn't always the three-piece ad man. But I was dressed so differently from him that I believed our sartorial contrast led to our night's troubles. I was looking gay-bohemian.

There was always something Mutt and Jeffish about Kev and me, especially in college, and I think we gathered more than our share of sideways glances and second looks. At least I think we did, for I was horrendously self-conscious, as was Kevin, and I used to imagine that because interracial buddies were relatively rare outside the few acres of the Colorado College campus, people must have thought we were cops or gay.

Anyhow, that night we were neither in law enforcement nor homosexual, but ravenous, and though the McD's was only seven or eight blocks away, it was, as I said, almost ten. And things clam up tight in Colorado Springs at about ten. "Know a shortcut," I told Kevin, and we slapped my car doors tight and blew out of the apt. complex. I went straight from Nevada, past Wahsatch, and hit the alley east of Wahsatch. I zapped down the alley, one two three, and we got to McD's in time to see them shut off the lights. "No biggie," I said and kept on down the alley toward this place called the Red Barn, an erstwhile western fast-food chain that served not only burgers but fried chicken and hot dogs. "Good deal," Kev said, "I'm in the mood for some bird." One more alley to go, and suddenly, I realize there's fog everywhere. It was so thick, I switched on my high beams, and of course, made things worse. Couldn't see a thing. I lowered the beam and crawled on until I got to Platte Street, and right across the street, there was the Red Barn—its barn-shaped roof and plate-glass double doors—under the pinkish yellow light pulsing from its red-and-white neon sign. Though it struck me as odd a few days later, at the time I didn't find it peculiar at all that there wasn't a shred of fog on the opposite side of Platte where the restaurant stood. We pulled up and walked in through the glass doors.

The long counter was to our left, and at the end of it, the register, attended by a teenage cashier. There was a line of about four people in front of her, three white teens, and a fairly tall, 30-ish ultra-black man, wearing a dark-blue pea coat and a watch cap of the same color, ragged beard, eyes so red, the first thing I thought was, Junkie. But as black people tend to do in places like Colorado Springs, I nodded to him, even mumbled, "Wuz happ'nin'," too, though I knew he wasn't close enough to hear me.

Rather than return the customary nod, he gazed at me with eyes both snide and severe, held his mouth the way we do when accosted by bad smells. His eyes were so red, Cha. Like plum meat. They made my stomach bunch tight. I stopped, flushed, turned left, faced the counter. Kevin, who'd been behind me, was now to my left, and we began to study the menu board, but for my own part, because of the sinister look the "brother" had given me, I couldn't focus on a thing. Kevin later told me he'd felt the same way, but not because of the black man, but because, little by little, we noticed that everyone in the place was staring at us. Everyone. And it was such a certainty that neither of us felt the need to turn our heads to the right, to meet the gazes of the kid behind the register, the kids before it, the red-eyed man, and behind the kids, the other customers, whom I neglected to mention, who sat at their tables and stared as though headless wraiths had floated in. Not a single one of them ate, moved, spoke. The very air stopped to observe us.

The first thing I thought was (and I tell you, I thought so many things in those first few seconds that time must have lain dead for ten minutes): They think we're cops, and the black man is robbing the place. no. stupid. self-hating. think we're gay. look how I'm dressed. clogs! for God's sake. woolly, short-waisted sweater. military trousers. no, they're afraid. to move. to breathe. jeez-God. they can't move. we can't move.

I looked out the joint of my eye at Kevin and saw his Adam's apple roll up and then down. He was so white his beard looked black. I felt nearly paralyzed but managed to say, "You see anything good?" Kev shook his head. "Me neither," I said. And without turning to face me, he said, "Let's get outta here."

We made a left face toward the door, and, of course, Kevin was out first. But I have the habit of pushing open pneumatic doors with my back, so I spun, looked at the room. Still not a soul moving in the restaurant. As I backstepped to the car, I could see, through the row of tall windows along the kitchen, a boy in paper hat and smock carrying a black plastic garbage bag. With every forward step he took toward the front of the restaurant, I took a backward step toward the car. Kevin, I believe, was already at the car, and he told me to hurry up. But as he was speaking, the boy saw us. He dropped the bag, stopped, and stared. My head thumped with blood, and I stopped walking. The boy walked up to the window with what I could only call fear-stiffened legs, because he rocked, rather than walked, to the window. He pressed his face up to the glass, cupped his hands around it, stared with big eyes. I raised my arm, pointed at the boy. "Kevin," I said, "look how this dude's looking at us, man."

"Let's just go, Bird!"

"Just check out this one guy."

"Let's go!"

So we went. Back the same way we'd come, in fact. I did it unthinkingly, and so back through the one foggy alley, back through the several clear ones, cross Wahsatch, left on Nevada. We never did get anything to eat that night. I sat with Kevin at his place and tried to get him to talk to me about it, but he spoke mostly in monosyllables. I told him all the things that had run through my mind: "You think they thought we were criminals, cops, gays? You know, Kevo, all those types that get people all het up?" Kevin told me I was way off. Then he told me, with his eyes, with the way he fingered his red beard, the way he sat jittering, smoking, rocking himself, saying, almost to himself, "Hmm, *that* was different," that what had happened to us was much bigger than I had known, much weirder, perhaps, than I could ever understand.

But I've only come to realize now that Kevin and I experienced a dream while awake, while hungry and sobered by October cold. I swear on what's left of my honor that it was real. See, Kevin knew this, and I did not. Now, I understand that his eyes were saying to me, brother, you just don't know. This is unique. This doesn't happen. Can't you see where we were? What we both did?

I went looking for answers, so—now here's the kicker, Cha. Here's the part where old sci-fi movies start playing that harmonium thing, or whatever—that singing insect that crawls up a baby boomer's spine—I drove to the place at the end of the term (eleven days or so later). I was going to sit down in the place, have a meal, watch people, interview them if I had to. I had my pen, my yellow legal pad. I was going to get the story straight and bring it back to Kevin, say to the man, "Can you believe how dumb we were? Check this out . . ."

But I found a locked door, dust-covered, greasy windows,

stools unscrewed from the filthy floor. I walked from the door to the kitchen, where the boy and I had met, and could make out rusted cutlery sitting atop the grease-matted grill, a bucket on wheels, a desiccated mop near it. I saw two years of desuetude, not a whisper of recent human activity or care. I backed away from the window in the same way I had, just eleven days before, and noticed that a whole glass plate on the right side of the door had been replaced with plywood. The wood was weathered gray, peeling and buckling. The big red-and-white neon sign had been decimated by stone throwers and wind, its gray neon guts exposed.

When I got back to the apartment complex, I raced up to Kevin's place, and when he let me in, I said, "You gotta go back to the Red Barn with me."

Kevin wasn't having it. Before I even told him my reasons, he said, "Look, that place gives me serious creeps, Bird. I'm not interested."

I told him about what I'd seen, and he seemed intrigued and uncomfortable for about two minutes, and then suddenly his face went blank and he looked bored. He said something like: "Bert, there's no explaining any of this. I guarantee you, the deeper you go, the deeper you'll be, and you'll have no place to go but deeper still. Think about it awhile, then absorb it."

I had no idea what you meant. Tell you the truth, Kevin, I just thought you were afraid. But you weren't. You just knew something I didn't, something that you can't explain in the literal sense. I don't mean to blame my troubles with Rose on the fact I never dreamed, but I've dreamed of her so much, I know that part of myself is trying to tell another part what I should do. But this is all too confusing and new for me to do by myself. I ask my friend Idrissa, and he just tells me that dreams mean you're asleep, but if that's true, then what you and I went through didn't happen. That it wouldn't have meaning. And I believe it does have less meaning without you.

I know you're hurting, man. I know you are, but I need your help. I need someone to tell these dreams to. I need your wisdom to help me figure out how to fix my marriage. You always put up with all my garbage whenever I'd break up with someone and find someone new. (I figure he's already told you, Cha, that I swung from woman to woman, like Tarzan and his vines, while we were in college. I suppose he's told you, ~~and maybe Rose, too,~~ that I'm a serial relationshiper, committed to one woman at a time, and then not.) ~~I don't mean to accuse you, Kevin, but if you do tell others, I wouldn't blame you.~~ Fuck, fuck fuck fuck fuck fuck *FUCK*. Kevin, I just realized I can't send this letter to you. What's the death of my ego compared to the death of Dylan? And to tell you the truth, I want things both ways. I want to save my marriage—I would even live with her (ironic as that word "even" sounds), turn over all my journals to her, let her into my dreams, if I could, but there's something here I have to do. I just have to. Don't tell my wife, eh?

Only semisincerely, the Best I Can Do—

Love,
Bert

————

He is both asleep and awake, hallucinatory with weariness. Hungry, too. He lies here burning, for the Kourmans are at it again. His eyes snap themselves shut. Abruptly, he is in flight, thirty-seven thousand feet in the air. The plane's body is a hollow sausage, held aloft by spatula wings. He dreams that he's dizzy with insomnia, rigid with hunger, yet he knows that he is back in bed, dreaming—and dreaming, he is awake. Both asleep and awake. This is something he has never experienced, a new kind of dreaming, and he hates it. He is miles high—no sense of movement—listening to the talking man, a journalist, he thinks. But he's afraid the man's words, at times, are warped by the wash of chemicals, the enzymes, the hormones that pull him toward a second sleep. Sleep inside sleep.

The journalist's features appear to him in disjointed flashes. They never fall together. Wide nose festooned with freckles, tired cat-green eyes, rust beard, small ears, short 'fro, small feminine hands. The man says, "Ever been there before?" and points to the floor, and Bertrand can see through the glass bottom of the fuselage. Out the windows it is still black, but below, he can see everything, the ocean, the crisscross of roads, vegetation tightly woven as moss. "Been here more than I can count, my man," he says against Bertrand's silence. "What you see depends on where you go. . . . Folklore, huh? Well, you gonna learn more than folklore, I'll bet." He pauses, squints at Bertrand. "So I guess you'll be living in the villages and whatnot, huh?"

He tells the man he doesn't know, but that he'll contact people at the University of Dakar and maybe the embassy, too. "Screw embassy people," the man says. "I know embassy people; ain't worth the time. Plantation mentality. Neocolonialists. They're the last ones you wanna ask about Africa. Strike out on your own. Take it in; drink it up. You'll like it. Can't help but. It's home, homey. Drink deep, young man. What you see depends on where you go. Lemme show you." He points to the floor and says: "Look how the colors squeeze tears from your eyes. All those people in lemon, saffron, watermelon, cobalt, gold, kelly, scarlet. Listen to 'em laugh; see their ivory teeth; listen to the sounds of Citroëns, Subarus, Muslim prayers, buses, car rapides; smell the cattle, the spermy ocean; feel the thunder of dance; breathe the ochre dust; talk politics with that group of khaftan-clad men. Not them guys. Those. Yeah, see?

"Yeah, I'm going to Banjul to cover the aftermath of the coup, good brother. You heard about the coup? Yeah, Jawara made a mess a things, am I right? Didn'e? I don't figure this Senegambia jazz gonna last anoth—ooh, look at those spiders. Good God! I wouldn't want one a them on my neck. Could strangle you with them long legs. Ooh, taste those citrons, those guavas, those little bananas; here, slip on that boubou, that grass-green number there. You look sharp, young blood. Make you look Africano all the way. Go on into it, go deep; chew that kola nut; smoke those Lucky Strikes; steer clear of those military men; eat that white, white rice." He points out thing after thing, and Bertrand can taste it, hear it, see it, smell it, feel it all. It's exhausting—poverty, palm trees, Brahma bulls, millet, gyros, pot. The people. Polyrhythmic drums and koras. Cafés, fetid jails. Cornrowed women, soccer games, reggae, soul eaters, Bata stores. Fresh fish, sweet clams, Gauloises, and Etoile de Dakar. Turkeys, goats, baboons, chickens bound tight as electric coils. Cobalt water, sixty-thousand-franc refrigerators. Kene, Mammi, Alaine. He does go on.

And he's not the only speaking traveler, now. There is this woman, too. A big beige woman in lime-green leisure, hair the color of ginger, blood fingertips. Luggage-large hips and thighs, a voice to bore holes through rock, a mole beneath the eye. She means to whisper, says, "Baby, you just don't know," says, "Them niggers sure can do," says, "Got dicks as big as wrists," says, "And black? Real black like lava stones," says, "tar pits, mine shafts, belts, and heels. Not that faded shit you see in Jersey. Make a woman out you, darlin' dear."

Bertrand is naked now and sitting next to the woman. He's erect, huge. The flight attendant rolls her cart just past Bertrand and the beige woman, and slowly disrobes, as the beige woman thumps her finger against Bertrand's erection. "Solid," the beige woman says. "Every woman need the solid thing. Wanna ride, sugar?" And the flight attendant straddles Bertrand. She rides him as the beige woman whoops, shrieks, and hollers: "Look at 'im. Look at 'im. Look at 'im go! Was I lying, girl? Go like that all night long."

"Whut we gwine do," breathes the journalist, "'bout loud-moufin cullid folk like dat dar?" Bertrand tries to smile, but it feels more like a wince. He sees that he is back in his clothes, back in his seat next to the journalist, but the sex across the aisle is still going on. The people across the aisle are standing around the couple as they continue to screw, and they're all holding drinks, making bets, rolling dice, throwing money on the plane seat, which is now a billiard table. The naked couple is Kene and Alaine. Alaine is smoking a cigarette as his wife rides him, and Kene is crying.

The journalist scrapes his beard just so, with index and middle fingers. He sniffs and says, in a perfect British accent, clipped and round and square where it ought to be, "They'll foul the continent, old man." Bertrand lists toward sleep, a sleep inside sleep, and everything slides across the floor of his brain. "Yeah," he says, "they will."

"You'll like it down there," the man says in his own voice. "You'll learn just who you are." And consciousness slips with flashes of light amid gray mist. Slips with a crackling sound like power lines at night. Slips, and he dreams his sleepless self.

Siesta Repast

Alaine is twenty paces from me. He has just stepped off the bus, noon lunch. It is my plan to take the bus to the airport restaurant, since I'm growing increasingly sore about the constraints of "family" life. I want to be alone. I want nothing. I know Alaine will certainly try to persuade me to stay home for the meal. He sees me, moves right to me with his slender, soldierlike stride, sunglasses, trouser creases splitting air like butcher knives. I rarely see him dressed this well. If I were curious, I'd ask him why. Velvet head cut smooth like a cue tip, goatee tight as macramé, glassy shoes, lotion thinskin glaze. And here I am all bushes and brown rice, general unkemptness, dashiki madness, chicken bound, weakneed. The heat suffocates me, softens me flesh to bone. You can't fight a man in these rags.

"Bertrand," he says, "where do you go? Doh lekk?" I tell him I have errands to run in town, but he "reminds" me that nothing will be open till three, when siesta ends. "Well," I say, "the airport stores stay open."

And as he lights a cigarette, he says, "Too expensive. What you need? I get it for you tonight." He removes his shades and focuses on my chest, rather than my eyes, and he says, "You spend too much money. We have got to start being more careful with the money."

I slowly close my eyes, inhale, and slowly open them. I say, "I think we need to talk about—"

"In fact," he says, looking me in the eye this time, "I think I should tell you something important. Come on, I buy you what you need in town. Later." I relent as easily as I thought I would. Must be the bound-chicken thing.

He leads, and I followed him across the road and past the little mom-and-pop store where I often buy bug spray, candles, canned milk, and meat, cigarettes and matches; past the big locust trees and the hedge of bougainvillea; past the shanty where an old man and his son live; past the twelve-room house where the Samb family live; past the mosque, where the muezzin is now calling the devout to prayer; down the sandy path that leads to "our" place. "Listen," Alaine says, before we enter the courtyard. "Listen," he says again, "don't, don't, *don't* tell Kene, but I am feared I might lose my job. I don't know of certain, but the political situation at my work is not good."

I am only vaguely aware of what Alaine does for a living, some kind of clerical work in one of the ministry offices in town. I do know that when he says "political," he doesn't mean his inability to suck up to the right people. He means that he's often held in ill regard for his national political views. He's a member of the Senegalese Democratic Party, which the dominant party, the Progressive Senegalese Union, deemed (along with every other party) illegal up to the midseventies or so. None of the lesser parties is still thought fully legitimate or acceptable by the dominant powers, and Alaine isn't shy about expressing his views.

He doesn't appear to be upset in the least, but it's clear that he's more than a little concerned. "We must be careful with money until things look better," he says.

"Well," I say, "I'm pretty careful as it is. You're asking me to give more to Kene each week? Is that it?" Why do I acquiesce this way? Why can't I show him how angry I am? There I was imagining kicking him all the way to the beach, screaming, "Motherfucker, I got two thousand fuckin' dollars left to get me through the next nine months, and you're asking me—the guy who paid for your fucking Kenmore—to be more careful with my money?" But instead I speak to him in a manner almost hymeneal. Me, the new Mrs. Kourman, hermaphrodite he-bride, obliged to be both fruitful and husbandly.

Alaine tosses his cigarette butt to the ground and steps on it. "Not now," he says. "The money is same as normal for now."

"Um, that's good, see, because—"

"Things are good now. The food is inexpensive because we fish. I buy a gun in town for hunting, too. It's old but very good. You can buy more bullets later. To pay me back."

OKaaaay, I'm thinking, while he's running his stupid, fucking mouth, I can buy underwear, which you can wear for me. I'll give you all my rubbers if you promise to let me use 'em when you've finished with 'em. I'll eat your goddamn digested rice. My anger is right here, right in my hands, my belly, my heart, but I can't pull it up. I stand here and listen to him spending my money, and I keep getting madder and madder, but listen, for the most part, as though we are in full accord.

He says, ". . . and the rent is, for me and my wife, very good."

"Can't complain. Thirty thousand CFA is extremely cheap compared to what I paid in the States. Back there I—"

He clutches me by the arm. His eyes are big. "You are paying thirty thousand?"

"Sure."

He releases my arm and raises his hand to his brow. "Wyyyy! Too much. Too much. For that little room, you pay thirty thousand?"

"It's not just the room, you know, but—"

"You pay what we pay for the two *big* rooms." He grabs my arm again and looks me dead in the eye. "You must talk to Monsieur N'Doye. He charge you too much. Too, too much."

"But Idrissa told me the price was fair for, you know . . . He said the price was good. And it's nowhere near what I was paying in the U.S."

"He do this to you?"

"Idi? Sure. Yes. He interpreted for me, but he didn't set the price. It's just that, you know, compared to what I paid back home, it's pretty reasonable."

"No, no, no, no, it's not. It's not reasonable at all. Idi know. He know! You must get you rent lower. He's take advantage of you. Too much. Too expensive. Idi know this. He know this. You have the smallest room. Even fifteen thousand is too high." He's getting extremely worked up, and, of course, so am I, only we express it in diametric ways. While he paces with his head lowered, his brow knitted as if he were feeling not only disgust but pain, I stand motionless, watching his squat shadow weave the ground like a fish weaves water. I hold my face without expression, if such a thing is possible, but my guts quiver, my teeth crack. I come this close to crying.

"Alaine! Bertrand! Come and eating!" Kene hollers from across the yard. She smiles at me as I step within a few feet of her. "I am use English," she says, smiling as pretty as love itself.

We have a dish I have never seen before, small eggplants and carrots, onions, and some kind of fowl in a bed of rice. The bird is small, about the size of a raven. Perhaps a bit larger, and its flesh is dark, almost the color of liver. "What's this?" I ask Kene, but it's Alaine who answers me. "Yassa," he says.

"I mean the fowl, the bird."

"Chicken. Yassa is chicken."

I poke at it with my spoon. "Smells good, Kene," I say in Wolof, but I make no attempt to eat it. All I can think of is the stupid red-eyed glare of the bound chicken.

"Mammi!" Alaine barks. "You can't just eat the carrots."

Mammi says, "The toubob isn't eating either."

"Mammi," Kene says, "he isn't a toubob; he's a black man."

"Eat," says Alaine.

Mammi forms a small rice ball in her hand and eats it. I lift a spoonful of rice and eat it, staring down at the chicken.

Kene peels a little chicken flesh from the thighbone, then takes some rice, and forms a ball. She holds it out to me. I hold out my spoon to receive the ball, but she gently nudges my hand aside, and says, "Open your mouth, Berdt." My gaze travels up her bare arm, to her collarbones, to her lips, to her eyes. "No thank you," I say. I glance at Alaine. His jaw ripples, his nostrils flare. He says nothing, just eats. "Is it the same chicken?" I say.

"Chicken is chicken," Alaine says. "Why is everyone being so stupid today?"

I say, "I just want to know where the thing's from. I mean—"

Kene lowers her arm. "Look, Alaine," she says, "we have two babies. You think I would poison you?"

Alaine drops his spoon onto the floor cloth, springs up from the floor, and slams into the master bedroom. And without a flicker of interest in her husband, Kene raises the rice ball and says sweetly, sweetly, sweetly, "Bertrand, doh lekk?" I open my mouth like some kind of automaton, and she feeds me.

chapter 4

Insomnium

Aug. 29, '85

Dear Rose,

I try particularly hard, these days, to keep my letters to you brief. Since I write so frequently, I should at least try to be concise. That's real hard for me to do. And maybe I should wait for you to write me again. I shouldn't keep answering your last letter over and over again. But here I write. Can't help myself, I suppose.

Rose, I don't understand this, as you once called it over the phone, "sudden, great love" I have for you any more than you do. Though it might seem so, though I might even fear it sometimes, it isn't obsessive. Overbearing maybe, too late perhaps, maybe even bizarre, and clearly one-sided now, but I'm not obsessed.

For the past several months I've felt that there is some one thing I did that I could take back, or some one thing I could say. But you can't undo sex, and words are clearly not doing the deed. When I left, I was so certain that you were deeply in love with me, despite what I'd done. I expected many letters from you. And I thought that each of us would do a lot of hemming and hawing, trying to figure out what we could do to straighten things out between us.

It felt so good to be sitting in those airports, this summer past, being paged to those white phones. It made me feel like God's buddy. My own mother wouldn't have called me at the airport, but you, Rose, you did. It made me want to write you every week. Why did you call me at Stapleton, and La Guardia, and say all those nice things if you didn't—I don't know what to say anymore. Here I am stuck with this great love for you, and I don't know what to say or do for myself.

Help me, will you? I don't even know how to write this letter. I'm in trouble here. The folks I live with, people I've lived with for the past two and a half months, seem like decent people, but I don't know if I can trust them. Same goes for my assistant, Idrissa, the guy I've been mooning over for all these months.

Good, you'll say. Serves you right. Maybe you'll know how it feels to trust, then suddenly to not trust. I don't know what I'm doing or saying in these letters to you. I'm alone here. I'm too much inside myself, too inside my head. I'd like to think that if I hadn't slept with Jewel, you'd be writing me every week, and we'd be OK, but I'm probably kidding myself. But, Rosebaby, it was just that once, and I owned up to it. I could have lied, said it was fantasy, accused you of being crazy. When you told me it didn't matter, I knew you were being kind. I knew I'd pay, too. I'm paying big.

I dream now.

A few nights ago I had this dream, and I want to tell you about it because I figure it might help me explain why I did what I did to you and to me. Here it is:

I was in Manhattan, and I was supposed to give this paper at some university nearby, though I don't remember the topic. It was a cloudy day, and I was thinking of it as a typical N.Y. day, as if I know what that is. Well, I was nervous about being in N.Y., intimidated by the whole thing: riding subways, reading before a black-clad, fedora-wearing, cigar-chewing N.Y. audience, and I freaked out and went back to my hotel.

When I got back, though, it was immediately evident to me that someone had been in my room. Then it was apparent that the person was still there. It turned out it was the cleaning woman, young, tall, gorgeous, the same skin color as me, perfect build. For some foolish reason I began speaking to her with an Italian accent. We seduced each other and ended up making love on the floor. She'd never had a person go down on her, so I did, and she climaxed. I know this must be making you uncomfortable, but there's no sense in me expurgating a dream, Rose.

I dressed afterward and went to the university to give the paper, but never actually got there. Again I went back to my hotel, and there, in my room, I found the woman and her boyfriend, a light-skinned, tall, bearded man. He told me he'd heard me speaking when I checked into the hotel, and that I certainly hadn't had an Italian accent. I tried other accents, but they weren't buying it. They said, Just speak in your own voice. I did, but they didn't seem to like it.

Then later, still in N.Y., you and I went fishing in a polluted river. The East, I guess. I selected your fly and tied it on. I showed you where to cast. You caught one almost immediately. It was a stupefyingly ugly, diseased fish, whose gray-white skin was falling off, whose eyes were like white beads. It smelled like rot and motor oil, and I cut your line and let it fall back into the black water.

That's pretty much it, Babe. And since I'm not used to dreaming, you can't expect much from me in terms of my interpretive skills. I think it's pretty clear, though, what it means, and all I can say is I'm sorry for being what I've been and doing what I've done. Please, please, please forgive me, if you can, and I'll speak to you in my own voice from now on, and I'll take you to clear waters and lead you to pretty fish—rainbows, greenbacks, speckleds. We'll reel them in and let them go. I don't ask you to love me. Just talk to me.

Already I've gone on too long with this letter. But it probably doesn't matter. I'm sure you don't read the goddamn things anymore, all this microscopic scribbling on graph paper. It must look insane. None of it makes sense, and, you know, I hate dreaming. But it does make you think.

Please write me.

Love,
Bert

He walks the beach. He looks at things. The sun's crown is brass-orange on the horizon, and the ocean is coppery glass flecked, now and then, with mango, rose, violet, silver . . . actually, every color he can name, if he stares long enough. It's as though the world is blank, the world is white, and from that whiteness, color and shape intermittently thrust themselves at the eyes. Watermelon, turquoise, sand, olive, cherry, sand. Sometimes white wings shred themselves from the air in a great flock, swirl and loop and dive. They might become a great amoeba, then a cloud. Salmon, pearl, forest, peach, butter, tar, sand. Four large pelicans rise from the strand like mushrooms, huddle on the darkening beach like hoodlums. He looks at them, he looks at everything, really, as though he means to collect them, store them away till he can better see and understand them while he sleeps. Sand, smoke, cherry, grape, lemon, sand. Take them to the black wall of sleep, hold them up as you would hold cleary marbles between your eye and the light. It makes more sense to him now. Seeing, hearing, tasting, touching, smelling make more sense now.

As he nears the pelicans, he hears Idrissa call his name. He stops but doesn't turn toward Idrissa. He doesn't move. He watches the pelicans. He watches the seagulls. He closes his eyes and sees odd things, unfamiliar things, both dark and bright, sharp edged and curved, the fabric of future dreams, perhaps. He opens his eyes and turns to see Idrissa galloping toward him. It strikes him as odd to see Idrissa running, never having seen him run before. Idrissa ambles, he plods, he lopes, on occasion he even struts, but run, no. He turns away from his assistant and gazes at the four hoodlums again. Perhaps in the clear black of night they will be four witches at a cauldron or a snowstorm on the beach. Perhaps he'll carry one on a subway, or eat her eggs, or run in terror from her. Whatever she'll be, however he'll see her, she'll be no less real than what she appears to be in clear light, for she'll be shot through with him, his needs, his fears, his memories. *My bird.* His creation. *Mine.*

Idrissa claps a hand on his shoulder and says, "You need to go home." He sounds excited and sad and weary, all at once. Despite Bertrand's desire to tell him to screw himself, he turns and says: "Some tribe somewhere on this continent, my good buddy, says something like, 'Home is not where I am born, but where it goes well for me.' In my case, I'd say, 'Home is not where I live, but where I live alone.'"

Idrissa folds his arms over his chest and jerks his head toward the village. "It's a bad time for proverbs, Berdt. You should come." And he does, despite himself. He cannot, for some reason, maintain his resentment. *Dreams must melt resentment.* He supposes that it's because what he sees in the clear light is only half of what is to be. There's nothing and no one to judge until we have slept on things.

Kene slaps Alaine so hard his eyes tear up. Her Wolof snaps through the room like a ricocheting pellet. Alaine slaps her left ear twice. He's been smiling, but his smile is only half there, on the lower part of his face, masklike. His red eyes glare hard, sharp, semimurderous. Again he slaps her twice on the left ear, and grabs her arms, which are chopping hard. Alaine tries to pin both her arms under his left arm and tries to slap her again, but Idrissa wedges himself between them and folds his arms around Alaine. Bertrand sees that Alaine is bleeding beneath one eye, and fingernail welts run from his left ear to his beard. Inwardly Bertrand is saying, "Idrissa, what's going on? What's this all about?" But there's no time for asking what's caused all this, no real way to gain purchase on the flying arms, but he lays a hand on Kene's shoulder, slips an arm around her so that his forearm presses her breasts, his thigh her hip. But before he can say, "It's OK, it's OK, calm down," before he can press his lips to her nape, breathe in her fragrance of charcoal and rose oil, before he can ignite himself, before he can tell her she would be his first, his only, the corporeity of his dreams, she spins, knees him in the balls, and arcs across the room as he goes down. He sees the tan soles of her feet, the multicolored pagne skirt blur to a brownish haze as she bolts away. She plucks an empty wine bottle off the sideboard, spins around, and hurls herself back toward Alaine, who won't take his eyes off his wife or relinquish the terrible half smile.

He feels himself rise from the floor and tackle Kene as she crosses in front of him. Her warm, soft fleshiness, her ball-sapping strength, her perspiration, charcoal, rose oil body. He feels something burning beneath his heart. His teeth are clenched. He might cry if he can't hold on. The bottle scatters its green wash across the floor, and green teeth bite his elbow and forearm. Kene rolls away and rises. Alaine breaks away from Idrissa, and husband and wife tumble into each other, scratching, slapping, cuffing, tugging, ripping. Idrissa grabs at Alaine's right arm, misses, grabs for his left. Alaine twirls and pulls away. He dashes to the foyer and out the door. Kene lunges after him. Idrissa and Bertrand follow only to the door and no farther. They watch the couple plunge into the night. Bertrand turns, as if by instinct, and he sees Mammi, the little one, sucking on the second knuckle of her index finger. Her face is wet with tears, but she is silent. Bertrand approaches her, reaches for her, but she backs away. "I'll get Madame N'Doye for her," says Idrissa, and he steps out the house.

————

The house is quiet now, and I am in bed. I'm crushed with fatigue, and Kene's belt to my testicles, and the poor meal I shared with Idrissa tonight, make my stomach queasy and liquid feeling. My elbow and forearm burn, and I'm sure there's still glass to be plucked from them. Of course there had been no dinner tonight, so I walked to the mom-and-pop store with Idrissa to buy fruit, canned meat, and bread. We took our time going there and took our time returning. Somewhere between the course of going and coming, Idrissa told me that the fight had had something to do with Kene's anger over Alaine's Belgian mistress and his dismissal from his job. I think he picked up something about Kene fooling around, too, but I doubt that. Besides, if she were the type to fool around, I'd like it to be with me.

When we returned, we found the Kourman family, and Kene's best friend, Oumi Samb, sitting on the porch, silent and sullen. We made no greetings, and no one greeted us. Kene was dressed in rather formal attire, boubou, headwrap, newish sandals. Oumi was dressed similarly. It was clear that Kene had every intention of leaving. Idrissa sat with them, but I walked inside the house. I saw two suitcases. I turned toward the door and said, "Idi, may I have a word with you?"

I wasn't angry, and I had no idea what I was going to say to him. Idrissa stood and joined me inside. I nodded to the couch, and we sat down heavily as old men. I sat back, crossed my legs, and then I noticed I was jittering with nervousness. "I talked to Alaine the other day," I said, "about the arrangement you helped me make to get this room." I pointed my thumb over my shoulder. "He told me I was paying too much. Way too much." I paused to let the words sink in, to read his face for signs of discomfiture, but Idrissa remained taciturn. I felt anger rise up from my belly, but before I said another word, Idrissa folded his arms and leaned back, tipped his head to the side, and said, "It was too much money for you?"

"That's not the point."

"You said it was three hundred fifty dollars lesser than what you paid in the U.S. You were happy with the price?"

"Idi, that's not my point."

He crossed his legs, stretched an arm across the back of the couch. "Tell me the point," he said.

"I guess I . . . I guess I thought we were friends."

Idrissa looked thoughtful for a moment. He squinted; he shrugged. "Sure. Sure, you and I are friends. But now I must ask you what your point is. I don't understand you."

"Alaine says I'm paying too much for the room. He said you knew that from the start. He said you should have helped me get the place for a cheaper price. That's what a friend would do, Idi . . . goddamn it."

"The rent was not too expensive until Alaine said it was, true?"

"Wait a minute—"

"You were happy until Alaine said these things, true?"

"Idi—"

"Alaine has made you angry with your friend, true?"

"Wait a second. Wait a second—"

"With me you had peace. With Kourman you are not at peace. Why you doubting my friendship? Why you trusting a guy who would break your peace, and not me?" He pointed to his chest with his right hand and turned his left hand, the one resting on the couch, palm up. The sclera of his eyes were red with exhaustion, his brow knitted. He said: "You told me that . . . that the university was paying you, and this other foundation, too, who pay you. I didn't think it was your own money. You spend so much. You give to everybody. What I always tell you when you ask about money? 'Up to you; it's up to you.'" He began nodding. "Yeah," he said, "yeah, but all the time you put this responsibility on me to tell you this and that, and I keep telling you the same thing: 'Up to you.' Can I tell you everything? Am I God?" According to my dreams, all I know is _I'm_ not God.

Before I could answer, the Kourmans and Oumi entered. Kene and Oumi each took a bag. Then Kene held out her hand to Mammi, and Mammi clasped that hand. But Alaine firmly took Mammi's other hand and said in Wolof, "She stays here." Kene pulled. Alaine pulled. They jerked the child back and forth, making her head snap side to side. Idrissa rose from the couch and approached the four with his hands raised. "Not good, not good, not good," he said. I stood and entered my room, thinking, Tonight, let them be his family.

As his bed whirls him toward sleep, he hears Kene shriek. He hears her wail. It is a restful, peaceful, lulling sound, so used is he to it now. They are making love with a fervor that's beyond the usual intensity. She yowls like a night creature. He hums stupid, atonal music, and the bed barks, juddering across the tile floor. He feels tumescent as a football, as he knocks the narrow walls of

Kene in a bed of green glass. She grips him so tightly he feels the
pressure around his neck, on the tip of his nose. She comes two,
three times, and then he himself lets go. Only then does he feel
the sun beat down on his face, and see the green glass crushed to
fine powder on Kene's breasts. He removes the pillowcase from
the pillow and gently sweeps the glass powder away. She brushes
her index finger against the hollow at the base of his throat, collecting sweat beads under her nail, and she says: "Nothing can be
given; everything must be earned. Until now, you've been only
half awake. See how it goes?"

"I can see that," he says.

"You love me, don't you?"

"I do. I love you."

"Of course you do. You're a good boy. You do as I tell you."

Though no one says so, he knows that they are Chinese and
black, and that they are slaves being mated by two abusive white
men who run a farm high in the mountains of Colorado. Their
bed is in the open air now, and a breeze cools their skin. As he
dusts the powder from his lover's breasts, he feels his own hands
on his breasts, his penis inside his vagina; his hands reach down
to caress his own face. He feels the sun on his back and on his
face, his chest. They both sit up and gaze out and away. Their
overseer seems to be gone, but they are afraid to run just now.
They decide to wait till dark. Scrub pine, mesquite, pale blue
sage, and tumbleweeds all around them, they see their freedom
everywhere they look, for everywhere they look, they see themselves.

And again, later that night, Kene's howling and Alaine's voice-
less bedknocking transport Bertrand's dreaming head to a porno
theater in Denver. He's eating popcorn and drinking root beer.

Kene and Alaine are up on the screen, screwing porn-star fashion with lots of barking, dirty talk, and grimaces that are simultaneously angry, wry, and nauseated. First they do it doggie style, but Bertrand is annoyed that the camera focuses mostly on Alaine's large eggplant-colored penis, rather than on his wife's pendulating breasts. He's far from turned on, but the man sitting in front of him appears to be enraptured. The man's head is thrown back, and his eyes are half opened. Bertrand can't see his arms but knows he's stroking himself. The man rolls his head back and winks at Bertrand, so Bertrand rises from his seat and moves back four rows.

Kene straddles Alaine; the cowboy position, they call it. She bucks and shakes and rocks herself on the eggplant penis, but again, the camera stays on what Bertrand finds least erotic, Kene's upper back and her long beaded locks flying about her head. Then the Kourmans slip into the married position—Kene supine, Alaine between her thighs—and to Bertrand's frustration, the camera devotes itself to their faces, Kene's eyes brimming with tears, Alaine's with delight. The masturbating man five rows away starts to moan, his voice blending with the sex sounds coming from the speakers. Bertrand has had enough. He stands and walks up the aisle, but after walking and walking gets no closer to an exit and no farther from the screen.

Kene moans, hums, gasps, shouts obscenities, and Alaine pulls out and strokes himself, teeth gritting, sweat-slick head nodding like a junkie's. This is the money shot, and Bertrand wants out before it comes. But it comes, man and woman ululating like birds, and as their climaxing subsides they begin to kiss and stroke and coo to each other, to entwine their dark legs. It's this afterglow he finds most disturbing, and it's here, at the height of his discomfort, he realizes he's sleeping, and he can feel his teeth clamped tight. He perceives he's stopped breathing.

So he gasps for air and sits up in bed. He reaches up and pulls the light cord, and the sea-green walls of his room are tinged with yellowish 40-watt light. He is naked and covered in perspiration. His penis is hard and throbs painfully, and he feels as though he's been kicked in the groin. He lies back down, this time on his side, and tries to conjure up the dream's images so he can masturbate, but the pain is too intense. He reaches for his bag, removes cigarettes and lighter. He lights a cigarette but doesn't smoke it, just watches the smoke coil up to the ceiling and spread out like a cloud.

He takes up his pen and notepaper and scrawls, "Fifteen steps from here, but you'd think they were living in my head." Kene giggles in the usual way, and then she says something in Bambara, her native tongue. Alaine says something in French, and then they fall silent. "I think I hate them."

The house pulses with quiet, except for Kene's occasional postcoital purr, the susurrus of limbs against limbs against bedclothes. Might as well be in bed with me, loud as they are, he says to himself. Maybe earplugs. Maybe tapes. Get me some tapes, ask Rose to send me my jazz. Betty and Ella, Grant and Trane. Waller. Dying to hear some rock, too. Donald Fagen, Neil Young, some Tull and Clash, Kate Bush, and Cockburn. He writes: "I left American music behind because I thought it'd force me more deeply into Senegalese culture. Fuck that. I need noise. This is killing me." The Beatles, Shriekback, the Femmes, Stan Clarke, Bootsy, Prince. Patsy Cline, for God's sake, Rickie Lee Jones; maybe some radio, record some radio for me. KUVO, with all that salsa, reggae, jazz, or KRDO with Paul Harvey, Larry King, and all that yack. American radio, and her voice, too. Telling me she forgives me for what I want to do. What I aim to do. Anything to block those sounds.

He hears Alaine chuckle, then say, "Ndeysahn," meaning,

Lord a' mercy, Oy vey, Ain't it a bitch. Wonder if they ever consider how I feel. Feel trapped in my room till they're done is what I feel. Feel like crying. He shrugs. Maybe should. If he could tell them, he would say he finds their lovemaking unbearable, both because it's annoying—Kene's roar, the insectile scream of their bedsprings—and because it makes him imagine that he is missing something essential. The anthropologist in him tells him the very idea is absurd. Racial theory, he'll tell anyone who asks him, has been discredited. And even before college and graduate school, before he even knew what anthropology was, he scorned those who believed in the sexual superiority of black people.

He thinks of the white kid with the ragged mustache and photo-gray lenses he worked with when he sacked groceries back in his high school days. The kid said to him once, "I hear you're not really a man till you've drooped a black chick." Bertrand was a virgin but resented the kid's very presence so much he answered, "Only the really really dark ones."

But when he hears the Kourmans in bed, especially when they thread their way into his dreams, he doesn't wonder so much about the tirelessness of black genitalia but about things entirely external to the body. Once Idrissa smiling, subtly shaking his head, said to him, "Colette is a good girl, but a black woman, a black man, in the bed?"

"So what's the difference for you?" said Bertrand.

"It's in the heart, man. You're in the same soup, you see?"

He dresses in shorts and flip-flops, takes up the pen, the journal, and pads from his room. It's his habit to stand at their door for a moment at night on his way to the toilet or on his way to gaze at the moon and stars. While he may not wholly tolerate the sounds of their bedknocking, he loves to hear the sounds of marital sleep—two dreaming heads, two breaths, the odd somnolent murmur of two. He likes to believe that if he and Rose had slept so, night after night, that, despite his blackness and her paleness, they might have become one.

He doesn't let himself feel his disappointment that Kene and Alaine have somehow made up after their interminable slugfest, and he won't let the reason for the disappointment rise to consciousness. He won't let himself say that he wants Kene. He won't look at his own looking—her smooth throat, the silk-fine hair on her coppery skin, the way her naked copper feet step soundlessly across the tile floors, the lips that must be soft as breasts, the breasts made to fill his hands, the ass like a heart, the ass like a plum, the muscles in her arms. He won't see himself seeing the way those arms flex when she pulverizes couscous, or sweeps the floor, or lifts her six-year-old, or punches her husband upside his head.

The whole time they'd been fighting, the whole time he and Idrissa had been trying to separate them, to dodge their flinging arms, to subdue their fury, he'd fantasized Alaine thundering off into the night and Idrissa following to bring him back. He imagined the neighborwoman carting their little girl away to safety, leaving him to console Kene. He won't let himself see any of this—though he sees it well enough in the hinterparts of his consciousness—and he believes he would never again sleep with a man's wife.

Alaine may or may not be his friend, but because he knows him, he'll keep his passion where it is coolly recondite. He moves from the foyer and onto the porch, and sees that it is misting; he's surprised that the frogs aren't singing. Rainy season must be ending. It'll cool down. Flies will thin out, mosquitoes'll fuck off, the village'll dry up, he hopes. He thinks of how the weather back home will soon be. Amber light in the afternoons, short and sharp. Chinook wind drying the air sweet and cold. Everything beneath the sky brown, yellow, conifer green, the sky, blue as a postcard sky, as Rose might put it. Then snow.

He thinks of snow, Bunny and Sally in their red coats, his green pj's, the puzzle piece. Whenever he thinks of snow and black girls, he thinks of Bunny and Sally Terry. That's where it started, he believes. A little boy's shame and embarrassment. Such a small, inconsequential thing to grow so large. And so long ago—1965? '66—he can't understand how it could still matter.

His mother would sometimes sit for the Terry family, but he believed the girls' parents brought them because they wanted Bertrand and Bunny to marry someday. He was only nine, but he loved Bunny, her quick black eyes, and shoulder-length hair. Bobbie socks. Saddle shoes. Jumpers. White gloves at church. He even liked her little sister, or at least tolerated her for Bunny's approval and affection.

The Terrys were military people, stationed at the Air Force Academy, but living in town. They seemed settled but, like all military families, were destined to move at some point, and that winter came the point. The last visit, only two weeks to go and then Captain Terry would take his family to somewhere near Chicago. No more baby-sitting the girls, no walks to school, no white-glove Sundays. Bunny or Sally. So this last night really wasn't about baby-sitting, but what could they call it? Boys and girls didn't slumber-party together, so call it baby-sitting, let the girls spend the night. Only two weeks and ya'll be gone for Lord knows how long. No, I don't mind; of course I don't mind. Bertrand loves those girls, too.

His sister? Up in her room sulking, I guess. Don't matter. Bertrand's the one spends time with them, and he's—

What? Ain't it the truth, child. Thank you. Yours, too; most boys'd be yanking girls' pigtails at that age. Be fighting like cats and dogs, child. I know what I was like as a girl, couldn't stand me no boys until you know what. But those three get along like peanut butter and jelly and whitebread.

What's that, honey? Huh? Oh say about four so the girls can have dinner with us. Oh, know what? we'll just take 'em home with us after church and on to school Monday. Uh-huh. Aw, no, no, no girl, don't be silly. Much food as I keep around for my two, you know I can feed your two. Naw-aw now, Belle, don't be silly. Huh? OK. OK. All right, girl. Bye-bye.

So after dinner, after television, that Sunday, the girls went down to the family room in the basement, and they decided to spin Marvin Gaye and Tami Terrell records and work on a cardboard puzzle. Bertrand was sent to bathe and dress for bed before he was allowed to join them. When he did join them, he noticed they were still dressed in their church clothes, and he asked them where their nightclothes were. "Daddy said we couldn't stay," said Sally.

"How come?"

But neither of them knew, and so they turned their attention to the puzzle there on the cool cement floor. Bunny and Bertrand gossiped about mutual friends and acquaintances at school. They were in the same grade but different classes. Sally kept trying to get them to focus on the puzzle. The girls had done well with it. They had most of the sky on the right side finished, and the castle was half done. Bertrand started in on the rose garden, but Bunny tapped his hand and said: "You know what you can do? You can look for that piece of sky there. We been trying for a long time and just can't find it. You're good at the parts that are all one color."

Bertrand felt his face and neck grow warm, and he wanted to tell Bunny that she, too, was good at something, but decided this would be silly, so he merely shrugged and said, "Not that good." He stretched for a blue piece on their side of the puzzle and ripped the already sizable hole in the underarm of his robe. "Oops," said Sally without looking up. Bertrand removed the robe, tossed it on the orange couch behind him, and sat lotus style. He picked up another piece, considered it, put it down. He repeated this action, moving with easy calm. But by increments, he noticed that the girls were giggling, softly, behind their hands. He knew it had to do with him but pretended he didn't hear them, tried to surreptitiously inspect himself to see what he was doing wrong. He gathered it must have been his slumped shoulders since all his life he had been exhorted to stand and sit straighter. He squared his shoulders, unbent his spine. Suddenly he found the missing piece, and in his excitement, he whooped and rolled onto his back, and this made the girls shriek with laughter.

"You better put your robe back on, Birdie," said Bunny, and she was pointing at his crotch. When he saw the hole in his pajama bottoms, he lowered his head, shrank into himself. His whole body pounded alarm and shame. His ears were hot. He didn't cry, but Bunny seemed to think he was crying and—though she was still chuckling—she placed a hand on his shoulder and said, "It's OK, Birdie. I'm sorry."

"Yeah, me too, Birdie."

But he was so knotted up in embarrassment, he couldn't move for a spell. The hole, he knew, was the size of his hand. They must have been able to see his ass and his balls. *Shoulda never took my robe off.* When he finally lifted his head, he couldn't look either girl in the eye but perceived that they'd stopped smiling.

"Are you guys poor?" said Bunny. "It's OK if you're poor."

"Yeah, we don't care."

"No we don't. Jesus loved the poor. Do you want to put your robe back on?"

"Maybe you should."

Bertrand didn't know whether his family was poor, but when he finally spoke, he said that they were because he believed that if they thought so they wouldn't dare laugh at him anymore. Yet he could hardly fathom the bigness of his shame. Ordinarily, he would laugh embarrassment away. If he tripped and people laughed, he would let himself in on the laughter by tripping himself several times more. He'd roll around on the ground, cross his eyes, make like his head was awhirl with cartoon birds and stars, but here, now, he felt something so far beyond shame that he has to this very day yet to find the end of it.

———

So It was snowing the next day, and they were easy to spot in their red coats, the tall and short twins, always dressed alike, almost always together outside of school. When I would see them, I'd give a quick wave and cross the street or the playground; I'd get lost in trees or packs of boys, or duck behind cars, mailboxes, corners. I'd hide from any red coat, after a while, and any black girl. I hid from them everyday for those two weeks, as though they were she-demons. They finally moved away, but I carried the subterfuge from those two weeks onward. Hid from all the black girls, which isn't so hard to do at a parochial school in Colorado Springs. Hid from Carlotta Baylor, Maureen Tandy, Velldree, Kim, a half-dozen girls whose names I never knew. Pretty soon, I stopped going to catechism. Maybe I believed they had all been there that night, all knew the secret, would skin me with laughter if I let them get close enough. I know for sure I believed that Bunny and Sally had told them all.

But why did I continue to hide from black girls after St. Mary's? It's crazy, makes no sense, unbearably silly. It was my asshole, and everybody's got one. Maybe it's just an excuse. Maybe I just went whitegirl crazy. Too much TV, too much Colorado Springs, where they tell you your sister is "pretty for a black girl," where polite people, even here in 1985, still refer to black people as colored. My reasons for avoiding black girls became . . . fuck, even Uncle Tom was married to a black woman. What happened to me? Why didn't it happen to the other black guys at school, Robbie and Clinton and them? They dated both, and even Alan MacVee, the gay dude, dated blacks, whites, Hispanics.

Did I begin to think white girls are prettier? Sexier? Who could be prettier than Norma Jean Vessey or that girl in jr. high? Did I begin to believe white girls understand me better because I spent my life knowing their ways better than ours? I always told myself that color makes no difference, but it does, like age, personality, religion, class, culture. Maybe I've been lying to myself, to cover my ass. Maybe all the reasons I've avoided black women have nothing to do with what I've always claimed. I used to tell myself I didn't feel it was so exciting to pursue black girls when I was in school because the matchmaking white girls would virtually assign you to the nearest black girl as if the two of you were a separate species from themselves, pushed my way because of her color and mine and nothing more. It made no difference to anybody if she was pretty or not, intelligent or not. It never occurred to anyone we might not like each other.

So maybe I turned to white girls because I believed I wanted to make my own choices, but except for Rose and Daisy Israel, I always chose those who were both neurotic and plain, the kind I thought I deserved, perpetuating the myth that a black man will be attracted to the homeliest white woman because what he wants from the relationship is to sexualize his sense of inferiority. But maybe what I wanted all along was to hide a little boy's shame.

———

He lays down his pen, rises from the porch, walks back to his room and dresses. He will go to the Meridien Hotel, which is a ten-minute walk from his room here in the village. He'll call Rose, ostensibly to ask her to send him some tapes. But somehow, he will find a way to tell her how much he's grown since he's been in Senegal. He'll tell her she hasn't a thing to worry about. She'll be home from class now, and perhaps a little tired. It'll take some doing to keep her on the phone. Though he tries, he can't keep from rehearsing the conversation in his head:

This is expensive.

Our marriage is worth it.

How's your research?

I've done nothing. Not a thing. I think about you.

Do you have a girlfriend yet?

That's not funny.

Funny like the rubbers I found in your bag?

They're for your visit, like I said before.

You made that up. I could tell. Anyway, I can't have kids.

I've had all these insights.

This is expensive.

See, when I was a kid I let a little embarrassment turn into this big, neurotic thing. I—

I can't have kids.

... them see my ...

You packed rubbers. Why did you pack rubbers?

So you see, obviously it's a certain kind of intimacy I've learned to—

Intimacy? Intimacy? Are you joking? You're joking, aren't you?

... fear, you see? They got too close ...

We don't even sleep in the same room.

... that I've always found unbearable—

You're gone. Where are you? Gone. Thousands of miles away. Don't—

Now, goddamn it, Rose, listen to me!

Don't—

This is important!

Don't talk to me about intimacy, Bertrand, till you explain the rubbers first.

The mist still swirls through the sky, and the streetlamps along the hotel road make coronas of yellowish-lavender vapor twenty feet above his head but cast little light down below. As he walks along the road, he mentally ticks off the things he will say to her. Being here gives me insight, he'll say, It's helped me untangle things. I can see now that I've been full of unconscious fears, little-boy fears. I don't need to have sex with a black woman. Besides, I never said I did, just said I hadn't, and you assumed I would.

He shivers as he enters the conditioned air of the hotel. He's surprised to see so many people in the lobby, to see that the bar, the Blue Marlin, is still open, that there are some two dozen patrons there, drinking and talking in low voices. He approaches the desk clerk and asks him why there are so many people down here at well past four in the morning, and the clerk says: "The upstair electricity is broke, sir. The rooms are too hot for sleeping, so we open the bar and serving food. May I help you, sir?" The clerk twirls a pen between his fingers and looks at Bertrand with a skeptic's annoyance.

"I'm wondering if I can use the phone."

"You are a guest?"

"No."

"The only phone I can let you use is already occupy. But you may wait in the bar, sir. The bar is cooler than lobby." The clerk points with a pen to the bar, says, "I will send a boy to you when the phone is empty," and Bertrand turns to make his way there as if following an order.

As he approaches the bar, he sees Medoune, an English teacher at some lycée in Dakar. He doesn't know Medoune well

but knows that he and Idrissa are well acquainted and had a
falling out a year ago over something that Idrissa never discusses. Medoune never wears African clothing, not even at the
mosque. He favors rugby shirts with the collar thrown up, navy
slacks, expensive sandals, sweaters thrown over his shoulders
with the arms tied loose across his chest. Tonight he is clean, as
usual, from toenails to fingernails; his shades, dark and pol-
ished, sit atop his tight Afro. Every weekend he prowls the
whole hotel complex, the lobbies, the rooms, the beachfronts,
with pantherine ranginess. Besides French and English, he
knows Italian, Spanish, German, and a little Russian. He knows
women, too, but can seduce them with or without his language
prowess.

A man named Saliu sits to Medoune's right. Bertrand knows
Saliu by little more than name, but he believes the man owns a
fairly large fishing vessel and is retired from the Senegalese navy.
The seat to the left of Medoune is empty, and a white woman
occupies the seat to the left of the empty one. Bertrand doesn't
look at her. He shakes hands with the men and sits next to
Medoune. "Up late, I see," says Medoune.

"You too."

"Good time to find the girls." Medoune grins and elbows
Saliu, who grins back at him and hoists his beer. "Nice, eh?" says
Medoune, thumbing toward the white woman. He cups his
hands out in front of his chest and says, "She makes her sweater
better, eh, Bert?"

"She's pretty," says Bertrand, but he will not look at her.
Instead, he keeps his eyes on Medoune's eyes.

Medoune turns his head right. "I would say she's German, eh,
Saliu?"

"Yes, Allemand. A big girl. Germany."

"Or Dutch, maybe," says Medoune. "Definitely not French.

Look at that ass. If she were black, you couldn't tell the difference between her and a Senegalese woman."

"I'm flattered," says the woman. She's American. She has
blue-green eyes, eyes of a winter feline, eyes that remind him of
mint and hail, or what the sky looks like from eight miles above
the earth. He sees what he sees and is so disappointed in himself
he feels his heart sink to his stomach.

"I'm sorry," says Medoune.

"Ha-ha, English girl!" says Saliu. He tips his head back, laughing. "English girl. Haaaa, Medoune, you are embarrass!" and
then he says in rapid Wolof: "My my, 'When thou seest the palm
tree, the palm tree sees thee,' don't the old people say? You can
blame the American for this one, boy. I'll bet he knew the whole
time, the young mongrel. Like knows like."

"Shut up, Saliu," Medoune says. "You ever stop to think these
people might speak like us, too? *He* does, for sure. He's the
anthropologist, remember?" He looks at Bertrand. "You do know
Wolof, don't you?"

"I speak a little Wolof. Forget it, Saliu. But I didn't know she
was American." He turns toward the woman. "I'm Bertrand.
This is Medoune. He's Saliu."

"I'm Sue Klemmer."

She offers her hand to each man, and when Medoune takes
hers, he says, "I'm sorry. We were just saying how good looking
you are."

"I said I was flattered. Your women are the most beautiful I've
seen. Here and in Romania, anyway."

Medoune says, "You like to travel, do you?"

"I always have. My dad was navy, and my husband flies for
Swiss Air."

"Navy!" cries Saliu. "I am navy, too."

Her smile makes delicate crow's-feet at the corners of her eyes, lines around her chapped mouth. Bertrand puts her at forty-three. "The beard gives you away, Saliu," she says.

"What did she say?"

"She says you look like a sailor," says Medoune, then turning back to Sue, says, "Well, I just hope you're not angry."

"Nope."

"If you're not, then you *can't* be an American," says Bertrand, and the two Americans laugh, lean toward each other till their shoulders touch. Though Medoune is smiling, Bertrand knows that he doesn't get the joke, but Bertrand doesn't want to appear to be horning in on Medoune's quarry, so he stands to leave. He'll go back to the lobby. But Sue presses his arm and says, "Wait, where are you going? I'm dying to talk American for a while." She offers to buy each man a drink, but Medoune and Saliu beg off, claim they were leaving anyway, and as Medoune shakes Bert's hand good night, he winks at him, leans into his ear, and sings in a whisper, "Good lu-u-u-ck!"

We had a wonderful conversation, Sue and I. Talked till seven in the morning. Never did call home. We talked about Senegal, because it was her first time here; Argentina, because she and her husband spent four months in jail there in the mid-70's; earthquakes, because she is from San Francisco; homosexuality, because her brother is gay; the Red Brigades, because she can see their point; Anwar's assassination, because I told her it made me sadder than the deaths of the Kennedys and King; South Africa, because you can't live on this continent without talking about South Africa; violence in America, because South Africa always leads to talk about America. I told her everything I could about home, pop culture, etc.

I learned that she is 38 and despises Germans, partly because her husband is Austrian. She doesn't believe in God. She works for FAO, so she's been nearly everywhere in Africa. She's about five foot five, and she likes Stork Beer. She reads a hell of a lot. She doesn't smoke or curse, and she likes to watch men. She spoke without blushing or looking away, and the eyes pinned me in my seat. I kept wanting to tell her I had to make a call, but how could I? I mean, there she was in the flesh, opening up to me like an oyster, and over there, way the fuck over there, was Rosie in her long johns, her glasses, a book in hand, a tapping foot, her trembling mouth telling me how much I have hurt her just because I packed rubbers and just because she knows I'm a virgin to black women.

Why should I have left the bar to face the little-boy shame, when here is this Venus accepting me on credit? She spoke to me in the way Rosie used to, without inhibition, without—like, she even told me she'd had a breast reduction when she was twenty-three, and as she spoke, she drew circles and squares in the air around them. I stroked them with my eyes till the nipples grew firm, and her blush darkened the overtanned skin on her chest. She told me how terrible it had been to have her body as a little girl in the sixties. "I'd done pretty much everything, sexually, by the time I was sixteen or so," she said, and then she paused and thoughtfully scratched a mosquito bite on her thigh. "Why I never burned out on sex, I don't know."

I'm taking her to see Goree Island on Friday if she shows up. She's supposed to be here by ten. I hope she comes, but I have my doubts. Maybe she thinks I'm some kind of nut. She can probably smell my lust all the way from here. ~~I'm attracted, but.~~ Tired. Bed calls. Call or write Rose ASAP.

chapter 5

Phantasm

N'Gor village
Sept. 1 or 2

Dear Rose—

Instead of collecting proverbs in Yoff village today, which I should have done, I went to Dakar with Omar the tailor, Idi's friend, to buy palm wine. As you know, I'd craved palm wine ever since I read Amos Tutuola's novel *The Palm-Wine Drinkard* in college. I wish you'd read that book. It's so strange, like a dream. Tutuola never attempts to describe the taste, color, or smell of palm wine, but because the main character, Can-Do-Anything, can put away 225 kegs of it per day, and because he sojourns through many cruel and horrifying worlds in order to try to retrieve his recently killed palm wine tapster from Deadstown, I figured palm wine had to be pretty good. And I figured, what the hell, what the hell, I've got a brain tumor anyway. Yoff can wait. Well, I don't know what's wrong with me really. I don't have any brain tumor. I'm not in pain, and I feel pretty good. But I'm having weird "episodes" I can't describe, except to say that I'm sleeping too much. I haven't seen a doctor. I'll wait till I get home. That'll be in a week or two.

So I'm coming home, but not before I do and see a few things. Vacation-wise, you know? I doubt you care. Do you care? You don't care. You've written me twice in all these months, Rose, a cold epistle about your final exams, your mom's hysterectomy, and the unusual June weather—and your nine-word F.U. scrawled on notebook paper. You're not even reading this, right? These words are still in the envelope, I imagine, and the envelope is in your sock drawer, where we keep the dildo and the "love oil." So what does it matter what I say? I write you all the time, and you don't write me back. So let me tell you about yesterday, OK?

'K.

I was wide awake, but as Omar and I boarded the bus, I dreamed palm wine dreams. It must be pale green, I thought, coming from a tree and all. Or milky blue like coconut water. I had it in mind that it must hit the tongue like a dart, and that it must make one see the same visions Tutuola himself witnessed: a creature big as a bipedal elephant, sporting two-foot fangs thick as cow's horns; a creature with a million eyes and hundreds of breasts that continuously suckle her young, who swarm her body like maggots; a town where everything and everyone is red as beef; a town where they all walk backward; a town full of ghosts. Tutuola must sleep a lot or very deeply.

I really had no business going, I know. I'm at least a month behind in my research, though I've been getting caught up. But I excused myself from work by telling myself that since I had no Wolof proverbs on the subject of drinking, I'd likely encounter a couple that day. Still I took my pad, pencils, and tape recorder along, knowing I wasn't going to use them. And I didn't. Who cares about pithy sayings and made-up stories, when stuff like this happens. *Here's* a story for you!

On the ride to town, I could scarcely pay mind to matters that usually fascinate me. For instance, I often carefully observe the beggars who board the buses and cry for alms. Their Afro-Arab plaints weave through the bus like serpents, slipping between exquisitely coifed women and dignified, angular men, wives of the wealthy, daughters of the poor, beardless hustlers, bundled babies, tourists, pickpockets, gendarmes, students. A beautiful plaint can draw coins like salt draws moisture. Some beggars not only sing for indulgences but also sing their thanks. Jerrejeff, my sister, paradise lies under the feet of mothers. A heart that burns for Allah gives more light than ten thousand suns. Some of them sing proverbs from the Koran. Be constant in prayer and give alms. Allah pity him who must beg of a beggar. Some of them merely cry something very much like Alms! Alms! And some of them rasp like reptiles and say little more than "I got only one arm! Gimmie money!" and the proverbs they use are usually stale, stuff I've heard nearly every day. They annoy me, but even so I often give them alms, and I sometimes record them. I guess it's because I like being in a culture that has a good deal more respect for the poor than our own. And I guess I try hard to appreciate art forms that are different from the ones I readily understand. But, honestly, as I say, yesterday I could think of little more than palm wine. It would be cold as winter rain. It would be sweet like berries, and I would drink till my mind went swimming in deep waters.

We alighted the bus in the arrondissement of Fosse, the place Omar insisted was the only place to find the wine. Preoccupied as I was with my palm wine dreams, they weren't enough to keep me from attending Fosse. It's an urban village, a squatter's camp, a smoke-filled bowl of shanties built of rusty corrugated metal, gray splintery planks, cinder block, cement. It smelled of everything: goatskin, pot, green tobacco, fish, overripe fruit, piss, cheap perfume, Gazelle Beer, warm couscous, scorched rice, the sour sharpness of cooking coals. People talked, laughed, sang, cried, argued—the sounds so plangent I felt them in my teeth, my chest, my knees. A woman dressed in blue flowers scolded her teenage son, and the sound lay tart on my tongue. Two boys drummed the bottoms of plastic buckets, while a third played a pop bottle with a stick, and I smelled churai incense. Two little girls danced to the boys' rhythms, their feet invisible with dust, and I felt them on my back. I really mean this, Rose; the whole day was in me, on me, around me. I was a video recorder, you might say.

A beautiful young woman in a paisley wraparound pagne smiled at us, and I rubbed Omar's incipient dreadlocks, his wig of thumbs, as I call them, and said, "Hey, man, there's a wife for you." Omar grinned at me, his amber eyes were crescents, his teeth big as dominoes. "She too old for me, mahn," he said.

"Oh please, brother, she couldn't be older than eighteen."

"Young is better."

"Whatever. Letch."

I don't really like Omar. He insists on speaking English with me even though his English is relatively poor. Even when I speak to him in so-so French or my shaky Wolof, he invariably answers me in English. This happens all the time here. Everywhere I go, people want to speak English, and my personal proverb has become "Every English-speaking traveler will be a teacher as much as he'll be a student." I suppose if his English were better, I wouldn't mind, but there are times it leads to trouble—like yesterday; and times when the only thing that really bothers me is that it's Omar speaking it. Omar the tailor man, always stoned, always grinning, his red-and-amber crescents, his domino teeth, his big olive-shaped head, his wolfish face, his hiccuping laugh jangling every last nerve in my skull. He perpetually thrusts his

long hands at me for cigarettes, money, favors. "Hey, I and I, you
letting me borrow you tape deck?" "Hey, I and I, jokma bene
cigarette." He's a self-styled Rastafarian, and he has the notion
that since the U.S. and Jamaica are geographically close,
Jamaicans and black Americans are interchangeable. I'm pretty
certain I'm of more value to him as a faux Jamaican than as genuine American.

He was constantly in my face with this "I and I, mahn" stuff,
quoting Peter Tosh couplets, insisting I put them in my book. (I
can never get him to understand the nature of my work.) More-
over, it took him three and a half months to sew one lousy pair of
pants and one lousy shirt for me, items I was dumb enough to
pay for in advance. From the day he measured me to the day I
actually donned the clothes, I'd lost twenty-odd pounds. (Constant diarrhea and a fish-and-rice diet will do that to you.) But I
wasn't about to ask him to take them in. I only have a year's worth
of fellowship money, after all.

Omar always speaks of his great volume of work, his busyness,
the tremendous pressure he's under, but each and every time I
made it to his shop to pick up my outfit, I'd find him sitting with
four or five friends, twisting his locks, putting the buzz on, yack-
ing it up. "Hey, I and I, come in! I don't see you a long time."

In northern Africa they say, "Bear him unlucky, don't bear
him lazy." But I bore Omar because he's a friend of my assistant,
Idrissa, who's spending a week in Thiès with his brother. When
he comes back, it'll only be for a couple days. His girlfriend sent
him an erotic letter and a ticket to Paris. And money. I went with
Omar to get the palm wine because Omar, who knows Fosse a
great deal better than Idrissa does, insisted yesterday was the
only time in palm wine season he would be able to make the trip.
(The "trip," for chrissakes, takes maybe twenty, thirty minutes by

bus.) He told me that Idrissa wouldn't be back till the season was well over. Since Omar is so "pressed for time," we wasted none of it getting to the city.

As I walked the ghetto with Omar, I reflected on how Idrissa often fills things in for me with his extemporaneous discussions of the history, economics, and myths about wherever in Senegal we happen to be. Idrissa is self-educated and garrulous. My kind of person. He's also very proud of his Senegalese heritage. He seems to know everything about the country. As Omar and I walked, I told myself that if Idrissa had been there, I would have been learning things. What did I know?

Next Day—Different ink—
On our walk, Omar seldom spoke. He seemed unable to answer any of my questions about the place, so after about ten minutes I stopped asking. We walked what seemed to me the entire ghetto and must have inquired at about 8 or 9 places without seeing a drop of palm wine. Each inquiry involved the usual African procedure—shake hands all around, ask about each other's friends, families, health, work; ask for the wine, learn they have none, ask them who might, shake hands, leave.

It was getting close to dusk now, and our long shadows undulated before us over the tight-packed soil. I was getting a little hungry, and I kept eyeing the street vendors who braised brochettes of mutton along the curb of the main street. The white smoke rose up and plumed into the streets, raining barbecue smells everywhere. I said, "Looks like we're not getting the wine today. Tell you what, why don't we—"

"Is not the season-quois," Omar said as we rambled into a small, secluded yard. It was surrounded by several cement-and-tin houses, some with blanket doors, insides lighted mostly by kerosene or candles. Here and there, though, I could see that some places had electricity. Omar crossed his arms as we drew to a stop. "We stay this place and two more," he said, "then I and I go."

"Aye-aye," I said.

Four young men sat on a dusty porch passing a cigarette between them. Several toddlers and under-fives, each runny nosed and ashy kneed, frenetically crisscrossed in front of the men, pretending to grab for the cigarette. Until they saw me. Then they stopped, and one of the older ones approached us, reached out a hand, and said, "Toubobie, mawney." Omar said, in Wolof, "This man isn't a toubob. This is a black man. An American brother." I answered in Wolof, too. "Give me a proverb, and I'll give you money." The boy ran away grinning, and the men laughed. I drew my cigarettes from my shirt pocket, tapped out eight, and gave two to each man.

"Where's Doudou?" Omar asked the men.

They told him Doudou, whoever he was, had left a half hour before but was expected back very soon. One of the men, a short, muscular man in a T-shirt and a pair of these voluminous trousers called chayas, detached himself from his friends and walked into one of the houses. He returned carrying a small green liquor bottle. I felt my eyebrows arch. The stuff itself, I was thinking. I imagined myself getting pied with these boys, so drunk I'm hugging them, telling them I love them, and goddamnit, where's old Doudou? I miss that bastid. The man in the chayas unscrewed the lid with sacramental delicacy, drank, and passed the bottle on. I watched the men's faces go soft when each passed the bottle on to his brother. I took the bottle rather more aggressively than was polite, and I apologized to the man who'd handed it to me. Omar winked at me. "You don't know what bottle is-quois?"

Omar has the irritating habit of using the tag "quois" after most of his sentences. He does it in English, French, Wolof, and his own language, Bambara. It isn't an uncommon habit in French West Africa, but Omar wears it down to a nub.

"Paaalm wiiine," I said in a low, throaty voice, the way you used to say my name after we made love. My God, what was wrong with me? I was behaving as though, like the Drinkard himself, I had fought the beast with the lethal gaze and shovel-sized scales or had spent the night in the bagful of creatures with ice-cold, sandpapery hair, that I'd done some heroic thing, and the stuff in the green bottle was my reward. As I brought the bottle to my lips, Omar said, "It's no palm wine, I and I."

I drank before Omar's words even registered, and the liquid burned to my navel. It was very much like a strong tequila. No, that's an understatement. If this drink and tequila went to prison, this drink would make tequila its cabin boy. "Is much stronger than palm wine," said Omar.

My throat had closed up, and it took me a few seconds before I could speak. All I could manage was to hiss, "Jeeezuz!" And abruptly one of the young men, a Franco-Senegalese with golden hair and green eyes, said, "Jeeezuz," but then he continued in rapid Wolof and I lost him. Soon all five of them were laughing, saying "Jeeezuz, Jeezuz," working the joke, extending it, jerking it around like taffy. My blood rose to my skin, and every muscle in my back knotted. I squinted at Omar, who looked back at me with eyes both reassuring and provocative, and he said, "He saying he like Americain noire talk. You know, you say-quois, 'Jeeezuz,' and 'Sheeee,' and 'Maaaaan-quois.' We like the Americain noire talk." His mouth hovered this close to a smirk.

I was furious, but I had no choice but to grin and play along. I lit a smoke and said, "Jeezuz" and "Jeezuz Christ," and "Jeezuz H. Christ," "cuttin' the monkey," as my dad would put it. My stomach felt as though it was full of mosquitoes. My hands trembled. I wanted to kick Omar's face in. His hiccuping giggles rose above the sound of everyone else's laughter, and his body jerked about convulsively. Yeah, choke on it, I thought.

But I didn't have to endure the humiliation long, for soon an extremely tall, very black, very big boned man joined us, and Omar said, "Doudou!" and fiercely shook hands with the giant. Doudou nodded my way and said, in Wolof, "What's this thing?" and I froze with astonishment. Thing? I tried to interpret Omar's lengthy explanation, but his back was to me and he was speaking very rapidly. As I say, my Wolof isn't very good. Doudou placed his hands on his hips and squinted at the ground as though he'd lost something very small. The big man nodded now and then. Then he looked at me and said in French, "It's late in the season, but I know where there's lots of palm wine." He immediately wheeled about and began striding away; Omar followed, then I.

The walk was longer than I'd expected, and by the time we got to the place, the deep-blue twilight had completely absorbed our shadows. After four or five months of living here, I've become used to following strangers into unfamiliar places in the night. But even so, I felt uneasy. I watched the night as a sentry would, trying to note every movement and sound. There was nothing extraordinary about the things I saw on the way, but I know deep inside I'll remember them twenty years from now as vividly as I see them right now: a three-year-old girl in a faded pink dress sitting on a porch; a cat-sized rat sitting atop an overflowing garbage crate; a man in a yellow shirt and blue tie talking to a bald man wearing a maroon khaftan; a half moon made half again by a knot of scaly clouds; Omar's wig of thumbs; Doudou's broad back. I wasn't thinking much about palm wine. Then we arrived.

It was an inconspicuous place, built from the same stuff, built in the same way practically every other place in Fosse is. Perhaps a half-dozen candles lit the room, but rather than clarify they muddied the darkness. I couldn't tell whether there were six other men in the place or twelve. I couldn't make out the proprietress's face or anything about her, for that matter. The only unchanging features were her eyes, an unnatural olive black and egg white, large, perpetually doleful. But was her expression stern or soft? As the candlelight shifted, heaved, bent, so did her shape and demeanor. At times she seemed big as Doudou, and at other times she seemed only five foot two or so. One moment she looked fifty; a second later, twenty-three. Her dress was sometimes blue, sometimes mauve. I couldn't stop staring at her, and I couldn't stop imagining that the light in the room was incrementally being siphoned away, and that my skull was being squeezed as if in the crook of a great headlocking arm, and that the woman swelled to two, three, four times her size, and split her dress like ripe fruit skin, and glowed naked, eggplant black like a burnished goddess, and that she stared at me with those unchanging olive-and-egg eyes. It's that stuff I drank, I kept saying to myself. It's that stuff they gave me.

Then with increasing clarity I heard a hiss as though air were rushing from my very own ears, and the sound grew louder, so loud the air itself seemed to be torn in half like a long curtain, until it abruptly stopped with the sound of a cork being popped from a bottle; then everything was normal again, and I looked around the room half embarrassed as if the ridiculous things in my head had been projected on the wall before me for all to see, and I saw that Doudou was staring at me with a look of bemused deprecation. I felt myself blush. I smiled rather stupidly at the giant, and he cocked his head just a touch to the left but made no change in his facial expression. I quickly looked back at the woman.

She told the guys that the wine was still quite fresh, and she

swung her arm with a graceful backhand motion before ten plastic gallon jugs apparently full to the neck with the wine. It was
very cheap, she said. Then she dipped her hands into a large
plastic pan of water on the table that stood between herself and
us. She did it the way a surgeon might wash her hands, scooping
the water, letting it run to the elbows. In the same water she
washed two bottles and laid them aside. Next, she poured a little
palm wine into a tumbler, walked to the door, then poured the
contents on the ground outside. I could feel excitement sparking
up again in my stomach. "Is ritual," said Omar, but when I asked
him what it meant, he ignored me.

The woman returned to the jug, filled the bottom half inch of
her tumbler with wine, and took two perfunctory sips. After that
she slipped a screened funnel into the first bottle's neck, filled
the bottle, then filled the second bottle in the same way. Omar
lifted one of the bottles, took a whiff, then a sip. I closely watched
his face, but his expression told me little. He arched both eyebrows and nodded a bit. The woman handed the second bottle to
Doudou, and he did pretty much what Omar had. I don't recall
noting his expression. Then Omar handed me his bottle.

Rose, it was awful. It was *awful*. It was awful. Though Idrissa
had warned me about the taste, I had had the impression that
they were trying to prepare me for the fact that it doesn't taste
like conventional wines. I was prepared for many things, a musty
flavor, a fruity flavor, dryness, tartness, even blandness. But for
me, the only really pleasant aspect of the liquid was its color,
cloudy white like a liquid pine cleaner mixed with water. It had a
slightly alcoholic tang and smelled sulfuric. It had a distinctly
sour bouquet, which reminds me of something I very much
hated as a kid. If you could make wine from egg salad and vine-
gar, this palm wine is pretty much what you'd get.

Really, the stuff was impossible to drink, but I did my best.

The ordeal might have gone more easily had Omar not been Omar—singing reggae music off-key, slapping my back, philosophizing in a language he didn't understand, toasting a unified Africa, then toasting the mighty Rastafari, toasting me, then Doudou. But the thing that made the ordeal in the bar most unpleasant was that Doudou glared at me for what felt like ten unbroken minutes. He stared at my profile as though my face were his property. I couldn't bring myself to confront him. He was just so fucking huge. He was not merely tall— perhaps six foot eight or so—but his bones were pillars, his face a broad iron shield. He gave off heat; he bowed the very atmosphere of the room. Wasn't it enough I had to drink that swill? Did I need the additional burden of drinking from under the millstone of this man's glare? Just as I was about to slam my bottle to the table and stalk out, Doudou said, in French, "An American."

"Americano," I said.

"Amerikanski," he said.

"That's right. We've got that pretty much nailed down."

"Hey," Omar said, "you like the palm wine?"

Before I could answer, Doudou said, "He doesn't like the wine, Omar."

"Who says I don't?"

Doudou cocked an eyebrow and looked at the low-burning candle on our table. He rolled the bottle between his fingers as if it were pencil thin. "I tell you he doesn't like it, Omar." Then he looked at me and said, "*I* say you don't." I felt cold everywhere. That small, painful knot hardened between my shoulder blades as so often happens when I'm angry.

"You know," I said, stretching my back, rolling my shoulders, "I'm not going to argue about something so trivial." Then I turned to Omar and said in English, "Omar, the wine is very good. Excellent."

Omar shrugged and said, "Is OK, I think. Little old."

Later on—Different Ink—
(My hands are getting terrible cramps. I hope to heck that if you're not reading these letters of mine, you are at least recycling them.)

We were silent after that, and Doudou stopped staring, but it got no more comfortable. Two men started to argue politics, something about the increasing prices of rice and millet, something about Islamic law, and when it got to the table-banging stage, Omar suggested we leave. I had suffered through two glasses of this liquid acquired taste, and Omar, much to my regret, bought me two liters of the wine to take home. I did want to go home and said so. But Doudou said, "You must stay for tea." Omar said yes before I could say no, and I knew it would be impolite to leave without Omar. We walked back to Doudou's place, and I saw that the young men were still quietly getting happy on the Senegalese tequila. Doudou sat in a chair on the porch and sent the young man in chayas into the house, and he returned with a boom box and a handful of tapes. He threw in a Crusaders tape, and immediately two of the men began to complain. They wanted Senegalese music, but Doudou calmly raised his hand and pointed to me. The men fell silent, and I said, "I don't have to have American music."

"Sure you do," said the big man. He leaned so far back in his chair that its front legs were ten inches off the porch, and the back of the chair rested against the windowsill. His feet stayed flat on the ground.

"Your French is good," I said.

"Better than yours," he said. He was smiling, and I couldn't see a shred of contempt in his expression, but that burned up the last of my calm. It was full dark, but I could see his broad smooth face clearly, for the house's light illuminated it. It hung before the window like a paper lantern, like a planet. Looking back on it, I can see that I must have offended him. He must have thought I was evincing surprise that he, a denizen of Fosse, could speak as well as he did. Actually I was just trying to make conversation.

When the bottle came my way, I tipped it and drank a full inch of it. "Thanks for the hospitality," I said. Doudou folded his arms and tipped his head forward, removing it from the light. "Amerikanski," he said. One of the men chuckled.

Omar sat "Indian" style a foot to my right. He rolled a very large spliff from about a half ounce of pot and an eight-by-ten-inch square of newspaper. He handed it to the man sitting across from him, the Franco-Senegalese with the golden hair. The comedian. "Where's the tea?" the man asked in Wolof. "Eh?" said Doudou, and then he pointed to the boom box. The man in the chayas turned the volume down. The golden-haired man repeated his question. Doudou's only reply was "Ismaila, get the tea," and the young man in the chayas rose once again and came back quickly with the Primus stove, the glasses, the sugar, and the tea.

"Omar tells me that you're an anthropologist," said Doudou.

"That's right," I said.

"The study of primitive cultures." Doudou said this as though he'd read these words off the back of a bottle. A dangerous sort of neutrality, as I saw it. It grew so still for a moment there that I jumped when Ismaila lit the stove; the gas had burst into blue flame with a sudden woof, and I found myself glaring at Ismaila as though he'd betrayed me. I cleared my throat, said, "That's only one aspect of anthropology..." I struggled for words. When I'm nervous, I can barely speak my own language, let alone another's, but I managed to say, "but I to study the living cultures." There, I thought, that was nice. I went on to explain that the discipline of anthropology was changing all the time, that it had less to do with so-called primitive cultures and more to do with the study of the phenomenon of culture and the many ways it can be expressed.

The light from the stove's flame cast ghost light over the four of us who sat around it. One of the men, a short man with batlike ears, sat behind Omar and me. He was in silhouette, as was Doudou, up there on the porch. The man with the strange ears tapped my shoulder and handed me the spliff. I took a perfunctory hit and handed it to Omar. "Ganjaaaa," said Omar.

"I knew an anthropologist once," said Doudou, "who told me I should be proud to be part of such a noble, ancient, and primitive people." He paused long enough for me to actually hear the water begin to boil. Then he said, "What aspect of anthropology do you think he studied?"

"Couldn't tell you," I said.

"Too bad."

"Maybe," I said, "he trying to tell you that primitive ... I mean, that in this case 'primitive' mean the same thing as 'pure.'"

"Really. 'In this case,' you say."

"I can only—"

"Was I supposed to have been offended by his language? Are you saying we Africans should be offended by words like primitive?" He placed his great hands on his knees, sat up straight. It occurred to me he was trying to look regal. It worked. I could feel myself tremulously unscrewing the top of one of my palm wine bottles, and I took a nip from it. My sinuses filled with its sour bouquet. "Well ... you sounded offended," I said.

"Who studies your people?"

"What?"

"Do you have anthropologists milling about your neighborhood? Do they write down everything you say?"

"Look, I know how you must—"

Doudou turned away from me. "Ismaila, how's the tea coming?" he said.

"No problems," said Ismaila.

"Look here," I said, but before I could continue, the man with the pointed ears said: "I get offended. I get very offended. You write us down. You don't respect us. You come here and steal from us. It's a very bad thing, and you, you should know better."

"What, because I'm black?"

"Black," said Doudou, with all the sarcasm he could muster.

"Is fine, I and I. Is very nice."

"What the fuck's that supposed to mean, Omar?" I said. "Look, I'm trying to help all black people by recovering our forgot things."

"Your 'lost' things," Ismaila said quietly as he dumped two or three handfuls of tea into the boiling water. He removed the pot from the flame and let it steep for a few minutes. One of the men, a bald, chubby man with a single thick eyebrow, rose from the ground and began fiddling with the boom box. He put in a tape by some Senegalese group and cranked it up a bit. The guitars sounded like crystal bells, the bass like a springy heartbeat; the singer's nasal voice wound like a tendril around the rhythm. As Ismaila sang with the tape, he split the contents of the pot between two large glasses, filling each about halfway, and dumped three heaps of sugar into each glass. While he worked, I kept nipping at the palm wine like a man who can't stop nipping at the pinky nail of his right hand even though he's down to the bloody quick. The more I drank, the odder its flavors seemed to me. It was liquid egg, ammonia, spoiled fish, wet leather, piss. The taste wouldn't hold still, and soon enough it wholly faded. The roof of my mouth, my sinuses, my temples began to throb with a mild achiness, and if I'd had food in my belly that evening, I might have chucked it up. Ismaila began tossing the contents of the glasses from one glass to the other. I could see that Omar was following his movements with great intent.

"What's all this about, Omar?" I said in English. "Why are these guys fucking with me?" I hoped he'd understood me, and I hoped that none of his friends would suddenly reveal himself as a fluent speaker of English. I also ended up wishing Idrissa were there when Omar said, "No worry, I and I; the tea is good."

"Things lost?" said Doudou. "That must mean you're not pure-quois, that you think you can come here and bathe in our primitive dye, legitimize your blackness to the folks back home."

Omar and I exchanged looks, our heads turning simultaneously. That speck of consanguinity encouraged me. It emboldened me. "Want some palm wine?" I said to Doudou. "It really tastes like crap."

The giant shifted slightly in his chair. He said nothing for maybe fifteen seconds. "How does it feel," he said, "to be a black toubob?" I felt my face suddenly grow hot. My guts felt as if they were in a slow meltdown. I took a large draft of the wine, and disgust made me wince. "By 'toubob,'" I asked, "do you mean 'stranger' or 'white'? I understand it can be used both ways."

Doudou leaned forward in the chair, and it snapped and popped as if it were on fire. It appeared for a moment he was going to rise from his chair, and everything in me tightened, screwed down, clamped, but he merely leaned and said, "In Wolof, 'toubob' is 'toubob' is 'toubob.'"

The blood beat so hard beneath my skin I couldn't hear the

music for a few seconds. I tried to breathe deeply, but I couldn't. All I could do was drink that foul wine and quiver with anger. I stared for a long time at some pinprick point in the air between Doudou and me. It was as though the world or I had collapsed into that tiny point of blackness, which, after I don't know how long, opened like a sleepy eye, and I realized that I'd been watching Ismaila hand around small glasses of tea. First to Omar, then to Doudou, then to the golden-haired man, then to the man with the bat ears, then to the chubby bald man with the unibrow. Ismaila didn't even look my way. I sat there with blood beating my temples. Their tea sipping sounded like goddamn shrieking birds.

Then Ismaila brewed a second round of tea, but I received no tea in that round either. When everyone finished, Ismaila simply turned off the stove and began gathering the cups and things. It was the most extraordinary breach of Senegalese etiquette I've seen in all the months I've lived here. No one, not even Omar, said a word. Omar, for his part, looked altogether grim. He leaned toward me and whispered, "You got no tea, huh?" I could hear the nervous tremor in his voice.

"It's no big deal, Omar."

"I and I, you tell him for give you the tea-quois."

"Skip it."

"Quois?"

"Forget about the tea. I got this." I raised the bottle and finished it.

"He *must* give you the tea."

"Omar, that big motherfucker don't have to 'must' shit."

Omar relit the spliff and said, "Is bad, mahn, is very bad." He offered me the spliff, but I waved it off and opened my second bottle. Omar often displays what one could call displacement

behavior when he doesn't understand me. He swiftly changes
the subject or says something noncommittal. You might think
that this is one more thing that bothers me about him, but actually I find it kind of endearing, for some reason. "Is bad, I and I.
He do bad."

"Fuck it."

The other men had moved closer to the big man. Two sat on
the ground, two squatted on the porch. They spoke quietly, but
every so often they burst forth with laughter. I drank and stared
at the bottle. "Listen in you ears, I and I," said Omar. "You must
strong Doudou. You must put him and strong him."

"Speak French, Omar."

"No, no. You must. He do this now and every day-quois.
Every day. Only if you strong him he can't do it."

I took this to mean that unless I "stronged" Doudou, he would
treat me badly every time he saw me, but I wasn't figuring on
seeing him again and I whispered as much to Omar—in French,
so there'd be no mistake. "And besides," I said, "as your country-
men say, 'The man who wants to blow out his own brains need
not fear their being blown out by others.'" I raised the bottle but
couldn't bring myself to drink from it this once.

"No, mahn, strong him. He do this and then 'nother man,
then 'nother, then 'nother man. All the time. All day."

"Sheeit, how on earth could—"

"Believe in me, I and I—"

". . . anything to do with how other people treat me, man.
Let's get out of here. I can't just—"

Omar clutched my knee so firmly I understood—or thought I
did—the depth of his conviction. "You make him strong on him
now, and it will be fine for you." Then he removed his hand from
my knee and touched it to his chest and said, "For me, too." It

was then that I realized that the incident with the tea was meant for Omar as much as for me. Omar had brought me as an honored guest, or as a conversation piece, or as his chance to show his friends just how good his English was. But why was it up to me, either as symbol or as a genuine friend, to recover his luster? I was the guest, right? I told myself to just sit there and drink, then leave. But suddenly, the men around Doudou burst into laughter again, and I distinctly heard the golden-haired comedian say, "Jeeezuuuz!" and I felt my body rising stiff from the ground in jerky motions. I walked straight up to Doudou, dropped my half-empty bottle at his feet, and slugged him so hard I'm certain I broke his nose. I know for sure I broke my finger. Doudou went tumbling from his chair and landed facedown on the porch. He struggled to get up but fell forward, his head rolling side to side. His blood looked like black coins there on the porch. All the men rushed up to him, except the chubby man, who shoved me off the porch. I went down on my ass but sprung up almost immediately. I was still pugnacious but in a very small, very stupid way. Omar removed his shirt and pressed it to Doudou's nose.

I said, "Is he OK?"

No one replied.

I said, "We can get him a cab, get him to a doctor. I'll pay for the cab; I'll pay the doctor." And someone told me in Wolof that I could go out and fuck a relative. I stepped closer to the lot of them, out of shame and concern rather than anger, but Omar handed his shirt to Ismaila, stepped toward me with his palm leveled at my chest. "You go now," he said.

"But I thought you said—"

"You are not a good man." He turned back toward Doudou, whom they'd moved to the chair. The man with the strange ears left with a plastic bucket to retrieve fresh water. They all had their backs to me. I stood there a good long while, sick to my stomach from palm wine or shame, or both. After some minutes, Omar turned toward me for the briefest moment and said, "Don't come again, Bertrand." He said this in French.

I left the little courtyard and immediately lost my way. I wandered Fosse for what must have been ten years. On my way, I encountered an army of headless men who chased me with machetes. Blood gushed from their necks like geysers. Later, I was eaten and regurgitated by a creature with 3000 sharp fangs in its big red mouth. It had the head of a lion, and its long snaky body bristled with forty-four powerful baboon arms.

Months later in this strange new world, I discovered a town where everyone ate glass, rocks, wood, dirt, bugs, etc., but grew sick at the sight and smell of vegetables, rice, couscous, fish. They captured me and tried to make me eat sand, but I brandished a yam I'd had in my pocket, and when they all fell ill at the sight of it, I ran away.

In another town I met a man who was handsome and elegant in every way, and I followed him to his home simply to jealously gaze at him. But while on the way to his own home, I saw him stop at other people's homes, and at every place he stopped, he'd remove part of his body and return it to the person from whom he'd borrowed it. At each place he'd leave a leg or an arm or a hand, and so forth, so by the time he got home, I discovered he was but a skull, who rolled across the ground like a common stone. It made me sad to see his beauty vanish so, and I walked all the way back to my empty home in Denver with my shoulders rounded and my head bent low. And when you asked me what I found on my long, long journey, I told you "Palm wine. But it wasn't in season, so I have nothing to give you but this story."

Love,
Birdie

Within a minute of laying down his pen, he's asleep, and in no time he's dreaming a return to America. He's back at college, but a great deal has changed. He walks, amid a large throng of students, across the quad, south, from the library to Armstrong Hall. It's a concert, a miniature Woodstock, replete with bubble blowing, nudity, hallucinogens, Frisbees, and whirling, head-whipping dance. He learns that folk music is back in vogue. They call it punk-folk, and it's sung by short-haired "hippies." The band occupying the stage sings what Bertrand knows is their hit song, "Mr. President," whose only lyrics are "ooooh, Mr. President, oooh, Mr. President / Why do ya havta be so mean?"

As he makes his way through the crowd, here and there he greets old friends and acquaintances. Some are happy to see him, some must be reminded of who he is, exactly. "Oh, yeah, I remember you. Didn't recognize you in the khaftan and big hair." He sees former professors, and people he knows from here, N'Gor village, and though he'd like to talk to each of them, tell them lies about all he accomplished in the field, he is anxious to cross campus, get himself to Rose's apartment.

He greets her at her door with a kiss, a smile, but before he even steps inside, she says, "I've decided you can be my primary sexual partner, but I'm going to be seeing other people." She says she needs to "balance out" her sex life as though she is talking about her studies or her diet. Bertrand breaks into tears and runs home to his parents' home, whines to his mother what he's been told. In no time, he is driving himself and his mother back to Rose's place. Mother and wife hug warmly and begin to talk about the importance of a woman's need to balance out her sex life; Bertrand weeps at the kitchen table, not even thinking to wipe his eyes on the white sleeve of his khaftan.

He awakens just as the afternoon light has begun to go blue, and he writes Rose a letter about the entire dream. He reads the letter and then smashes it into a ball between his palms, tosses it into his waste can. But after a while he removes the letter, smoothes it back into form, and slips it into his journal. He takes up his shower things, fills his room with bug spray, and closes the door.

chapter 6

Somnambulism

Been away from the village for a few days. I'm at Allasambe's place on N'Gor, and tonight I'll be seeing Idrissa, Alaine, and Kene for the first time in several days. Since their little brouhaha. Tonight Allasambe's having a party for his girlfriend, Nata, who's graduating from nursing school. I'm sorry I didn't take him up on this visit sooner. A ten-minute boat ride and it's ten degrees cooler, the breeze is nearly continual, it's quiet. Maybe I'll ask Allasambe if I can rent a room here.

The day after the fight was too weird, and I'm glad I spent most of it with Sue and slept most of the rest of it away. Alaine's face is a road-work of scratches on the left cheek, and his left eye is swollen almost shut. Kene has been smiling a great deal, and she doesn't have a bruise from what I can see. Mammi has been quiet, but she clings to both her parents, never leaves them alone together during the day. She rarely takes her eyes off them. It's clear they want to be left alone. I mean they don't want me around. They've even been speaking a dialect of Wolof I don't know. Anyway, I can only understand them when they want me to, so what's the point of my being around? I'll doubtless be heading back with them tonight, however, since tomorrow I'm to take Sue to Goree Tengen.

I've been so nervous about it, I've actually been able to get a little work done. Didn't mind it, though, when Allasambe sat down this morning, interrupting me. I kept expecting him to spring something on me: Kene's in love with you, and Alaine knows. Hey, Bert, I've invented a new strain of okra, and I'm looking for investors. I want you to meet my sister. I want you to meet my cousin. I've wanted to get you alone for weeks now, you nappy hunk of man, you. But over café au lait and a day-old baguette, over the sound of waves crashing in the distance, and the hiss of the Primus stove, he aimed his large eyes right at mine and said, "You don't look so good." And to that I had no answer. He chuckled. "Maybe you think I'm trying to sell you something expensive, eh?" and he held up his hand before I could answer. "I'm not selling anything, but I'm not giving anything away either." He paused and let it sink in, but my eyes must have told him that nothing was sinking. "I want to sell you a kind of protection, but I want you to name the price, a small, small price, for what I'm going to sell you is a gift, really."

He slipped his hand into his pocket and extracted something he purposely kept obscured in his closed fist, except I could see part of it, a leather loop about six inches in length. "Before I show you this, I have a story to tell you about myself, so you'll know why I care. And a little about my people.

"I know you know there are no secrets in a village. Everyone knows about you, all five or six thousand people who live in N'Gor village. And we have seen people like you come and go for longer than your own country has exist. Four years ago there was a Peace Corps man who went mad and disappeared. Years before that there was a French painter who died only fifty meters from where you now live." He slipped the thing back into his pocket, squatted, and wrapped his arms around his knees. "But it doesn't go bad just for strangers like yourself but for born inhabitants of N'Gor, too. I went crazy six years ago, myself."

"What happened?"

"Do you see the young boys who go about the village wearing those rough . . . those, those—"

"I think you mean 'gunny sack.'"

" 'Gunny'? I was going to say 'jute.' "

"They're initiates, right?"

"Yes. They have to wear those gunnysack khaftans until the circumcision wound heals. It's not easy. They're not allowed to wear underwear, so practically every time they move it hurts and itches. The pain is to keep them mindful that they have become men. And, truly, it is small, this foreskin pain, compared to some of the things the boys will have to suffer before they become men." He sat back on his ass and crossed his legs. "Keep eating, Bertrand. You're getting skinny as you sit there." I laughed, but he only smiled with his eyes. I dipped my bread into my coffee and ate.

"What we learn, I can't tell you, because it's secret, but during these days, we see things that you have never seen, go places you have never gone, do things you have never done. Only a rare man from here can grow up and forget these things no matter where he goes or what he learns in the lycée, the university, the mosque, the church. This is what we can never get your people to understand. When you meet an African man, especially if he's from a village, you should know that he is a house of secrets. If you laugh at his "old-fashioned" knowledge, he will appear to be laughing with you, but he is laughing at you. But I can't blame you for being confused, you people not from here. For one thing, a lot of the old knowledge is being destroyed, and for another, your minds are too weak to know what we do. The more you understand your ways, the less capacity you have for ours.

"But six years ago, even I laughed at our knowledge." He thumped his large fingers against his chest. "I was living with a Frenchwoman in Dakar, selling expensive things to people who couldn't afford them, making good money, driving a car, traveling to France four times a year, smoking marijuana twelve hours a day . . ." He raised his hand. "I don't criticize you for having a white woman as a wife. I only tell you this about myself because it is so, and because I would have had the same trouble if I had married a black Americana. She might have respected the old knowledge as my girlfriend did, but she would have understood no better. In our opinion, a toubob is a toubob, stranger is stranger. No, don't misunderstand my point, which is this:

"I went nuts, and it was the most fun I've ever had in my life. Everything went out the doors and windows. I laughed all the time, but the laughter made everyone afraid. You know why? Because I literally couldn't stop laughing. I laughed at my girlfriend's face. I laughed at my clients, at the ocean and birds, at my bowl of rice, and cars. My face hurt, and so did my neck and chest. I throbbed in pain, man, but I couldn't stop laughing. I was hospitalized for six months, but after two weeks, my doctor would have nothing to do with me. 'He's crazy!' he said."

It was then I noticed that though Allasambe is generous with his smile, he never really laughs. He chuckles a bit, a two-note sound, with a dip of the head, but he never guffaws or titters or barks. "So I was free," he said. "I could go all over the hospital, and everyone was afraid of me because I could break glass without touching it, and I could take people's food if I wanted to, and they couldn't stop me. My laughter was like, you know, magic. And nothing could stop it. Certainly not drugs. I never wanted to leave there. My girlfriend was long gone. She is now with a man from Thiès.

"Anyway, I was king of the hospital, until six men from N'Gor came to get me one night. I can't tell you how they saved me, only because I have no memory of it. I know I spent most of my time in the mosque and in my family home. I can tell you that these men told me that I was behaving the way I was because someone had intentionally taken my life from me. Someone I was close to. He got my job, my apartment, even my girl for a week or two. How he did, I couldn't tell you. Many people claim to do magic, and there are many theories flying about, but those who claim to have power usually have none. If you want to find a real man of power, look among the beggars. The greatest ask for nothing for their help and knowledge but a bowl of rice, and they dress in rags. The others are only entrepreneurs and thieves. They themselves know nothing, but now and then, they stumble upon a man of true knowledge and learn from him, buy from him, or steal from him.

"So my life was stolen from me, and it has taken me a long time to get it back. I have this job in summers and a part-time job at a new company. I have also tried to repay Allah for some of the things I did wrong to others. I can't pay my old girlfriend back because she won't let me near her. Anyway, it's too late. There are many I can't pay back directly. But if I do two goods for every bad . . ." He shrugged, got up to make more coffee, and as he worked at the Primus, said, "I can help you, and it will be good for me."

"You're talking about karma."

"Yes, karma. I know karma. Good, yes."

Then I asked him what he was trying to tell me, and rather than answer, he removed the object from his pocket and held it out to me in his open palm. It was a tere, one of those cloth or leather pouches that many people wear and carry here because they are said to imbue the bearer with protection or good luck or knowledge. They are said to have inside them herbs and other secret ingredients. The keys to their power, though, are the Koranic prayers written on special paper and wrapped around the herbs and things. I decided then and there to buy it for a small amount, and when I get back to my room, take my seam ripper to it, look at everything under my magnifying glass, record it all here. But as I looked at it closely, I could see the care with which it had been stitched. It would be like scraping the paint off a portrait to quantify its beauty, like dicing up a brain to find the source of dreams. I'll ask Idrissa to help me find tere makers. I'll get in that way, if it's possible.

I know a young student who works part-time where I bank in Dakar who bought tere from a man who purported to be a holy man, a marabou. It was supposed to help her pass an English exam, which, if she passed, would have gotten her a promotion at CitiBank. She told me the man claimed she wouldn't even have to study. Carry the thing in her purse, voilà, big job at the bank.

Never happened. She failed.

Allasambe's tere pouch was a goat-leather square of two-by-two inches and sewn to it was the leather band I had seen when he'd held it out before. "You tie it to your arm or leg, I take it."

"Your arm would be best, but it's good to hide it so people don't know your power, but truly it doesn't matter."

Finally, I asked him as nicely as I could to get to his point.

He said: "Someone close to you is trying to take all you have. You can't stop them from doing it without one of these. I don't know if this particular one works, and if it does not, we get you a new one. You have nothing to lose by wearing it. Pay me what you want."

"What if I don't want it? Look, if you're talking about the Kourmans, I have to say—"

Allasambe's expression didn't flicker when he interrupted me. "I didn't say the Kourmans. I didn't say any name. And I won't, because it . . . well . . . it doesn't make any difference. All that I'm saying is someone."

I asked him how he knew.

"Everybody knows. Everybody in N'Gor—the old women, the little children. Everybody but Bertrand knows. You don't know that you're in danger of belonging to someone. You don't need to know the person. What you need is this."

"Idi? Idrissa?"

"Name the price."

"Well, fifteen hundred, I guess."

Again his expression stayed the same. 1500 CFA is a mere five dollars; surely he wouldn't have wasted all the breath for five dollars. "Here," he said, tossing me the pouch, "you can pay me anytime. Before you leave Senegal." I clasped the thing, felt his body heat still in it.

"I have that much in change right now."

"Your choice."

"Do I wear it now?"

He told me I could wear it whenever and wherever I wanted, but it "would be good" if I wore it all the time in the village and put it in my pillowcase at night. No hard sell from this man. I asked him what it would do to the person it's meant to protect me from, and he said: "It won't hurt anyone. It will protect you by making your will stronger. Someone is doing magic on you, it's clear. I would say that they will be angry when their magic, or whatever you want to call it, doesn't work on you. We can never tell how people are going to react to the things we do." He nodded his big head and smiled.

I shouldn't have sighed so impatiently, but I did, but still his smile didn't stiffen in the least. I said, "Allasambe, you know I'm having a hard time with this. I mean, you know . . ."

He lifted his brows and shook his head, and I was a little relieved to see what might have been a shade of pique color his face. His perfect calm is unsettling as hell.

"Oh, I know, my man. I know where you're from and what you do for a living. I've lived in the West. How do you think I lost my mind? But think of me as a professional counselor if you want to. Take my advice, and the tere as the symbol of my advice. There is someone in the village whose entire association with you is false. You don't know it, but this one robs you, little by little. The stealing is so small and grows so slowly that you can't see it. You don't have the eyes to see it. I do; others do." He held out his hand. "Well?"

I offered him the coins, but instead of taking them he bent over and closed my hand with his long fingers. "Keep the money. It's just ritual, a way of showing respect. If you are not willing to pay for it, you are saying it isn't worth anything. But you put value in it when you pay."

"Wish I'd paid more," I said.

"You are not the first person to say that." He stood, slung his hands into the pockets of his chayas. "I guess you need to work, eh?" Allasambe paused, cocked his head a little bit, and said, "What exactly do you do? What are you researching?"

"Stories," I said. "I'm looking for stories that practically everyone knows, and I want to compare different versions."

"Why?"

I told him I wasn't really sure, and I felt pretty dumb when I said that. But I really don't know anymore. Lately I've been feeling like structuralism and morphology is stuff for chumps who have too much time on their hands. What's the difference between me and some dude who hangs out in a bar, listening to the same sorry-ass stories night after night? Who cares if four of them have the pickpocket stealing food, and seven have him stealing money? Let every individual teller and every auditor create his or her own story, at every moment in time. Let no story be told or read or heard the same way twice. The important thing is that someone's listening while another's speaking.

"But a job's a job," I said. I couldn't look him in the eye.

"Ligayi moi bax-tchunit," Allasambe said.

"I know that one, Ally. 'Man was made to work.'"

Allasambe pointed his left at me and smiled, but it was a sad smile. "I'll tell you a story, since you want stories." He sat down with his heels close to his ass, arms wrapped around his knees. He slowly rocked back and forth, the way a little boy would. He remained quiet for a long time, and I tried not to see this long silence as a kind of performance, in and of itself—the long pause, before the story, that stops the very air and fills the auditor with a great expectancy—but the anthropologist in me is forever grappling with the rube, and he's always grappling with the would-be writer, who believes in art because of its beauty.

"Do you have a foreskin?" he said, and I was so surprised by the question I laughed. He stopped the gentle bobbing and gave me a quizzical look. I blushed, of course, said that I do, and he nodded and went on. "Then you're still a boy, and I am your elder. So you must listen carefully and not interrupt.

"Here in Senegal we're always seeing American black people who come here as though they are coming home. It still surprises many of us because you come from such a perfect place. I know. I told you I've seen the West. You people have everything, but you come here, to eat in this poor place where there is not always enough rice and couscous. The books in the libraries are tattered—pages are missing—but you come here for knowledge. You call this home, but most of you would not dream of staying.

"But there was this one man who came here to stay. He was from California, and beside from the details of the story, I don't know anything else about him. Well, he was fat, and he was like you, still with the foreskin. But he lived in a village, instead of Dakar, as most of you do, and he was like a sponge with learning Senegalese things. He became a Muslim, and he never ate American food or wore American clothing. He ignored French things, too. But he was still a boy, like you, and so this man decided to become initiated, you know, to become a man, you see.

"But this isn't an easy thing to do. He had no family here, especially no mother and father. He was old, too, maybe thirty, and men of knowledge believe that a man his age, with no family, cannot possibly become initiated because he is too full of ways that are opposite of ours. It's like when you take hot glass and pour cold water into it. The glass will crack. The marabous he approached told him initiation would either kill him or make him crazy. You must understand, Berdt, that becoming a Muslim is easy when compared to becoming Lebou or Wolof, or Bambara, or Peul. To be a Muslim means only remembering what we really are, remembering our true state of being, and behaving as a Muslim is a matter of the heart, keeping the five pillars. There is the Shahadah, the first pillar of Islam. There is no god but God, and Muhammad is the messenger of God. The second is Salah, prayer, from man to God. Then there is Zakat, which is something they say you like to do. Do you know what that is?"

I told him I had no idea.

"Giving alms, man. In this way, you're the best Muslim in the village."
He almost laughed this time, and had I laughed with him, he might have
crossed over.

"So anyway," he said, the next is Sawm, which is fasting at Ramadan,
and the last is the Hajj, which everyone knows, because of Malcolm X
and his . . . what is the English word?"

"Pilgrimage."

"Yes. He is famous because of his pilgrimage to Mecca. Hajj is the
pilgrimage."

Allasambe paused here, but it didn't seem to be for effect. He
unfolded his arms and sat lotus style. He patted his pockets for cigarettes, but finding none, cocked his head and looked up at me, said, "Fifteen hundred CFA and one cigarette for the tere?" I lighted one for him
and one for me. He inhaled, blew, and nodded.

"But this man," he said, "wouldn't give up. He didn't know that you
can't do with blood what you can do with faith. He went from marabou
to marabou, village to village. He was desperate, I guess, because he
wanted a woman. You see, unless she is a prostitute, or, you know, not
so good, our women won't sleep with a man with a foreskin because, you
see, it would be like sleeping with a child. Some say it's dirty, too."

"So I've read." I felt myself inwardly whither. I hadn't given this matter
a second's thought.

"Uhm-hm. He wanted to marry. He didn't have the money to get the
operation from a white doctor, which a few people said he should do.
They said, 'Go to a white doctor. No one will ever know.' But he wanted
to be pure, I guess.

"So he went to a place not far from here, where there . . .
mmmm . . . it's not far from here, and there is a marabou there who
isn't a Muslim or a Christian, but who, they say, isn't a good person. OK,
so he went there, and he was taken to a place in the bush and told to go
into this, well I don't know the English word. Hutte?"

"Hut?"

"OK. So it was late, late, late, and there was no electricity there, as it is here in the village, so it was dark as it was before the sun was born. He was there in his underwear only, and, and it was hot. The false marabou gave him things to eat and drink that only an enemy would give you. The false marabou gave him these drinks and such and made him say prayers, but they weren't prayers anyone here has ever heard of. Nonsense words, I think. The American was told that these things were to clean his insides and remove from him all that he brought with him from the States. The American got very hot in his body and vomited, vomited, vomited. Everything came up from him, and he said he was burning, burning hot. The vomiting wouldn't stop, and neither would the burning, which was beginning to concentrate in his . . ." Allasambe pointed to his crotch. "He vomited till it was only water coming from him, and his . . ."

"Crotch."

"Yes, it was so hot that he took away his underwear and felt there, and felt nothing but hair. Nothing but hair! The vomiting kept going, and he felt something large in his stomach, and up, up, up into his throat, and then his mouth. It was his foreskin and everything else."

"You mean his genitals?"

"Yes."

"Up through his crotch, into his stomach—"

"And out of his mouth, and onto the ground, and after that, I'm sure he screamed a great deal when he felt them in his hands in the way no man should feel himself. They say he fainted and did not wake up till the late afternoon. He looked for his genital, but it was gone, as well as his mind, and, of course, so was the false marabou."

No beauty in this story, but I'll always remember it. No truth either, I'm sure, but it's the most remarkable telling of the Cock Thief I've ever heard. I could feel my pulse thudding in my neck. My toes were curled. Every version I've ever heard involves some mysterious guy, coming from nowhere, shaking men's hands in greeting, and disappearing. The men go to take a leak and find their willies gone. It's told from North to West Africa with all the usual elements, but Allasambe's version blows them all to shit.

I usually ask my informants, after they've told me a story, where they heard it, from whom, and whether they believe it, but I was too knocked out to keep my cool. The rube in me sort of won the tussle. All I could manage to say was "Is it true?" and all he did was smile and say, "I'll see you, Bertrand," pronouncing my name the French way. "Stay strong." He stood, shoved his hands into his pockets, then slipped his right back out and shook my hand. He walked outside and down the path to the beach.

The party gathers just before sunset. There are seven of them in addition to Bertrand and Allasambe: Nata, Allasambe's slightly heavyset girlfriend; Medoune, the panther; Alaine and Kene; Idrissa; Oumi, a tall, round-faced woman who, Bertrand learns, studied business at New York University; and a young half-French man named Raymond. All the women are dressed in colorful boubous and head wraps. The men wear untucked short-sleeve shirts and lightweight slacks, except for Bertrand, who always wears jeans and tucks in his shirt. He carries the tere in his pocket.

They begin with drinks at the island's only bar, the Terenga N'Gor. By candlelight, the men drink beer, Oumi sips wine, and the other women have soft drinks. The conversation ripples around their table in a kind of patois of English, Wolof, and French. There is a great deal of laughter. Bertrand tries to make eye contact with both Alaine and Kene, but they won't receive his gaze. He squirms a bit. The fuck did I do to you guys? But he looks at Alaine's puffy eye and softens. Maybe they're not looking anyone in the eye.

Allasambe has brought one of his boom boxes, and he's brought all the American music he has: Santana, Chic, Dylan, Coltrane, the Stones, Al Di Meola, the Clash. Bertrand is surprised and delighted by every choice, but from beneath her wrinkled brow, Oumi tells Allasambe she's sick of American music. She glances at Bertrand, so he smiles at her and says, "Guess you weren't crazy about the U.S." He doesn't know what else to say.

She cocks her head, rather than turn to look at him. "Let me just say I'm glad to be back home." When she does turn full around and look him in the eye, he is surprised at how pretty she is. He'd been judging her by her nasally voice, her seemingly perpetual frown, but when their eyes meet, her face momentarily softens, and she says, "Actually I got used to it. New York isn't bad. I'd like to work at the UN someday . . . but, you know, it's good to be home. Where are *you* from?"

"Denver."

"Colorado."

"My family lives in Colorado Springs, but I live up there."

"And your wife?"

"You must have been talking to Idi."

She smiles and turns to Allasambe, says, "At least you can play some reggae; do you have reggae?"

"No reggae. Wait till we go to my place. All African music, I promise."

Medoune leans across the table and taps Bertrand on the arm. "Hey, I have a question for you. Do you know Faulkner?"

"Crazy man," says Alaine. He nervously lifts his motor cap off his brow for a moment, then tugs it back down.

"I've read him. One book, anyway. Why?"

"I don't know what he means by 'cracker.' One of my students asked me about the word, and all I know is the British meaning, you know, 'He's cracker or crackers.'" Medoune twirls his finger around his ear.

Bertrand leans closer to the table. "Your students are reading Faulkner? In high school?"

"Sure."

Oumi leans forward. "American schools are terrible. Except the universities, you know." She leans back and talks to Kene, who is to her immediate right.

"A cracker," says Bertrand, "is a poor white person or any white person, really."

"Ahhh," says Medoune. "I see. American crackers are white."

"French, too," says Oumi.

Alaine snorts, and his eyes glance off Bertrand's. Alaine adjusts his cap.

Bertrand looks back at Medoune and begins a minor dissertation on the etymology of the word as a racial epithet, telling them that he'd studied the concept of race as an undergraduate, and his greatest interest had been in the area of racial terminology. He discusses with them the terms "white trash," "rabbit," "ofay," "greyboy," "pink," "yak," "honkey," and "whitcy." About midway through his talk, he notices a lone white man, curly headed, bearded, and thin, sitting at the bar. He can tell the man is within earshot by the way his blush shows under the yellowish track lights above the bar. Bet he thinks I'm doing this because he's here. Poor bastard. Bertrand is sorry for the man, annoyed too, and sorry there is no way of telling him he hadn't known he was there, that he doesn't hate him. He's just one guy. A moth in the tar bucket.

He remembers when he and a date had gone to the Star Bar in Colorado Springs. They had just sat down to their first beer, when a small, stooped, white man stepped from behind the bar, wiping his hands on his apron. "Hey, bro," the small man said, "no offense."

"What?" said Bertrand.

"We don't mean nothing by that kind of shit. We just call each other nigger sometimes. Didn't even know you 'uz back here. I'm up 'ere calling Bruce a nigger, and he goes 'boink boink' with his eyes, like, and he goes, 'There's this big, tall bro over there, Mike,' and I go, 'Shiiiiit.'"

Bertrand smiled at the man and decided to pretend that he had heard, and that he'd understood, and he'd be merciful, but inwardly, he was annoyed and put off. The man offered him and his date free beers, but Bertrand said, "We'll be late for our movie." When the small man walked away, he and his date discussed the incident over their beers, and when their bottles were empty, they left. All the way back to his car, his date stroked his arm, squeezed his hand, apologized for white people, and though he considered milking the moment, playing up the pity, he decided against it. "Nigger's just a word," he said. But the rest of the evening turned sour. He never dated the woman again.

Medoune's eyes follow Bertrand's, and he swivels in his chair to look at the white man. He turns back to Bertrand, pokes out his lips, closes his eyes, shrugs, says, "Go on," and Bertrand does, but he tries to keep his tone dry and his voice detached. He tries not to look in the white man's direction. He notices that all those who are fluent in English are listening to him, namely, Oumi, Medoune, Allasambe, Alaine, and Idrissa. Just as he is about to ask Medoune about Wolof terms, jokes, or sayings that refer to white people, Oumi slaps her hand on the table and barks, "Cracker!" She titters and then repeats the word, staring directly at the white man, who is leaning into the bar, his glass gripped tightly in his hand, his shoulders up around his neck. "Cracker.

Cracker. Hey, cracker. Cra-a-a-cker! You hear me. Dirty, stinking
white man."

————

I don't think Oumi quite gets the concept of the UN. After she killed
the bar scene, we walked up to Allasambe's place and had dinner.
Idrissa, Allasambe, and Alaine did the cooking. I gather that the men are
inclined to do the cooking here if the cuisine is other than Senegalese.
We had a Caesar salad, compliments of Idrissa, the Kourmans brought
a couple of baguettes and some wine, and Alaine and Allasambe argued
over how much garlic and white wine to use in the sea cucumber and lin-
guine dish they made. Whoever won out is a genius.

Nata ate, spoke, and gestured with an intensity I rarely see in the
women here. (Of course, since the Kourman-vs.-Kourman bout . . .)
She and Oumi were still laughing about the white guy at the bar. Idrissa
sat next to me, but we hardly spoke at all, "so how's it going," and that
sort of thing. I could feel his eyes on me, and I wondered what effect the
tere might be having on him, if any. I kept my eyes on the Kourmans too.
They'd livened up a bit at dinner, and they were annoyingly affectionate
with each other. As Idrissa would say, they were acting like French
people. Alaine, Medoune, and Raymond talked about soccer while they
ate, Raymond telling an extremely sad story about a member of the
national team who'd died from AIDS.

After dinner we played cards, danced, then walked down to the
beach and swam for about an hour. I hadn't brought trunks, and there
were none to borrow, so I swam in my underwear. I floated on my back
and looked up at the sky; the clouds, almost invisibly dark, were slowly
gathering, eating the stars by the mouthful. I imagined that I was in my
mother's womb, completely alone, swimming beneath her heart in dark
amniotic bliss. Until that moment, I always felt that the word "giddy"
should be used only by wealthy Victorians who swooned and got the
vapors, but now I see how no other word could describe the feeling. I did

somersaults. I splashed around like a six-foot baby. Medoune and I called to the women to join us in the deeper water. Most of the women were wading, hiking their skirts, of course, up around their knees, but Nata peeled down to her bra and panties and played tag with Medoune, me, and Raymond.

The wind stirred up, and it began to get too cold to be in the water, though I doubt the air was any cooler than sixty-five degrees. We trudged back up to the house, and while seven of us went in for tea and absinthe, Idrissa and I walked to the west end of the beach to sit in the dark and smoke some pot.

There was no moon. The ocean and the sky were one thin, gray sheet, almost invisible to the eye. I could barely see the waves skimming toward the strand of black, volcanic rock that clings to a good one hundred yards of the back beach. The waves were faint dark gray bands that seemed to grow wider, rather than closer to the strand. They grew like enormous black water balloons until they exploded in what looked like white flames against the rocks. It sounded like the heavy, slow gasp of ten thousand people, only to be ended by the sound of twenty thousand hands clapping. If you closed your eyes, it made you think you were standing outside the big top of a circus during the trapeze show. Gasps and applause in an endless succession.

Though Idrissa was with me, I felt solitary. I crouched close to the ground and closed my eyes to listen more carefully. I felt once again like I was in my mother's womb. I started thinking about my friend Kevin and his boy and his wife. I still don't know how to write him, whether I'm supposed to talk to him through Rose from now on. I thought about the first dream, too, wondered if it was about my mother, since I was thinking about all the womb stuff, but decided sure it was, though that's nothing very interesting. Kill your dad, sleep with your mom. Sure, sure, every good boy does Freud.

I heard Allasambe's soft chuckle. He nudged my arm with his knee. He'd been standing next to Idrissa for quite a while, I take it, because he said, "You looked to be asleep for a long time." He offered me the joint, and I took a hit, told him I can't fall asleep that easily. "Look there," he said, pointing straight up. I actually gasped when I saw the basket of stars where the clouds hadn't eaten all the sky. I was embarrassed when my friends started laughing. "You were asleep," said Allasambe. He told me how he would sleep back there some nights, that he always dreamed about the ocean and giant birds like eagles. I told him my dreams were full of crazy people doing crazy things and that I'd never yet dreamed of the ocean.

Then Idrissa said, "Hey, Berdt, Oumi goes for you. Why don't you ask her out?"

"'Cause I'm married. Besides, what makes you think she likes me?"

Both men laughed, Idrissa's usual giggle, Allasambe's breathless whisper. "Berdt," said Idrissa, "you can't spend all your time with men. A month or two, maybe, but a whole year?" He held a hand up to me and pulled me to my feet. "It's good to be serious, but you're too serious." When I was face-to-face with him I could see how drunk he was. He lowered his head so that he could look me in the eye. He weaved a little and couldn't focus. "If you don't get some love, you'll turn to Allasambe."

I laughed out loud. "Not in a million fuckin' years, my man. You mean 'turn into' Allasambe."

I looked at Allasambe, and he was grinning, laughing his silent laugh.

Idrissa said, "This is what I'm saying, man. You don't want to break glass with your eyes. Go ask her out."

"But I _am_ seeing someone. Kind of. I mean, there is this woman. Sue. An American."

Both men began to low like bulls. Idrissa slapped an arm around my shoulder, "Good, good. Two is better than one. Oumi on odd days and the other on . . . on . . . on even days. Ahhh, it will be good for you, Bertrand Milworth. And then, when your Rose come, bam! no girls. When . . . when . . . she goes, odd days and even days, again. Bam!"

"Come on," said Allasambe, "it's too cold to sleep out here, and it's getting late."

"Allasambe, this man needs love. This man has no love. Tell him to talk to Oumi."

"He will, my friend. Let's go."

He sleeps, but there are no dreams. It is the same black well of months ago, of his whole long life. His sleeping mind is half aware of the absence, and he struggles throughout the night to lift himself from the dead repose. He grits his teeth; his hands are clamped into trembling fists. He kicks the sheets from the bed, and now and then his eyes roll open, but the sleep will not rise from him, nor dreams come. His open eyes see nothing. He hears snippets of voices, as though someone is spinning a radio dial in his head. Nothing is clear. Nothing comes through. At one point his sleeping body actually sits bolt sharp in bed. He opens his eyes in time to see the door to his room open. There is someone standing there; a woman, he's sure. For a brief moment he's wide sober awake, terrified, fascinated, expectant. She remains there, backlit by the moonlight strained through clouds. She stands for what must be a full two minutes, and he wonders whether she can see him. He says, "Oumi?" She disappears by slow degrees, until he realizes she is closing the door, squeezing the gray light out of the room. The door closes with barely a sound. His head immediately grows heavy with drowsiness, and torpor rolls down his body. Again, he struggles to rouse himself, but he can't. He lies back down slowly as a leaking balloon, and consciousness won't come, and dreams won't come, and darkness presses into him and will not leave him till morning.

chapter 7

Succubae

This happens every time you go to Goree. You know you won't be able to describe it all in your journal, so following each visit you write almost nothing. Your passages on Goree are a mere catalog of abstract adjectives, and you could almost kick yourself for your lack of precision and objectivity.

Perhaps you should only try to describe one single part of it. The slave house, the barracoon, the ancient pale-rose-colored monster shaped like a horseshoe crab. Somehow you can feel the sweaty horror of the place the moment you step inside. You expect the walls to shed tears or blood. Your imagination tries its best not to go wild, but it does. You see the ghastly little pit where they threw in troublemakers—deep, black, windowless, hot. The place still throbs with old fevers, hisses with flies. There must be grooves in its interior walls from fingernails gone mad against the impenetrable darkness. The walls must be slick with the oil of seventy thousand sweaty backs. And on its floors, archeologists would find grains of rice gone hard and black as stones, indistinguishable, at first sight, from rodent droppings and beetle shells, the gobbets of dry blood.

You kneel and rest your hand upon the frame of the doorway, and swear you can feel the tremor of screams, curses, threats, bargains, begging. You cannot help but place yourself in the hole and stare out into the amber light at the young American and his pretty, white companion who stare back at you. You'd like to stop staring into the well, shut down the imaginative eye, but dreams give flight to such fancy. You're thankful for the tour guide's voice prodding you onward.

Then you're shown the square little room where they used to keep the babies. They fed them with flour and grease to make them fat and sellable. You look around yourself, thinking you might catch a glimpse from the joint of your eye of an infant spirit trapped inside. It would be a hot, red shadow the size of a cat. It would howl like a cat. Hunch in corners like a cat. You think you might catch a whiff of the feces, the vomit, the urine, the musk of freshly picked humanity. You think you might hear the wailing children, the crack of whips, heads and knuckles pounding walls. But you could admit this to no one, neither with your tongue nor with your pen. You don't believe in spirits.

And then you're shown that door at the rear of the barracoon. One single, open, arched doorway through which the slaves were brought one by one onto the small boats that would take them to the ship. They called it the door of no return, and you wrestle with yourself as to whether to capitalize the term, write "Tne Door of No Return," but you decide against it, believing that the lower case is less dramatic, less political, less redundant, more you. But despite what you think you are, the sight of it makes you cry every time you see it, and your companion wraps an arm around your waist, and though she herself is crying, she comforts you.

You and the beautiful white woman pass through the doors together, and now that you're out of the time machine, out of history, you stroll along and watch the sky, the water, the people. You fill her ears with all that you know about Goree, the slave trade, and Senegal, and you're surprised at how much you do know. Your head, you find, is full of the stuff of Africa, tales of Thioye the Parrot, Mbile the Deer, Diassigue the Mother Crocodile, who nutures her children by pretending to eat them, pretending they are worthless crumbs. You open up to the white woman, talk about your own mother, the tales of African life in a small, white world. "She was voted Mother of the Year in '67, the year after my first dad—my real dad—passed," you hear yourself say. You don't quite see how it is both the wretchedness and felicity in the sentence that force you to tell more stories: your father's death from cancer, your mother's remarriage in '72, your sister's two marriages, her two divorces, her lover who despises you, the niece you seldom see.

The white woman receives you, apprehends you like a sister, and tells you her own stories. You hear her say, "My brother, obviously, has a hard time fitting into the world, too. And so do I. We were the kids with beatnik, commie parents. I started reading the *Daily Worker* when I was twelve, I think. We had Paul Robeson and his wife over for dinner at least four or five times a year. I wrote my first book report in junior high about Ousmane's *God's Bits of Wood*."

Her stories spread the chambers of your heart. Your stories intertwine so well with hers that you begin to feel you have known her all your life. She is your best friend.

Though you resist the urge to wrap your arm around her and pull her close, you believe you *could* embrace her without her protest. You can tell her anything, and soon you hear yourself saying to her: "I don't know, I've never made love with a black woman. Never kissed one, or held her hand, or taken her to dinner or the movies. Only once or twice have I ever even shared a meal alone with a black woman who wasn't related to me. Never spent much time alone with one, except a kind of semi-aloneness with a lab partner in eighth grade and a lunch or two in high school." You describe the eighth-grade girl as tall and lean, with a round face, skin both dark and bright as cherry wood, hazel eyes, hair that seemed neither red nor black nor blond, but a plummy combination of the three, and Sue says, "She sounds gorgeous."

"She was," you reply, then tell Sue how you asked her to "go" with you. "But she told me to wait till after Christmas vacation. It was the most unique rejection I've ever heard of. I saw her on the bus, and everything, after that, but we were never in the same classes again. I never spoke to her again. I couldn't even look at her, really. The thing is, even though she was pretty, I asked her because . . ." A part of you retracts, freezes. The blood and nerves of your face heat up, and your heart beats faster. You'd like to change the subject, but how can you? You're forced to go on, but not before a few minutes of silent thought. Finally you say, "Don't know why I asked her, really."

You watch a beautiful young black woman, perhaps nineteen or twenty years old, stride from the water. Perfect, you say to yourself, but you don't mean the girl herself, despite her flaw-less black, black skin that sparkles with water, despite her long muscular flanks, her upright naked breasts with their inverted nipples, despite her diver-straight posture and shoulder-length braids that clatter with red and yellow beads. No, you don't mean her, so much, but the irony, the synchronicity of her rising from the sea like a hologram of your memory. You're sure that Sue, your white woman, sees the irony, too. You hope she says nothing of the young woman.

Sue says, "Don't you find them attractive?"

Though your impulse is to say, "Yeah!" as fervently and con-vincingly as possible, you say, "Depends on what you mean by 'attractive.'"

She points to the young woman. "Don't you think she's incredible?"

"What's incredible is I could never talk to her. I could never just walk up to her and tell her my name or ask her hers. I could watch her all day and imagine almost everything about her. I would stare at her from the time she came into my sight, till the time she left it. But I feel"—what will you say?—"almost as if I have no right. Pretty weird, huh?"

"Nothing's weird."

You're both silent for a long time. You both watch the young woman as she heads back to the water, where a young man waves her bathing suit top in the air and says, in French, "OK, girl, don't be angry. You can have it back!"

Sue says: "Nothing's normal either. If you want to get *me* to call you a freak, you can forget it. My husband and I have an open marriage. I sleep with women sometimes. I smoke hash every Sunday before church."

"I thought you said you—"

"I don't believe in God, but I love religious music when I'm stoned."

She takes your hand and presses her shoulder against your arm. You're a good deal more than aroused but can somehow see through the haze of desire that her gesture isn't sexual. "You're so alone," she says, and you nod. "Well, yeah, but—"

"Does your wife know about this thing with black women?"

"Oh, she knows all right."

"I take it it bothers her."

"Wouldn't it bother you?"

"It'd depend on the man. If my husband, you know, Mark, had never had sex with anyone but Oriental women, well—"

You stop strolling and slip your hand from hers.

"No, see, it's not the same with white men. Their own people may criticize them for being nigger lovers, if they date black women, but not for being self-hating freaks, turncoats, or, you know, enemies of their own history. A white guy's gotta be a rapist, or a child molester, or something, before people call him psychosexually ill. If he prefers Asian women, it's his predilection. If I prefer blondes, I slap the face of all black womanhood. But I'm not talking about a simple preference. I don't prefer white women or anyone else. I just don't know how to . . ." You pause long enough to hear the ocean wash the shore two or three times. "I can't get them to love me."

In a way, this sounds right to you, to a degree, but things are missing, and you know it: Bunny and Sally, or the Sadie Hawkins dance in eleventh grade when you rebuffed a pretty black girl's invitation with the lame "I don't have a driver's license." You turned away from her and moved down the hall before she could tell you what an irrelevancy that was. You neglect to mention Norma Jean Vessey, who went to your church, whose mother knew your mother, who said hello to you every day at lunch, even invited you to sit with her from time to time. You don't mention how, on these occasions, you'd tell her that you'd already eaten, or you weren't hungry, or only came in to tell a friend something, or had detention; how you'd leave campus on these days, go to the little convenience store on Wahsatch, and buy chips and soda (all you could afford) and eat in the gym.

For five whole months, the first semester of your sophomore year, she waited as patiently as nature, and never, no matter how often you rebuffed her, did the things you believed she'd do: roll her eyes, flip you off, storm off with her books clamped over her breast. And every time you put her off, she'd say, Maybe tomorrow, or, See you tomorrow, or, I'll try you tomorrow; always the pleasant moon face; always the patient tone. She seemed sad sometimes but kept at you. You wrote of her in your journal that year: "Don't know why I don't sit with her. Just rap with her for a few minutes; she's funny, smart, gorgeous, athletic. Goes to my church. Smells like cinnamon." It's the only passage devoted to her. Hardly devotion, the way you described her. Abstractions. At arm's length.

Then, the following semester, it turned out you and she took the same history course, World History II: The Renaissance to World War I, Mr. Kasl, East Hallway, room 102. You sat directly behind her, and as was the case every January, you had the flu with a bad cough. You sat behind her, puffing enough air to flatten her Afro. You grumbled apologies, winced each time her neck muscles twitched in response to your intermittent buffeting. You'd say, "I'm real sorry," and she'd quarter-turn to say, "S'OK," but seemed always intent on Kasl's lectures. Sometimes, without turning around, she'd hand you a lozenge, a cough drop, whip back a tissue held between index and middle fingers. You believed by now that she hated you, what with your snubbing, your sniffling, your coughing. You could anticipate her every thought: Go die of consumption, jerk. Jesus Christ, nigro, are you trying to part my hair? Hey, Milworth, I been feeling too healthy lately; could you please blow some more tuberculosis my way. You expected that soon, along with the cough drops and tissues, she'd be passing back razor blades, strychnine. She'd spritz you with sulfuric acid. But all she'd ever do was quarter-turn, say, S'OK, and You're welcome. You rarely saw her face. You believed she kept it from you so you'd not see the rage in her eyes.

When class ended each day, you'd scoop up books and notes and slip away before she'd even closed her notebook. But by the end of the second week, the height of your flu, you began to crave her cool attention so much, you didn't want your flu to go away.

And you grew to love her smoky voice uttering the terse OKs and thank-yous. You loved the thoughtful questions she'd ask Kasl about Martin Luther, Copernicus, the *Mayflower*, or Rousseau. Everything you didn't know about her got to you, seeped into you. You never knew, and still you don't know, whether her slow absorption into your guts was connected at all to your assumption she despised you, but you liked to think it did. You liked to think that the more she despised you, the more you could love her. You were unworthy, and that suited you fine. You could experience all the anguished love without so much as holding her hand or looking her in the eye. This is not so unusual for adolescents, and you'd outgrow it. But this was 1972, and young black boys were supposed to be men, in the sexual sense, and most of the handful you knew were. Like your friend Dennis "the Menace" Mitchell, who slinked up to you in the library one day while you were reading a *Time-Life* cookbook to kill some time. The Menace, thin, green eyed, goat bearded, pretty as a calendar Jesus, eased his ass into the chair across from you and said in a tone meant for the gym, rather than the library, "Say, Bird, my man, whussup? What you doing this evening, blood-stone?"

"Homework, I guess."

"What you reading?"

"Italian cooking."

"Ayyy, 'ut's a matta fuh you, paisan, you no like-a da collard green?"

"With gnocchi, yeah."

"Sound nasty, blood."

"What's a matta *you*?"

"You know Mary, wha's-name, Kimbrough?"

"That freshman with the—"

"That's the one. Dig. We pulling a train on that girl tonight. You wanna hook up?"

"That's OK."

"You can go first if you like. It ain't no force thing. She want to."

"I don't think so."

The Menace sat up straight, aimed his beard at you. "Hey, man, you ain't no virgin, is you?"

Of course, you were a virgin. You looked around to see people blushing, smirking, snorting, leaning your way as if in one of those Merrill Lynch commercials. "Hell no," you said. "I just like one-on-one." You spoke with your chin tucked to your chest, eyebrows drawn together, jaws locked, lips scarcely moving, as if to say, "Hey, keep it the hell down, man." But the Menace didn't read you. "Pussy's pussy, man. You know—poontang, ace, trim, stank, lip, boo-tay. You don't be turning that stuff down. Come on, Bird, you ain't no punk, is you? This girl's for free."

"That's OK," you said, flipping a page of the book. Ah, look. Fusilli and sausage. The Menace slinked away.

You remember this day so well because it was the day—twenty minutes later in World History II—when Norma Jean, after five minutes of playing your wind block, turned full around, laid her eyes into yours, and said, "If I ask you to lunch, you're not gonna turn me down again, are you?" Little creatures inside you screamed and scattered, your organs flattened like tapeworms, your brain gasified, your bones liquefied. You expected anything but this. Everything about her was what you didn't deserve. You were terrified. Thankfully your outer shell was the antithesis of your inner self.

"I would, but I didn't bring lunch money today. Maybe we can—"

"I'll pay, and drive, as long as I get to choose the place."

"The cafeteria's good."

She paused, smiled, shook her head, opened her mouth to speak, then smiled again. "Naw, too easy," she said.

You laughed. "No, I mean—"

She touched your hand. "I know. You know the Rainbow Grocery in Old Colorado City?"

"Brown rice and beans, eh?"

"You make it sound immoral."

"It's not that."

"We can eat at Griff's some other day. I'm an omnivore. It's just that I know all this good stuff, teas and stuff that might help with that cold, so I wanna take you to the Rainbow."

"I'm surprised you haven't punched me out."

"Day's not over yet."

"The coughing just—"

"You don't have to explain."

". . . all of a sudden. I can't—"

"I never get sick. You wanna go?"

To your surprise, you did want to go with her. You would have eaten through fields of alfalfa to be with her. But still you felt inferior, unworthy. Ask yourself, Where does this feeling come from?

You both had cheese-and-avocado sandwiches, kettle-fried chips so greasy they were translucent. She had green tea and you Dr. Brown's Cel-Ray soda. You had trouble eating the food, not only because it wasn't to your taste but because Norma Jean made you shiver so much you could barely open your mouth. Pretty? Yes, but never mind that—her clear skin, colored like a camel-hair coat, the widow's peak, the Indian cheekbones, lips soft as orange slices, the Mandinka nose, the one incisor tooth that tipped slightly into the bicuspid next to it, the black irises that contrasted with the sclera like onyx against bone china. It wasn't even her smoky voice or the fact she was older and smarter than you. You shivered as though you were outside in the slushy streets, under the frigid sky. Shivered so much she noticed and said, "With a fever like that, you really should be home."

Sue flattens her lips together and tips her head to the right. "How do you get anyone to love you? You don't. They love you, or they don't."

"I can't explain." You want out of this conversation, and as far from these thoughts as you can get, but they hold you in their crocodile mouths. "You must be hungry by now," you say, and your white woman friend says that she is, so you take the boat back to Dakar and, on the way, talk to her about the shawarma places you could patronize. You mention how sad Goree makes you and about the spirits they say live there. You wish to slip back into the encyclopedic riff and talk as though you were a tour guide, but by the time the two of you are in a restaurant, the steam wafting from your rice, she says to you, "Maybe you just tried too hard."

You know immediately what she's talking about. You pretend to be thinking her words over, but you're watching two Senegalese prostitutes laughing, drinking Gazelle beer. The darker, more slender one is dressed in a red sleeveless blouse and gold toreador pants. Her short Afro has been reddened by the sun. The paler one, colored like an American, wears a boubou of green and gold. Her head wrap makes her seem more dignified than the way she's carrying herself. She's hissing at the waiter, waving her cigarette hand at him. "Get your ugly head over here," she's saying to him in Wolof, and then she tips her head back, laughing loud and long.

You wish you could stop watching them. You wish you were staring into the holding pens on Goree again. You look at Sue.

Her eyes are almost artificial in their green blueness. You want to tell her you'd love to kiss her between her breasts, up her neck, to her ear, roll your tongue around hers. You imagine going back to her room at the Meridien and tucking yourself so deep inside her that you and all of history disappear.

"Did you say 'tried too hard'?"

"About a half hour ago, yeah."

You wonder if you could laugh this way with Kene, or if your Rose will ever smile in your company again.

"I don't think *trying* ever had anything to do with it."

"So your wife is worried about what you'll do out here, I guess."

"She hasn't got anything to worry about. I don't study African cultures so I can check out the action."

"I thought you said you were an anthropologist."

"Very funny." You throw a grain of rice at her. You're glad the two of you are laughing, for laughter is a wind that changes the course of conversations.

A waiter approaches you and says, in English, "What you need? Everything good? Your wife need more beer?"

"I'm fine but bring my husband another, please." She smiles at you, blushes beneath her browned skin.

The waiter spins away, and you say, "I've known black women who couldn't tan as well as you, whose eyes were almost as blue, whose hair was blond as a surfer's, but still . . ." You're surprised that it's you now following the thread.

"How long will you and Rose be apart?"

"At least another eight or nine months. Not long by anthro standards."

"I don't suppose you have the kind of marriage Mark and I do, open?"

"No."

"So if you sleep with someone else—"

"She expects me to."

"Any woman would. Men are men. I think any woman who would expect either herself or her husband to abstain for a year isn't being realistic. Or fair. You're both human beings, and you need to . . . Bert, let's go back to the hotel. I want to give you something."

All the way back on the bus, you imagine telling her, while the two of you are in the middle of groping, that you can't, you just can't. It wouldn't be right. You'll tell her it would be just too ironic to break your sexual fast on this continent with a white woman. You're so steeped in your own self-abnegation that you're not aware of anything outside your head. You neither see nor feel the bodies pressing against you. You see nothing outside the windows of the bus, not a single baobab tree, nor the small herd of Brahma bulls that stops the bus for seven minutes, nor the two wire-thin boys who drive them across the street. You don't see the sun, low and orange, or how the ocean swells like a sparkling sleeping breast, or how the sun casts pink light into the air, or the women selling boiled eggs, peanuts, and oranges on the roadside, or the long-legged children playing soccer with a ball of newspaper tape and twine, or the blue Mauritanian making his way from the mosque at Ouaccam village, or the teenage girls loping across the esplanade of Ouaccam, or the boys who accost them to flirt. There is nothing in your head but you and the white woman on her bed, writhing, and you telling her how very much you'd like to, but, no, it wouldn't be right.

"It wouldn't be right." These are the very same preemptive words you'd rehearsed for Norma Jean had she wanted to become your lover, but it turns out she didn't. She didn't want you at all. You found that out on the very day of the lunch at the Rainbow Grocery. After you'd eaten and exchanged personal histories, the two of you rose and walked the aisles of the little market. You felt honored to be with such a beautiful woman, so warm and funny and smart. She knew about all sorts of herbs, teas, and powders that made you sleep or brightened your eyes or improved your memory. She showed you candy made from yogurt, and this chocolatey stuff called carob, and tart, leathery taffy made from fruit. And then, suddenly as a gust of wind, she placed her warm palm on your arm and said, "Have you ever heard of Young Life?" and when you answered in the negative, she told you that it was a Christian organization for high school kids. She told you that since you hadn't regularly been in church for a couple years, Young Life could serve as a suitable alternative until you felt the call of church again. As blood pounded your eardrums, it dawned on you that she had pursued you these months in service of the Lord, and nothing more.

So the moment arrives when you are actually in Sue Klemmer's hotel room. The door is shut, and the room is lit only by the rose amber of the sun-sea light. Sue sits on her bed, removes her shoes, and lifts her purse from the nightstand. "Sit by me," she says, and she pats the empty space at her right. You'll be strong. Women aren't cigarettes. Let's be friends. We are friends. Sister and brother. She digs through her bag and removes her wallet, snaps it open. You sit close to her, but not too close. If this is to happen, she has to make the first move. There will be no first move. How vain of me, you think, how stupid I'm being. She'll offer you hash, since she doesn't believe in God. She'll give you a condom and tell you to pursue the 19-year-old you'd seen on Goree today.

She removes a photograph from the wallet and gives it to you. It is a picture of Sue at about the age of twenty-two, twenty-four. She wears a dark-blue dress and a graduation cap, white, with a gold tassel. Her hair is darker and longer than it is now, and there are more freckles on her nose than she has now. The picture confirms that her bosom was, indeed, as she told you a few days ago, much larger than it is now. A light-skinned black man of about forty stands next to her with his arm around her waist. "My dad," says Sue.

Your face burns so hot that perspiration beads your forehead.

"I'm not showing it to you to make you feel bad. I haven't been trying to play a trick on you."

The photo trembles there in your hand. And you can't think of a thing to say. You hand her the picture, but she gently presses your hand away and says, "I want you to have it."

"But—"

"I have tons of graduation pictures, tons of my dad. I want you to have it because I want you to remember me." She draws both her legs up onto the bed and sits cross-legged, hunches her back a little. She rests a hand on your thigh. "I love my dad with my whole heart. He's smart and funny, and as wise as . . . I love him so much that—Bert, what I'm trying to say is that I gave up being black a long time ago. That's why I left the States thirteen years ago and never went back. White Americans can be annoying as heck. Black ones can be defensive to the point of dizziness. I used to tell myself that I avoided most black men because no one compared to my father, and I used to think that black women resented my higher-than-high yellow presence, my flat ass and big tits and baby blues.

"But that's only partly true. There're a couple of other things, too. One is that a mulatto who's the daughter of a mulatto doesn't really count, when you get down to it. In college I think I showed pictures of my dad to practically everyone I met. I think that's why I still do it now; just never lost the habit. I had to prove myself, you see, but what's the point? I mean like, what's the point of being black if you have to flash an ID before anyone lets you in the door?"

She gently strokes your thigh, and your cock stiffens, your ears and nipples and mouth tingle, but you feel like crying too. You feel like throwing your arms around her and sobbing as though for the dead.

She says: "The other thing is that I began to feel, from the time—I've never told anyone this before because it sounds so ugly, but there were times when I distinctly remember feeling like I was better than other black people. And when I got old enough to realize how horrible that was, I had to get out of that place. Moved to Europe." She folds her arms together, then unfolds them, clasps her hands together, twining the fingers, then untwines them. Her hands rest there on her lap, right over left, like open shells, pink, curled.

She sighs and says: "Passing in America means hearing all sorts of nasty talk that black ears aren't supposed to hear, and there's just no getting used to it. It also means finding black people who love you for the right reasons and the wrong reasons." She pauses, reaches up, and touches your face. "I don't have to explain that, do I?" You shake your head; your vision blurs with tears. "I'm not saying that Europeans are free of bigotry," she says. "They're nothing of the sort. It's just that since there are so few black people where I live, I don't have to feel like I'm always on the outside looking in. . . . Well, I'm on the outside in Europe too, but—"

"Sue, I'm sorry. I can usually tell. I've *always* been able to tell."

She uncrosses her legs, leans into you, and enfolds you in her arms. "It's not your fault, Baby. It's genetics; it's culture. It's economics. We didn't make this world." She kisses you under your jaw three times. "Bert," she says, "if I weren't an ex-colored girl, I'd have loved to have been your first. But I don't count. There is a kind of end to blackness, and I'm it."

"No, Sue. I don't buy it, black is black. I mean, are you saying you're white?"

"Absolutely not, Bertrand. I'm invisible."

You do spend the night with her, but there is no sex. Your naked bodies turn toward each other, they soften and stiffen, redden and relax as marital bodies often do, but there is no sex, and neither are there dreams, for you. At six in the morning when you rise, your head hurts, and your neck is stiff. You and the pillow have left red marks on Sue's white skin, and she squints so firmly, you can't see the color of her eyes. Sue packs. You help her. You eat no breakfast, and the two of you take the shuttle to the airport. You wait with her till she boards the plane. You savor her kiss for a while, but you don't wait to watch the plane roll away. You take the number 7 to your little room in N'Gor village, which is only fifteen steps from Alaine and Kene's room, and go straight to bed. You sleep, sleep for eleven hours, in fact, but still there are no dreams.

During his sleep over the next twenty-three nights or days, he suffers night sweats and bruxism; he snores, speaks in French, Spanish, English, Italian, and a Wolof far more fluent than that which he speaks while awake. Twice he has awoken in a sitting position and heard a sound like frying fat or radio static that faded as his eyes gained focus. One morning he awoke standing in front of his door, dressed in underwear and flip-flops, hand on the knob. Shock coursed through him so swiftly, he stumbled backward onto his bed, dropped his face into his hands, and hyperventilated for nearly two minutes. He began coughing with a coarse violence, then fell to his knees, speckling the floor with spit. "Fuck," he said, or rather gasped, and for some reason he felt like laughing, but the coughing got hard again, and he lost the urge.

Sometimes, on the verge of sleep, he feels as though a body lies on top of him, its belly to his back, or it straddles him, and though he struggles to throw it off, he never can. He can't so much as twitch a finger. It's as though the body presses him into a sleep so black and recondite that he can scarcely breathe. One night he felt hands, four of them, six of them, delicately massaging his face and body. The hands felt dry and rubbery, very warm. He struggled to open his eyes and rise, but all that happened was that he felt his whole body become light as fog and levitate several inches over his bed.

Nearly every night his penis fills with blood, and on these nights, he rises from bed to piss, but he never passes more than a trickle. The erection hurts him, as though he suffers from priapism, so he never thinks to relieve himself by masturbation. His penis is a dead thing these days, cold and flaccid by day, cold and tumescent most nights. He rarely thinks of sex at all and wonders, now and again, whether he's coming down with something. He hasn't the money to see a physician and has no one to talk to about his condition, since the Kourmans, particularly Alaine, have grown icy and distant.

Sometimes at family meals (he rarely sits with them now) they speak to each other in flat, cool sentences and don't so much as look at him. The food has no taste to him, and he never feels full after eating. After a week of this, he begins to take all his meals at the airport diner, spending some two or three dollars per day. He counts his dwindling sum in his head as he chews (1802, 1800, 1797, 1790). And there, too, at the airport diner, the food might as well be clay, cotton, plastic, tinfoil, so devoid of flavor it seems to him. He is almost certain he's ill, but since he can rise and walk, and work, and sleep, he eschews medical help. And feels no pity for himself.

And for nearly every night of those twenty-three nights, he hears snatches of conversation just beneath hearing. He hears what may be his name. And depending on the night, he hears what may be conversations between two men, or between a woman and a man, or among a small gathering of people, and once in a while, a buzzing monologuist, whose voice is a blend of cicada and Brahma bull. Sometimes there is laughter, but more often than not the voices sound serious, even dolorous. There is a tinny quality to them, and sometimes he strains so hard to hear them he wakes up. And when he does, he'll creep from bed, cross the room, press his ear to his door, listen. He never hears a thing but Alaine's (or is it Kene's?) snoring.

Over the next twenty-three days or nights, he wakes up groggy or weary, depressed or semisomnolent, choleric or trembling with euphoria. Over his morning coffee, he'll screw as deeply into his mind as he can, but finds nothing but memories of the previous waking day and his plans for today and tomorrow. He feels his dreamlessness deep in his stomach—a literal hunger—or he feels it run up and down his ribs in a nervous thrill. It's the same dull anxiety he felt when Rose had confronted him about his tryst with Jewel Hefler. A "thin" feeling, he calls it, for his heart doesn't beat but ticks like a watch. His breath is shallow. He frequently swallows. He stiffens his body.

For each of these twenty-three days his work goes steadily, despite the fact that Idrissa is on holiday in France. He has found, in his tapes, two new proverbs and has found a seventh version of the story of the Disappearing Pickpocket, though he doesn't really care. No excitement at all in his heart or head. He writes no letters home and takes no trips to the post office to collect those he may have received. He writes nothing in his journal. No point in that. No point in much of anything, really.

And on the twenty-fourth day, the most alarming thing of all happens when he finds himself waking up in the shower, his flip-flops on his feet, a bar of Dial soap in his hand, a washcloth in the other. He is whistling a Milt Jackson number, "Darbin and the Red Fox." His crotch, underarms, and hair are soaped white.

His first reaction, when he discovers he's not in bed but in the shower, is a bark, a sound he has made only once before, when he was in the dorm showers in college and someone flushed without calling out the customary warning. The water scalded his crotch. He barked.

"Sorry, Bird," the flusher called.

Though here and now the water is the usual sixty degrees, his short, sharp bark takes him immediately to that other event in the dormitory shower, and for the briefest moment, he is more there than here. His confusion is so piercing that he drops both soap and cloth and cups his hands over his crotch. He falls against the wall. In the time it takes to draw one breath, his consciousness splits farther apart: he's in bed in black sleep, he is in two showers, he is somewhere between two places and nowhere at all. But in seconds everything resolves into a single reality: Bertrand lying fetal, the cool water thundering in his right ear. He's mad with fear and anger, hands over his genitals. He's had enough. He'll go home, check into a hospital. Fuck this noise. Fuck a Ph.D.

He stands up and rinses; the water feels gelid to him, and he shivers, despite the warm air, despite the fact he's grown accustomed to cold showers. He knows his shivering has everything to do with his agitation. His muscles are sore and his teeth clamped together. He walks stiff-leggedly from the stall, dries himself, wraps the towel around his waist. He sits down just outside the bathroom on a cement step. He sits for at least an hour, thinking so intensely he scarcely moves.

chapter 8

Pliny Says, "It Is Evident That Horses Doe Dreame."

Thought rises from your head like steam. You wonder what's eating your brain. You think about killing yourself before you start pissing your trousers or hollering filthy words at strangers. You think about cutting everything loose. You'll go to Italy and move next door to Sue Klemmer and have sex with her every day. Or you'll grow dreadlocks, hang out on Denver street corners, and scare middle-class people. Or they will find you dead in your little room, your pen in hand, transcripts up to your knees.

Your room. Since it is a Saturday, you wonder how you can get back to your room without facing the Kourmans. You aren't sure what time it is, but since it is morning, Alaine will still be in bed, Mammi and Kene cleaning or marketing or cooking. You know you can't bear behaving as though nothing has happened, and that's exactly what you'll have to do if you meet them. But what can you do? There is only one entrance to your room. The windows are barred; there are no rear or side doors in the house. You have to walk the little path from the bathroom to the front porch, up the steps into the foyer, then the common room, and through your sea-green door. You have to say nangendeff and chitchat in your weak Wolof.

How did you get here? Are you here? Maybe you strutted out here naked, right in front of woman and child, or maybe you'll find you've killed them, eaten their hearts, and put their heads in the freezer. Something like a smile moves across your face, and you shake your head. You won't think about that, but you do admit that, given the circumstances, anything is possible. Get up and go. There's nothing else to do.

The first thing he sees is Kene, sitting on the couch, quietly weeping. When she sees him, she begins rubbing the heel and back of one of her hands against her eyes. "Nangadeff, Berdt?" she says. He clutches the waist of his towel and steps closer to her. "Nangadeff, Kene? Ana Alaine?" he says.

"He is no home from a lot of nights," she says. She opens her palm, producing a balled-up tissue. She slowly spreads it open with her thumbs and forefingers, then blows her nose. "Mammi is at N'Doye house."

Bertrand tells her in French she need not speak English, so she replies in French, "He's been gone several nights. I'm just very upset is all."

"Look, let me put on some clothes, and—"

"You do what you like. It's all the same to me."

"I just . . . you know." He shrugs, cinches the towel more securely around his middle, takes two steps, and sits next to her, knees together, toilet kit and washcloth on his lap. He's afraid he'll watch her mouth too closely as she speaks, pay too much mind to her bare feet and her throat, so he looks at her arms. She is scented with rose oil, and with her own particular spice, and were it not for his lingering disorientation—his fear that a mere blink might transport him back to the shower, or the bottom of the sea, or a rodeo in Colorado—he would let himself fall into the heat and smell of her body. But if this is a dream, he thinks . . . but he stops himself. I'm not dreaming. I can't dream.

He can see that she is vulnerable, open, fretful. Her fingers are threaded together, her nostrils flare and retreat, her chest is flushed; it looks almost like suppressed passion, but he won't fool himself. He believes she can barely stand him, and he knows Alaine would cut off his hands if he put them on her. He tells himself that if he so much as shows a flicker of interest in her body, Alaine is sure to step into the room and read his face as easily as he'd read a clock.

Neither of them speaks for nearly a minute, until he remembers the Senegalese etiquette of men speaking first with regard to certain serious matters, even in this home, with its feminist leanings. "If you want me to look for him," he says, "I do it."

She gives him a sharp look. "I *know* where he is."

"He's . . ."

"He's with the garce, that Belgian, white, Belgian garce. Oh, I know ex*actly* where he is."

"Garce"? Bertrand runs and rolls the word through his mind but knows he doesn't know it. "Garce?"

"Female cur; I don't know the English."

"Bitch."

She stabs her finger at him. "Bitch, yes, bitch," she says in English. "She is une bitch-garce."

"My French is evil. I'm sorry."

"It's bad. Say, 'bad.'"

"No, I think evil's a better word."

She chuckles a little and shakes her head. She sits back and folds her arms. She crosses her legs and looks at him, says, "You look bad today, but at least you're up. How do you feel?"

"'Evil' is still the right word, I think."

HE SLEEPS / 163

Kene smiles and says, "You're funny. You're funny." Her arms and legs are still wrapped up, but her smile seems genuine to him. Bertrand is aware of his own soapy smell. He feels his nakedness. He won't let himself see that he is trying to charm her, and to conceal it more fully from himself, he says, "If you tell me where he is, I will go and return him."

"Bertrand, you can't do that! He's a man. Men are free. You can't tell him what to do."

"*You* can."

"Theory is one thing, cocks and pussies are an entirely different matter."

This stops him from speaking for a good long while, and he watches her rock her foot and slowly shake her head. Then he says, "What I am trying to say is that you are his wife. You have natural and legal rights. You have a baby."

"Daughter!"

"Do you really need to—"

"Sorry."

". . . my French at every turn. I'm trying to—"

"Sorry, sorry. You're right, I'm just angry. I understand what you're saying."

They are quiet again, and Bertrand feels his nakedness so acutely that it becomes unbearable. He says, "I'll be right back; I'm just going to my room and dress." But when he looks up at her, he sees she's weeping again. The tears fall heavily, but she's not sobbing. Her anger is back in full flower.

Kene says: "Is there something wrong with me? Nothing much. So why does he hate me? You men make all these promises. When you talk, mangoes fall from your mouths. A woman gets drunk from all the sweet stuff, but when you're finished, everything tastes like filth. Why is this?" She tightens her arms across her chest and sighs. She opens her palm and stares at the wadded tissue paper. She sighs again, perhaps because she sees it's used up, and she tosses it to the floor. Bertrand picks up his washcloth, wrings the soapwater from it right onto his lap, and hands it to her. "Thanks," she says, "you're a good boy." She dabs her eyes, blows her nose, and then sobs with such sudden ferocity that Bertrand feels the urge both to shrink into himself and to wrap her in his arms. But he remains rigid, alternately looking at his clamped-together knees and her convulsing back.

Finally, he can bear it no longer, and he gently places his right hand on her back. He is vaguely aware of his desire to communicate to her every dream he's had about her, but he won't look at his own thought. If the thought were a physical thing, he would be squinting at it till the image blurred. He wrestles with himself, tries with all his strength not to stroke her back. He won't rub small circles along the pattern of her blouse or bend close to her ear to drop ripe mangoes into it. He keeps his hand flat and very still. Last thing she wants is my chest on her back. I should get dressed. I really should. But he does not move.

As her crying subsides, he feels her back muscles stiffen, so he lifts his hand, and when he does so she sits up, looks him dead in the eye, and says, "You're not going to answer my question?"

He gives her a blank look.

"You thought I was being rhetorical? Well, I wasn't. I want you to tell me why you men talk one way but never, ever, ever follow your own words." She pins him with her eyes to the point he feels his innards coil up. He stops breathing. If Rose had looked at him that way, he would have hanged himself. He wants to look away, to go to his room, dress, leave the house. He looks at her mouth as though it's everything he needs, fruit, flower, and sap, and imagines touching those lips with his fingers. He would touch them lightly, stand, and leave. Why do men lie? God help you, woman, to be with someone like you. He'd say this, and he would walk away.

"Women lie too, you know," he says. "Everybody lies now and then, Kene."

"Sure, sure, even when your auntie's dress is so ugly it hurts your eyes, you tell her how beautiful it looks on her. When your daughter asks how she got in your tummy, well, you tell her you found her under the great baobab tree, or that her father gave you a kola that makes babies. You tell your mother that you were at the library and not with your boyfriend. You say you aren't jealous of Madame M'Baye's garden. But men say, 'I will come home to you every night, and feed your child, and breathe in your dreams while you breathe in mine,' and none of it is true. Men don't lie to protect themselves or spare feelings, but to use and throw away. I'm asking you why."

"I don't know! I don't know!"

"Aren't I beautiful?"

"Sure you are. Very."

"I cook, right? It's good, right?"

"I like it, you know, but the men I know don't—"

"Mammi's a good child, right?"

"I'm no judge of—"

"Bertrand, what's wrong with me? Shit! I can't order him to love me. I can't make myself become two, three women, whatever it is he wants. I'm twenty-five. I'm educated. I work. I'm a good woman. Where is my money? Where are his hat and shoes? Under that white bed! In that white apartment." She folds up her arms and legs again. She blinks back her tears.

"Kene, it's just . . . you know—"

"Oh, I know, I know. I know you don't know. You don't know snake piss."

"I need to get dressed."

"Answer my question."

"I got my own questions!"

"Then go." She kicks the coffee table. It skids a foot or two away. She's clearly dissatisfied that she hasn't overturned it so she leaps up to kick it again. Bertrand rises to clutch her shoulder, but his towel slips and he withdraws his hand to catch it. The towel hangs between his palm and his crotch like a long white loincloth. Kene giggles.

"I really need to dress."

She laughs. "Sure, sure. Sure you do. You think you have something I haven't seen before? You're hanging on to yourself the way the boys do when they learn about the Cock Thief."

His eyes widen, and as he rewraps the towel, he says, "You mean the story of the disappearing penis?"

"No, the Cock Thief. And it's not a story, it's true. Spirits take them. My mamaw's uncle had his cock taken. This was maybe sixty years ago, around World War I. He fought for France and came home a hero, but came back without his cock. And no, it wasn't shot off; a woman took it, what he says passed for a woman."

"You mean he was impotent?"

"I don't know. What's the difference?" She watches him cinch his towel with the eyes of a woman observing a sickly infant: pity, disgust, love. She says, "Are you hungry? I can fix you something and tell you about it."

"You don't need to cook."

"Then take me to lunch. Just so long as I'm back before my friend brings Mammi home."

"I will take you if you will tell me the story about this thief."

"What, you can't say 'cock'? You're such a baby."

"A fool, too, but I'm older than you by nine years."

"I'm older than you because I have Mammi."

"I like the way Africans think. What would you call that, merit years?"

"Nice turn of phrase, Baby Man."

He looks down at his waist. I'm flirting. I'm fucking flirting. He is only a hair's breadth from permitting himself to think, With a black woman. He feels his blood move in waves to the surface of his body. "Hey, Kene, have you heard a story about an American who's made to vomit up his penis?"

"It was supposed to have happened to a man who lived here, but that was before we came. That story is also supposed to be true, but I don't believe it. Why are you so interested in these stories? Are you afraid? Been having bad dreams? As much as you sleep, I'd guess they were very good ones."

"I haven't been sleeping all that much. More than is normal for me, I guess. I haven't been dreaming at all. For maybe a month or so."

Kene looks at him for a long time. Then she looks away and sits down. She studies him with an expression so serious he feels himself flush. Kene folds her arms, and she looks pensive again, the way she had when he'd found her.

"What's wrong, Kene?" He sits next to her, keeps his hands on his thighs.

She says nothing, her mouth slightly agape, the bottom lip hanging low and sweet as fruit.

"Kene, what's going on? Is it Alaine?"

He is fascinated by the subtleties of her tears. When she's angry, her tears gush from her eyes. He would guess they were hotter than the ones falling now, which slide down her cheeks like the afterspill of hot water down a teakettle's spout. He presses her arm with the palm of his hand, squeezes, and she lets him; in fact she leans into him and says in a throaty whisper, like Mahalia Jackson hitting low notes, "I gave you those dreams.

Almost every single one." The timbre of her voice alone, the perfect modulation, the blending of a variety of feelings—love/anger/pride/blues—is enough alone to push through his ribs and fill his breast with a lucent weightlessness. His body shakes from too much fear and too much joy, and he throws his arms around her neck and weeps with her. "I know you did," he says. He kisses her along her throat, up to the ear, and she rolls her face toward his. They kiss until she turns her face away and says, "I know you know, Baby Man. I know you write them down. They were good, good, *good*, good dreams."

He reaches up and touches her bottom lip. "You know everything about me."

She stiffens a little. She leans back from him. She blinks. "Of course I know," she says. "You belong to me."

Bertrand nods. "I do. How do you do it?"

She draws her head back sharply, squints. "You do it." She smiles. "You want me."

"But the dreams. The dreams, you see . . . I don't dream. I mean before you—"

"Everybody dreams, Baby Man, you just didn't see them."

"Yeah, but—"

She abruptly but gently pushes him against the couch back with her shoulder. She lies against him and folds her arms over her breasts. He wraps his arms around her. "My husband is the kind of man who doesn't believe in the things his own people can do. He's really that way. But you, you pretend to be that way. You don't fool me. Alaine thinks he's God, but you only think you think so."

Bertrand flinches when she says that, but settles almost immediately. He knows; she knows. He wipes tears from his eyes and clears his throat.

Kene wiggles a little, settling into Bertrand's embrace. "You're not a handsome man, but I like you. You have more natural goodness than Alaine. But I'm not saying I'm leaving him for you." She shrugs as though suffering a momentary chill. "But it pisses me off that they took away your dreams. I had no idea. Those swine made you an automaton. Made you sleep and sleep-walk. I should have known that tere was for something like that. You've been so sick."

"I've been fine."

"And I should have known why so many of them have been coming to check on you. I thought they were helping you. I really did." She chuckles. "Poor Baby Man. You're so easy to love because you're so sad."

He doesn't feel so loved right now, but he won't relinquish their embrace. He squeezes her a bit, says, "Who came to check on me? I'm not sure what you're talking about."

"All your friends. A few of their friends. A doctor. You've been sick, silly one. Apparently you haven't looked at yourself."

"I guess I've lost some weight. I haven't felt like eating."

"Oh, really? I hadn't noticed." She laughs. "You eat two bites and go back to bed."

"Did we ever actually make love?"

"You were in no danger of giving me a baby, but I imagine we did."

He remains silent.

Kene says: "I mean no, not physically, but I enjoyed it. You smiled a lot, talked back to me sometimes, but you seldom made sense. But for the last few weeks you've been dead to me. I thought you'd grown as tired of me as that stupid man. You stop dreaming, and Alaine leaves. When he left, you were all I had."

"But you just want an affair so—"

She nods. "Well, yeah. Don't be silly. I'm in no position to leave him. I'd lose my child. Lapsed Muslim that he may be, he'll still claim his parental privileges and rights under Islamic law.

Mammi's the issue of his seed, and I am his little vessel. You've lived here a while. You know how it works."

"But the dreams—"

"What's the big deal? You liked me already, and you want *every*one to love *you*, which I do, by the way. It was nothing for me to sit at your bedside and tell you stories and kiss your mouth and ears and rub you between your legs. I gave you things in your food to help you sleep better—Alaine and Mammi ate it, too, so don't think I was trying to poison you."

"So—"

"Let me talk. Let me say this, because I know what you want to know. You know what I did? I talked to you. I just talked to you about all the things we could do with my body and yours. I can feel the way your heart's beating under my shoulder blade that you think I do magic. But that's because you want there to be magic in this world. There is, lots of it—and Alaine believes every bit as much as I do—but what I did is no more magic than the philosophy of Carl Jung. You're attracted to me. You're here alone, and everyone knows you have no girlfriend. Oumi can't stand you, and your American girlfriend, the one you met in the bar? Well, she's gone, isn't she?"

"She was just a friend."

"Men."

"I thought Oumi—"

"You thought wrong."

"But Idi—"

"What do men know?"

"I guess not much."

"Less than that. Anyway, you and your wife are in trouble. I know, I know, so why look at me that way? People talk. Why didn't you bring her with you, by the way?"

"So Alaine is jealous, I suppose, and he want you to—"

"He 'wants,' 'wants.' But I don't know what he wants. I thought he'd start paying more attention to me when it was so clear to him that you were. Instead he calls his 'bitch' friend from Belgium and tells her to come live with him. Can you believe that? And he uses the fucking phone in his fucking boss's office. He gets fired."

She rubs Bertrand's arm, then pats it. "Who gave you the tere? Idi?"

"Allasambe."

"Same-same."

"What does it do? I mean—"

"It apparently does something. It makes you sleep a lot, it seems. I don't know how it works, but it apparently leaches something into your skin when you sweat or bathe. It's probably full of lead or something. I should have known. Why did you wear it in the first place? What were you scared of?"

"You, I guess. Both of you."

"Fucking Idi."

"What about Allasambe?"

"Here, take this damned thing off."

Bertrand fumbles with the clasp, until she pushes his hand away. She deftly removes it and tosses it onto the coffee table. "He told me it would protect me," says Bertrand, "from whatever you guys were doing to me."

"*We* weren't doing anything. I gave you those dreams." She sits up and looks at him. He feels his right side grow cool, and he thinks about going into his room to dress.

"Bertrand, your so-called friends have been interfering with your life in a serious way. I'm not the one who made you sleep like a dead man."

"I don't understand you."

"If I were you, I'd go back home. At least get out of this part of Senegal. No. Go home. Your wife needs you, I'm sure. Why did you leave her there?"

"You're saying I was sick?"

"Aren't you?"

He nods, thinking of the shower. "I guess I am, but what makes you think Idi and Ally have had something to do with it?"

"Because they gave you the tere, didn't they?"

"Ally did."

"Same-same, like I told you. I know they have, because since you went to the island, you've been dead to me. You didn't even recognize me when I came to your room then. You called me Oumi."

"The night of the party."

"Yeah, you remember now, eh?"

"But why?"

"You're the man, ask them. Tell them you know. Shit!"

"Be right back," he says and retreats to his room.

You toss your towel onto the bed and look down at your genitals, lift your penis with your right hand but don't clasp it. You scratch the pubic hair, then sniff your fingers: soap and you. Perspiration streaks all the way down to your flanks or falls straight from your armpits to splash on your feet. You feel a little queasy, vibrate, all nerve endings, you are. You touch your penis again. Nothing. Dead. You feel excitement in your solar plexus but nothing in your balls. Your hands feel hot, your lips, your nipples, even your ears feel slightly distended with blood, but you're a ghost from your navel downward. You dress and return to the common room. And right after you notice she has returned the coffee table to its place, you see Allasambe step in from the foyer and into the common room.

"Nangendeff?" he says.

"Manginirek," says Bertrand.

"Bonjour," says Kene. "Ça va?" Before Allasambe says another word, Kene says, in Wolof, "He's not here."

Allasambe points to Bertrand, says, "I came to see him, actually. But don't worry, Alaine will be back."

"So you've seen him," Kene says.

Allasambe shakes Kene's hand, then Bertrand's. He smoothes his chayas and sits. "Yes, I saw him yesterday. He'll be home in a day or two."

Kene pushes her lips forward, as if kissing the air; she arches an eyebrow. She sighs, dovetails her fingers, and sits, and now Bertrand knows she is annoyed. "Are you trying to make a joke?" she says.

Allasambe nods. "Sure, I'm joking." But he says this without smiling or looking in any way nonchalant. He is grave, in fact. He shrugs, tips his head to one side. "Bertrand," he says in English, "I want you to come for tea or a beer."

Bertrand feels uncomfortable with "code switching," as he would call it, particularly after the intimate words he has exchanged with Kene. He tries to shift the conversation back to French, answering, "Yes, tea would be a pleasure. Is tomorrow good?" Formal as though read from a Berlitz book. He's trying to show Kene that he, too, is annoyed. But Kene rises and walks to her bedroom without saying a word, and she shuts her door with a quick and firm snap.

Both men turn their gaze from her to each other at the same time. "I don't think she should be by herself," says Bertrand.

"Careful, man."

"I don't get you."

Allasambe smiles. "I know that you do." He nods ever so slightly.

"You don't think I'm after her."

"Alaine thinks you are. He says you've actually caught her."

Bertrand shoves both hands down into his pockets, rises up on his toes. "Is that why he stuffed that couch with the bird?"

"Come to the island, Bertrand."

"I don't know what you think is going on, Ally, but we were just going to lunch."

"Bertrand, come to the island, or Alaine will try to kill you."

Everything seems quiet for a good long while, an uncanny moment in a village of five thousand, even in the dozy hours of the siesta. Several seconds go by before Bertrand understands that the silence is from the blood that beats against his eardrums. "Alaine claims you stained his wife's sheets."

"What?"

"You'll be OK on the island, but we really should go now."

"What he's saying is so far from reality. . . . Look, the woman's right there, right in that fucking room. You go ask her. You go ask her if I ever, *ever!* laid a . . . You ask her if we ever had . . . I can't believe this shit! Go ask her."

Allasambe rests his chin in both palms, and he closes his eyes. He remains in this position for a minute or so, silent as grass. Bertrand says, "Go ask her," at the same moment that Allasambe opens his eyes and says, "I put the bird in the sofa."

"What? What did you say?"

"I put the bird in the sofa."

Bertrand looks at the Kourmans' bedroom door and then sits back heavily on the very sofa. "Well, I don't care about that," he

says, though he does care, and he knows he cares. He's certain
Allasambe can see his heart rocking his whole body.

"Idi told me to do it."

"Then he's a fucking liar."

"He was just trying to keep my friend from killing you."

"Why are you doing this to me? Why are all you guys doing
this to me?"

"I'll answer your questions when we get to my place. Idi will
too."

"So he's back."

"Been back for two weeks."

"Why hasn't he come around then?"

Allasambe lifts himself from his chair as though he were lifting
the world. He rubs his bald crown slowly, then looks at his watch.
It's then that Bertrand notices how tired Allasambe looks. Dark
rings beneath his eyes, and he's lost weight. He yawns, stretches.
"Idi has come to see you every day since he got back. He's seen you,
but you haven't seen him, apparently. You've been asleep nearly a
whole month." He yawns again. "Come on, he's got mail for you."

Bertrand stands up and folds his arms, and he's about to
become very grave, as heavy as he can be. He's about to protest
everything, point by point. He's about to tell these Africans
what's real. He goes to his room and straight to the rust-red
day sack where he keeps his papers, tapes, tape recorder, pens,
pencils, sharpener, stamps, clips, scissors, stapler, staples, staple
remover, nail clips, nail file, tweezers, stopwatch, Swiss knife,
letter knife, sewing kit, Band-Aids, ointment, string, smokes,
lighter fluid, brass Zippo, Ronson flints, measuring tape, adhe-
sive tape, cassette tapes.

He zips open the sack, and sees what he sees, and hurls himself back into the common room. He dashes the sack to the floor,

right at Allasambe's feet, and growls, "Where's my fucking journal!"

Allasambe raises his hands, the amber palms facing Bertrand, and says, "We have it on the island, OK? We've read it. And . . ." He pauses here because his voice falters as though he can't get enough air, then says, "We've decided you need our help, OK? You need our help, man. Alaine is going to kill you if you don't stop with his wife."

"I—"

Allasambe slumps a bit, deflates. He won't look Bertrand in the eye. "We have your letters, too, Berdt. One from your wife, and the other person we don't know." Now he does meet Bertrand's eyes. "We'll give you them when you come."

Bertrand's crying now in very much the same way he'd found Kene a while ago—hot, slow tears of rage and humiliation, the kind that prevent or lead to bite marks on other people. He nods his head so slightly that not even he himself can tell if it's really moving, then he says, "All right, all right, all right, lemme get my other bag and we can go."

chapter 9

Narcolepsy

Naturally you're tremulous as you board the dinghy to the island. You twitch and jitter as though this exceptionally temperate afternoon bleeds ice. The cold, of course, is inside you. Feels as though a cold stone rests in your belly, benumbing the other things you're feeling, or wish to be feeling: the anger, the indignation, the self-pity, the slightly febrile sensation that courses your skin, and the hunger, which sucks at your rib cage. You think again and again of eating a hot meal with the beautiful Kene. You should be full of sweetness, but you're nowhere near it now.

But despite your nervous gut, you're profoundly drowsy to the point of miasma. As the boatman ignites the engine, your head tips forward, then snaps up, and you find yourself two minutes farther from the village. It's a mere ten-minute ride, but each time your lolling head rises you can see greater distance between the boat and the mainland yet the island appears to grow no closer. The trip should feel like half the time it normally takes, given your intermittent naps; instead, it seems to take four times as long. Perhaps it's because your mind is traveling in a direction opposite the boat's. You find yourself coursing back to the village, back to the airport. A backward flight to New York takes you to Denver, and your car, in reverse, takes you all the way to Wood Avenue, where you float like a ghost into the sweet pinkness of your wife, your whole world. You would never say this; you can scarcely think it, but you miss the white world. It's your world, after all.

Small Colorado towns you understand. Women with freckles you understand. Dry air, fir trees, Chinook winds that scale down mountains, you understand. You understand the fleers of white men, the flares of black women, the head shaking, the tongue clucking of black men. These things you understand. Your skin is callused against such sere deprecation and withered air. You can't recall the last time you felt estranged from black people or unabsorbed by whites. Dreamlessness is no metaphor. It's your life. Why dream, when life is so cut-and-dried, so black, so white? Broad, clear skies, 330 sunny days each year, antiseptically clean streets, but filthy air—the very opposite of this world, where your life becomes, by degrees, imprivate, intimately coiled with a whole people, it would seem—moist and close as fucking. You go back and back, but what good does it do? You are, in fact, going forward.

No sense in speaking. The engine is too loud, and Allasambe is sitting astern with the boatman. Besides, what is there to say? If your word had meant anything to Allasambe, you'd be twenty minutes into your trip to the city with Kene, hoping to do what he's already accused you of having done. And why would you have? To get it over with? To be reborn? Something in between the two? She told you you had not, and suggested quite clearly she would not have. Still, you had your hopes. Part of your hunger is for pure knowing. Perhaps this is why food has had no savor for you as of late.

You look at Allasambe, his large cool eyes squinting away the light, his large-boned slackness. There seems to be no judgment in him. You'd like to think of him as your friend, but what friend would withhold your mail, your work, your personal writing? What friend would move so secretively at the periphery of your vision? Would try to appall you with an unsubstantiated, unbelievable tale of a man who spits up his own genitalia? You watch him as he speaks in low tones with the boatman. You imagine all they could be exchanging: ways to embezzle your last few dollars, or the blueprint of an enormous practical joke, or the weather, or soccer, or lunch.

The sky is bright, but the wind cool; the air smells of autumn, something you hadn't expected—that thousands of miles away from home, in this place where every molecule spins backward, autumn should smell like autumn. Your head drops. Green water. Your head snaps up, the water is cobalt, and seagulls skim it in the distance, then soar to invisibility in the high glare. Your head dips again. The engine purrs a lullaby. Sea spray in your face, and your head springs up. How unlike you, you who prides yourself in never nodding off in the dullest of classes, departmental meetings, bad movies.

"Hey, man," says Allasambe, as he gently places a palm on your shoulder. Your eyes click open, and you realize you'd been asleep for at least the last few minutes of the ride. The boat has nudged the shore long enough for him to have left the boat and stand beside you, ankle-deep in the surf. Allasambe smiles down at you, says, "I was going to ask if you wanted a beer, but it seems like tea is the thing."

"No idea I was asleep."

"You've been doing this for weeks."

"Why don't I remember?"

Allasambe shrugs. "Can you walk?"

"Why shouldn't I be able to walk?"

Allasambe offers his hand; you clasp it and hoist yourself up. Your head feels fairly clear. The boatman cuts the engine, and the sound and smell of the shore fill your senses as though the engine had been a veil against them. The surf thrums and hisses, the birds shriek, and the sea fills your whole head with its fragrance. You can taste seaweed, crabs, the silver fishes. Hunger sucks you into a knot. A breeze balloons Allasambe's chayas, and snaps the collar of your shirt, then dies off. "We go," he says.

They make their way to the path head, and once again drowsiness closes over Bertrand's scalp and forehead like a migraine. There is something about this path leading to the summer home that reminds him of the way he used to imagine Africa before he actually came here. The path is enclosed by trees with thick, shiny leaves about the size of a man's hands, low scrub, weeds, and flowers of every color. The path is resplendently green and wild, flitting with birds by day, rustling with bats at night. In short, it is the African jungle he'd carried in his mind's eye since childhood, not so much a place of mystery but of vanishing. But it is the only such strip of land he has seen in his short time here. The Senegal he's come to know in these five months is semiarid, mostly rolling grassland, interrupted now and then with naked baobab trees and patches of red earth that reminds him of his stepfather's native home of Harlem, Georgia.

Allasambe seems content to say nothing, but Bertrand won't have it; he taps Allasambe's elbow and says, "I suppose you guys have read my letters. What do they say?"

Allasambe stops and turns. He locks his large eyes onto Bertrand's and cocks his head a touch to the right. "We haven't read your letters."

"You read my *journal*. You read my *notes*."

Allasambe sets his arms akimbo, shrugs. "You were sleeping a long time. Too long, you know? We read those notes and things because we didn't know what else to do. We . . . do you want to sit down?"

"I'm fine."

"So we can talk. There's no hurry. The guys are praying."

Bertrand throws up his hands, looks around, and sits on a small boulder just off the trail. Allasambe squats and folds his arms around his knees. A cool breeze blows down the path, rattles the leaves on the trees, as those on the ground scud between and around the two of them. Allasambe closes his eyes against the dust, and Bertrand lowers his head, closes his own eyes, and he again feels the magnetic pull of sleep. He fights it off as best he can, but it lingers like the aftertaste of wine. The wind dies off, and Allasambe wipes his eyes with the side of his index finger. He clears his throat, says, "We didn't know what else to do, Berdt. We needed to know how you were feeling in the days before your sickness, perhaps find medical information, that sort of thing."

"And?"

"And nothing. What do you mean?"

"You read the whole thing, obviously."

"Actually Alaine did."

Bertrand clinches his toes together; the painful knot creeps between his shoulder blades, but at least his head is fully clear now.

"That's why he believes you've been sleeping with his wife. Anyone can see how strong you are feeling for her."

"They're feelings. Dreams! I didn't act on them."

"This is what we hope is true."

Bertrand clasps his fingers together and nods a few times. "Oh, it's true all right. You're wasting your time and mine. That's my personal stuff. Just give me my shit, and I'll get out of everyone's hair." Bertrand can't help thinking about Allasambe's story about the fat American who is tricked into vomiting up his own genitals. He actually thinks the word "genitals," perhaps to render the accompanying image less vivid. Did Allasambe tell him the story to warn him or scare him away? But he considers the fact that Alaine could not have read the journal more than two or three weeks ago, if what Allasambe has said about his deep sleep is even close to being true. Allasambe told him the story long before Alaine would have had impetus or opportunity to read the journal. He chides himself for forgetting, for a moment, that folktales are more powerful or less so, according to context.

"Allasambe, when was my last entry?"

"In your papers? I can't remember. We'll look."

"No, what *we'll* do is give me back my papers so I can go. Alaine's English is lousy. He—"

"You mean bad?"

"I do. Since when do a person's . . . OK, you know I admit—"

Allasambe raises a hand. "He brought the papers to me because he couldn't understand everything."

". . . the way I felt must have . . . What?

Allasambe repeats himself.

"Then why the fuck didn't you tell him, Ally? Why didn't you tell him which entries were the dreams? I mean, I use yellow paper for my journals, graph paper for everything else. I mean—"

Allasambe spreads his arms wide. "Tell him what, Bertrand? Only you can tell us the truth, eh? Alaine, you see, says the details are too true."

"What details!"

"When we find Alaine and bring him here, we'll ask him. I didn't have a chance to ask him. When I was in the middle of reading something, he kicked my Primus across the room and left."

"Reading what? What passage?"

Allasambe shrugs.

Bertrand springs to his feet. "That stupid motherfucker! Stupid goddamn motherfucker! He's using this as some kind of smoke screen to cover his own sins. He's the one having affairs. *He's* the one! What, is he afraid she'll divorce him? Take his kid and his money away from him? Trying to turn it all back on her is what he's doing, Ally. Kene told me what he's doing. Says he has some Belgian woman shacked up in Dakar. Did you know that? Do any of you all know that?"

"Bertrand—"

"Maybe I am sick. I don't know. Maybe I've been asleep since the plane hit the tarmac, but you people got to be stone-cold unconscious if you let that son of garce mess with your minds like this." He's pacing now. The knot between his shoulder blades burns, so he rubs it. "They had this fight. I'm sure Idi or someone told you about this fight Kene and Alaine had. She found something. A letter, and he wanted it back. Probably from the white woman. She found him out, and she was gonna leave him that night, you know that? Had her walking shoes on and she was just about gone, but they had a fight over the kid, and they had . . . You read my journal; you should know all this. Maybe know more than I do.

"Since the fight, I've tried to stay out of their way. I didn't want to be involved in the first damn place. What the fuck do I care about their crap?" He stops pacing, looks straight at Allasambe, who won't return his gaze. "I've been working,"

Bertrand says. "Hard. To make up for all the time I've pissed away worrying about my own marriage. And I've been having trouble with sleep, I admit . . . trouble . . . I wake up like . . . it's hard to explain." He folds his arms across his chest and bounces up on his toes. "There's nothing to explain. Let's just get my stuff so I can go."

The path to the house is sometimes broad, sometimes narrow, sometimes rocky, sometimes muddy. It's close to a quarter of a mile from the beach, and mostly uphill, but it's not an especially arduous walk, yet Allasambe breathes heavily and walks with an unsteady gait. "You've been sick," says Bertrand.

"I have."

"Malaria?"

"Worry. Malaria season is finished."

"Tell me about it."

But before Allasambe can reply, if he had intended to, they are met by Idrissa about fifty yards from the house. "Bertrand Milworth. It's good to see you awake," Idrissa says. Idrissa looks good. He's put on as much weight as Allasambe has lost, and apparently his girlfriend has spent money on his wardrobe. He's dressed as if for a party, perfectly creased blue serge trousers and a pale olive shirt, matching black belt and sandals, both shined and stiff with newness. He has a cigarette tucked behind his right ear and smells of Bertrand's aftershave.

Bertrand nods, shakes Idrissa's hand, but says nothing.

"Everyone is there," says Idrissa.

"Everyone? Just who are we talking about?"

Allasambe says, "The men I told you about. The ones who want to correct the problems."

"My problem is they have my things."

Allasambe turns toward Idrissa. "Alaine is there?"

"He's coming. Doudou found him and will bring him before dark."

Bertrand is surprised to see all the familiar faces sitting around the picnic table on the veranda, sitting in chairs in the common room, standing in the kitchen. There is Medoune, the Panther, whom he almost doesn't recognize because he's wearing a khaftan, as are Saliu, Omar the tailor, Monsieur N'Doye, his landlord, and three elderly men he has seen about the village but doesn't know. Only Idrissa and Allasambe are dressed in Western clothing. Bertrand shakes every hand but won't look anyone squarely in the eye. But all of them, even Omar, seem calm and warm and respectful, even well mannered. He feels naked before them. He immediately realizes that there is no possibility of his collecting his things and taking the 2:15 boat back to the village. He believes they are gathered to punish him, to side with Alaine against a home-wrecking interloper. Did he not write somewhere, at some time, of his intentions to seduce Kene? He can't remember. He is too afraid to bolt. There is something about the men's quiet, almost professional detachment that spellbinds him.

The very air of the place is still, grave. He assumes that the wilder ones, Omar, Saliu, Medoune, perhaps even Idrissa, have hewed back their natural impulses because of the older men. Bertrand sidles up to Idrissa, who has drifted into the kitchen, and asks him why everyone seems so formal. "It's two reasons," Idrissa says, "Ramadan and respect for you." Idrissa winks. "But it's not Ramadan for you, man. You can eat if you want to."

"I'd like that. I really would, but—"

"The letters."

Bertrand nods. "I don't suppose you could give me my other papers. I'd really appreciate it, Idi."

Idrissa folds his arms behind his back, his sergeant major pose, Bertrand calls it, and shakes his head. "They need them." Bertrand can tell by Idrissa's gestures, his mien, his posture, that he shouldn't make trouble. Yet he can't let things go. He whispers, "You lied to me."

"I know."

Bertrand's whisper becomes harsh. "I know you know!" He feels someone move close to him. It's Allasambe, who says to him, "Do you remember the room you stayed in the night of the party?"

Bertrand nods.

"Your letters are in that room. On the dresser."

"I'll bring you food," says Idrissa.

You had scarcely noticed a thing about the room when you slept here that first dreamless night. Small, but larger than your room at the village, clean, but not fussily so. There is a double bed with a faded Indian print spread, a wicker wardrobe, two chairs—one wicker, one wooden, painted gray. There are two windows, barred with ornate wrought iron. No exit, but through the door. There is a bureau arrayed with the usual things: colognes; a small plastic cup filled with buttons, pins, needles, thread, and paper clips; two brushes; and a nail file. And placed conspicuously away from these things is a small plastic tray, holding nothing but the letters with your name on them.

You take them up. Sealed, but how to tell if they haven't been steamed open, read, resealed? Impossible to tell. The first one contains the document you'd been dreading; the print on the envelope, the thickness, the whiteness say you need not even read the return address: Some Big Fat Name, Attorney at Law. It's cold to the touch, so full is it of legalese and accusations. You have no stomach for it. You search the room until you find a rubbish can. There it is, by the head of the bed and in the corner.

You toss the envelope in, sit on the bed, and rip open the letter you've been waiting for for over four months.

———————

September 29, '85

Dear Bert,

Indian summer came suddenly and early. It hit two and a half weeks ago and shows no signs of letting up. But Colorado weather does what it wants, when it wants. The sky is a postcardy, cloudless blue, smooth as a baby's forehead. I spent the afternoon at Poor Richard's, drinking coffee with lemon and catching up on the letters you've sent me. Then I drove to your sister's apartment to pick up my copy of the Kozol book I'd lent her—God, when was it? A couple X-mases ago? They invited me to stay for dinner, so I did stay, and we had a wonderful eggplant parm that Chloe made, some good red wine, and an amazing Caesar salad. Syria and I played Uno for a couple of hours, and when she went to bed, we grown-ups talked till about ten, and I filled Rita in on what you've been up to as much as I could. Then I went home and to bed.

Tomorrow, my mother and I are going to see *Vertigo* at Poor Richard's. They're showing movies in the rear, now that the Flick has been replaced by that god-awful Showboat, where they've been showing these repulsive "family-oriented" films. This week's dreck is *The Music Man*, and all next month they're showing *Frankenstein* (oooooh, scary). There will be an October full of other unspooky movies from the thirties at Der Showboat. I would actually like to go see *Cat People,* but I just can't bring myself to enter the place. Poor Richard's Feed and Read is better than nothing, but the benches and metal chairs are more suited to undergraduate and under-thirty tushes. And if you want to see anything relatively new (*Fanny and Alexander*, etc., etc.), you still have to drive to Denver.

Movies have been just about my only out-of-the-house activities since your departure. I've had no desire to drive any farther than my east-side mechanic's garage. A lot of this has had to do with the habits I formed while working on my thesis. I needed to keep things as uncomplicated as possible.

My thesis is in, by the way, and Drs. Buchness, Cooney, Garvey, and Costigan have signed off. I'm finished! But since I'm about a half year behind the rest of my classmates, and hadn't had a teaching job in the district before I went to school (as over half of them have), I'm stuck with subbing for at least the rest of the year, which I just can't bear. But bear it I must, since starvation and eviction are decidedly unfashionable these days.

Just so long as I'm not called up to Mitchell High too often. If that happens, I may just be going out of style, like it's going out of style. There's this cretinous gym teacher who has asked me out several times, though I've done nothing to encourage him and have barely said more than ten words to him. He's completely awful—the crew cut, the red neck, the fat calves, the blue, squinty, flinty eyes of a football cowboy. To make matters worse, he's of German descent. Imagine me bringing this storm trooper home to meet my parents. Dad would have a stroke, and Mom would have to be committed.

So I'll be subbing and seeing movies, and starting my fall garden, but thanks to this amazing Indian summer, the tomatoes and squash are still producing more than I or my neighbors can handle, and my kitchen is practically green with all the herbs. I brought your folks around 8 lbs. of yellow squash when I dropped by to say my good-byes to them last week. I left my band with your mom. She seemed quite upset. I think she wanted more detail as to why we're divorcing, but she didn't press me. (I've returned my grandmother's diamond ring to Mom, by the way.) I'm tempted to wear some sort of "ambigu-band" on my left hand to keep the Herr Futballers at bay. I have no interest in dating anyone anytime soon.

You should be getting papers from my lawyer in a week or two, and I'd appreciate it if you could sign them promptly. Despite everything, I've decided to go with the "no-fault" variety because of its simplicity. Besides, I know you're strapped, so my dad has paid for the whole thing. He sends his regards, by the way, and says you can take a year to pay him your half. Just send the check or checks to him.

Take Care—
Rose

P.S. Dylan's funeral was sad and beautiful. I talk to the both of them about once a week, see them in town now and then, and sometimes they smile, even laugh. They'd both like to hear from you, though I doubt they'd answer with more than a note or a postcard.

There it is, the feast your hungry breast has waited for, these several weeks, served without salt, without spices, without the bounty of herbs from her garden. You had been prepared for anything: "I love you but," or "I hate you because." Not a single reference to a single letter, no mention of your dreams or hers, not a single reminiscence. Not even some nasty invectives about your black girls. The letter might as well have been written by an old high school chum you scarcely knew and hadn't heard from in years, or a kindly old aunt—chatty, lukewarm, discursive, quaint, offhand, and risible as a Woody Allen heroine. You wanted passion, but she gives you the weather, old movies, Herr Futballer, take care.

Take care. Your wife of nearly five years requests you to take care. You fold the letter, and as you slip it into the envelope, your vision blurs with tears, and soon you're sobbing, curled up on the bed, weeping hard the way mothers do when they lose their children, or wives do when their husbands cheat on them. You deserve her dispassion, you think. Cut off, disremembered. How perfect. How perfect. These tears are too much, don't really even belong to you but to her. So you try to crush them back, but the effort makes you cry all the more, so you give in to them.

———

A tap on his shoulder rouses him from another unforeseen sleep. It's Idrissa, with a small covered bowl and a spoon. "Everything good?" Idrissa asks him, and despite the cold stone in his gut, Bertrand says he's fine. "Good, good. We thought you should eat something. We're all fasting till night. We're going to pray, then we eat, then we begin." He offers the bowl to Bertrand, but Bertrand points to the bureau. Idrissa sets it there, then sits in the wicker chair. Bertrand sits up, rubs the sleep from his eyes. "Why'd you lie to me, Idi?"

Idrissa toys with the cigarette behind his ear. He looks grave, nervous. "I wanted to help you."

"Explain."

"I'm not supposed to smoke now, but I think I will. Do you have fire?"

Bertrand points to his day sack, which sits by the bureau. Idrissa bends over, zips open the front pouch, removes a box of matches, and flames up his cigarette. His face may seem grave, but his hands don't tremble. "Berdt," he says. "You don't know much about women, do you?"

"Depends on the woman, I guess."

"I know more."

"Let's say you do."

"They're like Mother Crocodile."

"I'm not in the mood, Idi."

"You're not going anywhere. Get in the mood."

Idrissa's words alone would have been enough to make his heart leap so, but his eyes are sharp enough to open veins. "Am I in jail?"

"You're under protection; that's all. None of the men out there is your enemy. I am not your enemy. But you can't go anywhere till things are clear." He drags and blows. He nods. "OK, Mrs. Golo . . . you know what that means, right?"

"Monkey."

"She send out her five children one day and told them to bring back eggs—any kind of eggs—from the bush. The children came back, and she said to the first one, who brought back eggs from a guinea fowl, 'What did Mrs. Guinea Fowl say to you when you took the eggs?'

"'Oh, man, she cursed and screamed and spit at me. She said she would kill our whole family!'

"'Good,' Mother Golo said. 'Give me the eggs, and we'll eat them.' Then she asked the second child, 'What did Madame Boa say when you took her eggs from her?'

"'Oh, man, Mama,' she said, 'she hisssss at me and told me that she would crush our bones and eat every one of us in our time.'

"'Good,' Mother Golo said. 'Give me the eggs, and we'll eat them.' And so she asked the next two childs . . . children the same thing, and they answered all in the same way. Then she said to the last child, 'Tell me what Mother Crocodile said, little one.'

"'She didn't say anything, Mama.'

"'Not one word?'

"'Not anything at all.'

"'Nothing?'

"'All silence, Mama.'

"'Then hurry and take the eggs back to Mother Crocodile, for those who talk and talk and talk do nothing more, but those who are silent are dangerous. Take them back now!'" Idrissa stubs out his cigarette against the floor and lights another one. "That's how women are."

Bertrand has heard the story before, long before he came to Senegal, but he considers all that Rose's letter did not say and decides not to antagonize or argue. Context, he says to himself, is everything. So he bites his tongue, though he's anxious to ask Idrissa why he couldn't have been straight with him, why he couldn't tell him of all the intrigue.

Idrissa says nothing for a while, as though he's waiting for the little story to sink in. Finally, he says, "Kene and Alaine brought their fighting from France, where they met in graduate school. I think the Belgian woman has been with them, like a second wife, since then. Kene fought and fought, like Mother Boa, and Mother Guinea Fowl, and all the rest, but Alaine never took her seriously. She took money from you, yeah, but she also took your honor."

He lifts his hand before Bertrand can reply. "The chicken I told Allasambe to put there was to keep you . . . I don't know . . ."

"Asleep?"

"No, no. No, no. To turn your mind from Kene."

"Didn't work."

"We were trying to help you, man."

"'We'! What's all this 'we' shit?"

Idrissa stubs out the second butt, points index and middle fingers at Bertrand like a gun. "You ask too many fucking questions. You have no respect. Why don't you listen!"

Bertrand feels his blush down to his stomach. "I've never heard you use that kind of language before. I can't understand why you—"

"Some of us believe you didn't know what you were doing. Some of us believe you knew."

"Idi, you were supposed to be my friend. Why the hell didn't you just tell me that it looked to you like I was getting to close too Kene? You could have told me Alaine was watching me."

"Would you have listened?"

"Yes! Of course I would have."

"You never listen to me."

"Bullshit. I'd have been lost without you. You must have read that in my journal."

"I didn't—"

"What?"

"It's too late. Why did you sleep with her?"

"Fuck!"

"Then why did you make it look like you did? I'm sorry, man. I'll do everything to make it fair. We'll listen to what you have to say. We'll ask questions. If they decide you have acted by your will, we will let Alaine do what he wants to do. We have to."

"Is this a federal law?"

Idrissa runs his hands over his face and sighs. He locks his fingers behind his head and sighs once more. He is silent for at least five minutes. Bertrand won't look at him. Finally Idrissa says to him, "If you are true, you can do whatever you like, go home or whatever. I think Allasambe would let you stay here if you want to."

"Idi."

"Speak."

"Who took my dreams?"

"We did. But better to ask, who gave them to you and why?"

Bertrand throws himself from the bed, and Idrissa slowly rises from his chair, tranquil as smoke. "This isn't fair!" Bertrand says. "None of this is fair!" He won't tell Idrissa, not anyone, what he spoke of with Kene. So he sits down, says: "I don't find her all that attractive. I just missed sex. I missed my wife. I'd hear them screwing, and you know how it is. But black women don't do anything for me."

Idrissa looks at him for the first time with the disgust Bertrand has always suspected most of his brothers and sisters have always felt for him. But then Idrissa seems to inwardly check himself, and his face relaxes, and for a moment, compassion eclipses that former aspect, which may have been Bertrand's own projection anyway, and as he moves toward the door, Idrissa says, "Eat, Berdt, and I'll come for you when it's time."

"Idi."

"Yeah, man."

"Do you believe me? You believe I never touched her, right?"

Idrissa clasps the door handle and faces the bureau. His gaze seems inward. He nods once or twice and turns around without letting go of the handle. "I think you touched her. I think you touched her, yes, but didn't know. I think it's a little sad."

He leaves the room and closes the door without a sound.

You are alone for hours. The first thing you do is eat the food Idrissa brought you. It's much better than food has tasted for some time. It's room temperature so the okra sauce is gelatinous, but it's well seasoned, and the fish is fresh. You eat everything in the bowl, then scrape up every dollop of gravy with your fingers and lick them clean.

You're drowsy again, so you lie down. As you roll into sleep, you hear the men begin their prayers; their basses and baritones remind you of church, so you dream of church. You are a boy, dressed in a suit you wore between fifth and seventh grades. The suit is tight; the cuffs barely conceal your socks. Your mother taps you on the arm and says, "It's your turn, son. Go ahead. Go on." You know she means for you to go to the altar, which is a cave, actually. You climb the stone steps to the cave. You are supposed to go into the cave and say good-bye to your father. You walk for what must be several dozen yards, but you can't find the bier on which he lies. You call him, and he answers. Still you can't see him. You call, and he answers, but you're no closer. You hear a choir of voices singing strange, beautiful music. Then Idrissa calls you from your slumber.

"It's time," he says.

I dream this: A dark room, lit only by guttering candles. Warm gusts blow through the windows and whip these lights into beautiful/ugly shapes on the walls, on the serious African faces sitting around me. I dream this one man, a marabou by the name of Gueye. Older than dirt, walks with a limp, has one good eye (the other seems to have a cataract, white as a pearl and perpetually teary), and he carries around a staff the length of two baseball bats and the girth of one. As he interrogates me, he brandishes it like a scepter and punctuates his words by striking its end on the floor. I know by instinct not to show this man the least bit of disrespect, to show every smidgen of deference I can muster.

A man I know, a man named Allasambe, the man who seems to be my chief advocate, I suppose you could call him, argues with Monsieur Gueye about his or anyone else's right to conduct this whole affair. (Idrissa, an old, old friend, seems helpful, too, but he appears far too intimidated by Monsieur Gueye, I think, to contradict him.) I seem to remember Allasambe claiming Monsieur Gueye made him sick because of his obstreperous disrespect.

Despite my fear, I nod off again and again, only to be woken by the hammering of the staff against the floor, and once by a slap on the ear. The men are smoking, shaking their heads, grumbling, mumbling. I dream a formal Wolof, which I can barely understand, which is nothing like the dialect I've picked up while here. And I dream someone sitting behind me with his foot on the back of my chair, pushing, pushing, pushing, pushing, pushing, until I begin to feel as if the whole thing were taking place on a raft on the open sea. I dream a knife sharp enough to lay open the throat of a goat without it flinching, without it feeling a thing, resting on the coffee table between me and the marabou. The knife burns orange, copper, silver, blue, green, depending on how the candlelight chooses to reveal it from moment to moment.

They use my own journals as their principal evidence against me. This sounds familiar. Perhaps I've dreamed it before.

Anyway, they use my journals, mostly the other dreams I've recorded. There was this one I had this summer past about being home and climbing a glass mountain with both the men Rita had been married to. We ended up in a strange, ugly, swampy land that swallowed both of my ex-brothers-in-law. I found a stream and followed it. The water became sweet and clear and led to Dad's garden. Then I walked into the house, went to bed, and the door opened, and in walked a woman. I remember only her breasts and her words. "You're not God." Which is a favorite phrase, it turns out, of Mrs. Kene Kourman, the woman I have been accused of screwing. She says it, according to Mr. Kourman, the plaintiff, after he has given Mrs. Kourman an especially intense orgasm. I happen to know she says it in other contexts as well, and I said so to the men. But no one believes me.

Mr. Kourman also cites certain particulars about his wife's anatomy I had referred to in my dreams: the moles on her back, the tuft of fine hair on her tailbone, a feature, they tell me, rarely found on Senegalese women. And the color and shape of her nipples and breasts. But the most damning aspect of the evidence was what they called my obsession with African women. The interrogation went something like this:

You write that before you came here you had had no relations with black women.

No, sir.

Never?

You read so yourself.

Indeed we have. So you came here to find a black woman.

No, sir. I came here to collect stories, sayings.

Why didn't you visit a prostitute?

As I said, sir, I came here to—

Or find a half-breed like yourself?

I'm not a half—

Good question, sir. And mine is, why didn't he marry one of his own kind?

I fell in love with Rose.

Who's that?

His wife, sir.

I see. But, apparently, young one, you never sought women of your own kind.

Sir?

Yes, Allasambe.

It says somewhere in here that he wasn't found to be attractive to his own kind.

Because he is so ugly?

No, he doesn't say that. He doesn't seem to know.

I *don't* know! It just happened. It just happened.

You'll speak, young one, when you are spoken to.

Yes, sir. Yes, sir.

Now then. You never sought women of your own kind, is that not so?

Sir, I can't think with whoever it is behind me pushing my chair.

Why, I ask you, did you not seek your own kind?

I've been unsure, sir, all my life. It could be coincidence.

Eh?

He's using French, Monsieur Gueye. Bad French. He means "harmony of all things."

Thank you, Allasambe. So you . . . you always found yourself following your natural impulses and ignoring tradition.

No, sir. No, sir. That's not what I mean at all.

He contradicts you, Allasambe.

No, I—

Then you prefer the white ones.

No, sir. I just—

Excuse me, sir—

Yes, Doudou.

It's obvious that he hates anything *like* black skin. Look at my nose. Look what he did to me.

Doudou (says Allasambe), he hit you because you are naturally obnoxious toward toubob people. Everyone knows this.

(This causes general chaos for a while, with accusations and counteraccusations flying about the room. I can understand very little. Finally, the one-eyed man gently taps the staff against the floor till the argument ceases. He locks his eye on me.)

So, young one, you came here to cleave to a black woman, one of our women, because you wished to, what, learn something new? . . . Allasambe, read me the section where he talks about his reasons for choosing white women.

Give me a few minutes, Monsieur Gueye. (Minutes pass, and someone wakes me.) Here it is, right here, sir: "I always chose those who were both neurotic and plain, the kind I thought I deserved, perpetuating the myth that a black man will be attracted to the homeliest white woman because what he wants from the relationship is to sexualize his sense of inferiority"—

That's it. That's enough. Thank you, Allasambe. So you felt inferior and were looking for a way of feeling superior—

There's a little more, Monsieur Gueye.

No, no, that's fine, Allasambe. Don't make me lose my trail of thinking. So you wished to destroy this inferiority you feel. You could not do so with your own people because they, too, are inferior to you, or they do not like you. So you come here, of course, because the African women are the pinnacles of sexuality.

Monsieur Gueye.

Yes, Idrissa.

What about the things the woman herself might have done? What about the chicken, her war with her husband, the fact that she has fought with the other women because they say she is immoral and a witch?

There is no question that these things are true, Idrissa, but we are before a man who had been more than willing to ride her, it seems to me. Isn't it so that he continued to sleep with her not only when the charm was removed from the house but during his long sickness? Did he not buy a refrigerator for her? Did you yourself, Allasambe, not find him, today, prepared to take her to Dakar for God knows what?

This is crazy! I never slept with her. I never touched her! How many fucking times do I have to say this? And that chicken was—

Silence, young one. I am talking to your defender.

Is this some kind of trial, sir? (Everyone laughs. I know it is obvious, but you'd have thought I'd juggled balls with my ass.)

·

Anyway, as I was saying, for God knows what? Here is a man who has no natural love for his own people, and no love even for his wife's people, who plays the suitor to a woman who is already married, and does so right before the eyes of her husband. Here is a man who needed no prodding. Not from Kene, who, if she is a witch, could have chosen a real man. Did he need magic to make him feel his lust? You all know that those suffering under love charms feel both compulsion and disgust for those who bend their will. But he writes again and again only of his adoration for her. Where in his papers did he talk about any disgust? And, furthermore, did not his own white wife command him to find a black woman? His own wife, whom he could not satisfy, with whom he refused to live? When even a blind man sees a tree with his hands, no one can tell him it is a weed. He sees what he sees. Yes, Kene used charms, but the question is, did she need them?

Monsieur Gueye.

Yes, Omar.

And is he concerned with this meeting? Look at him. He is almost asleep.

Monsieur Gueye.

Yes, Allasambe.

I think the tere we gave him to break the trances may be the reason for his sleeping sickness.

That may be true, young man. You did mention that before.

I think he means no disrespect.

Perhaps not. But even during his long sleep, did we not sometimes find his room perfumed by a woman?

I would say those were the times he was least aware of his actions.

True, true, but it seems to me that he wanted her under every condition, we could say.

May I say something?

Go ahead, toubob.

Did I ever write about my respect for Alaine's marriage? I did, and if you'll give me my papers, I can show you.

Give him the papers, Allasambe.

I dream that I flip through the pages with my sweaty hands and look for a passage that I think would help me. I can't find anything. Everything I read seems to suggest that I really did want the man's wife. I did, and I didn't. What I really wanted was to be in a relationship that the world wouldn't despise.

I dream the trial for two consecutive nights, which, I suppose, is unusual. Or perhaps I dream that I dream for two nights. I am hungry, tired. They won't let me sleep or piss, or eat or drink, on this second night. The man won't stop rocking my chair. My eyes snap closed every couple minutes or so. My head hurts. There were questions, sure, but mostly assertions disguised as such:

When did you realize that you were lacking perfect love?

What did your mother do to you to drive you from her lap?

Why did your father not take you into his rooms and teach you the ways of your people?

Do your parents not burn in their hearts for having a son who sleeps with whites and a daughter who sleeps with women?

Have you ever slept with a man?

These little black girls who were sometimes in your mother's care, why were you so afraid of them? Our little boys learn to play with girls from the time they're weaned.

Why did you attack our brother Doudou?

Why, if Alaine's wife had supposedly enchanted you, did you try to court the white American? By the way, is it so that she is also married? Do you prefer married women because another man supports them?

Does your wife sleep with other men when you are away?

If it was Alaine's wife who enchanted you for money, why do

you give so much money away to everyone else? Such charms are to soften your will only to the charmer.

Is that so, Monsieur Gueye? I heard different.

Quiet, Idrissa. We know he gave you a lot of money, too.

Fuck you, Omar.

Stop that! I will say this only once, Omar and Idrissa. This is a serious matter. If you cannot comport yourselves like Lebou men, you will leave.

Yes, Monsieur Gueye.

Sorry, Monsieur Gueye.

Very well, then. Where was I? Oh yes. Yes, yes. I'm sorry. I hate to ask so many times, young toubob, but tell me again how you could have seen Madame Kourman's moles if the details of this account aren't true?

May I see the journals again, sir?

Of course. Of course. Medoune. The journals, please.

I can't say they read my journal uncarefully. Far from it. They've parsed every sentence—underlined, circled, asterisked. When I have the thing in my hands again, for those brief, fruitless moments, I see French and Wolof translations and transliterations scribbled in the margins. Question marks litter the thing like schools of spermatozoa. There are even corrections of spelling and grammar. Such humiliation. I thought of Harriet the Spy, and the character Jack in *The Shining*, and every forcibly "outed" gay man or woman. My face burned with shame, not only at the fastidious denuding of my soul but at the paucity and insignificance of my research. Did I have sex with Madame Kourman? No, at least I don't remember having done so. Like Jimmy Carter in the *Playboy* interview, I can only admit to lusting in my heart. Poor Jimmy, poor Jack, poor Harriet the Spy. Poor me. I am hungry. My intestines are knotting into themselves like a tortured serpent. I am weary, and the person rocking my chair won't stop, and every time I complain about it they tell me to pay attention; this is an important matter. Why am I changing the subject, focusing on trivialities? Don't I know they have my life in their hands?

No, I did not know this. I have barely had the vaguest idea of what's going on, but when they raise that last question, I'm out of my seat and across the room so fast, I'm sure they're astonished. A matter of life and death? I throw my fists at anyone who comes within a foot of me. I kick, I bite, but there are too many of them. Too many. They tackle me, tie me up, and badger me with still more questions. Asking me if I tried to run because of my guilt. That sort of thing. Good God. This dream. Too much.

I confess to everything. I don't even hear half of what they're saying. I just confess, and because I do, they enjoin Alaine Kourman from taking my life.

The men leave in twos and threes, silent as God. Each time I blink, a few more are gone. I don't know where they could be off to. No boats run between the island and the mainland after dark. But then I don't really care. I'm still tied to my chair. All I know is that I'm not going anywhere, just yet.

The only people remaining with me are Alaine, Doudou, Omar, Idrissa, and Allasambe. They untie me and order me to disrobe. They tell me to lie right there on the cold floor. Four men, friends and enemies, hold down my legs and arms. I am sobbing, begging them not to do this to me. I look at Idrissa, then Allasambe, and plead with them to help me. I choke on my snot, and Idrissa takes my shirt and wipes my face. Someone splashes cold, cold water on my genitals, and I thrash and heave, but I'm too weak to break even a single grip.

Open your mouth, someone says, and a rolled-up rag is shoved between my teeth.

Bite hard, someone says.

Do I scream? Sure, I scream. I fight like fire and wind. My muscles and bones snap, and they have to sit on my limbs to keep me halfway still. Allasambe is actually in tears, but he doesn't seem to be close to letting me go.

Easy, easy, easy, easy, easy with him, someone says. Perhaps it is Allasambe.

Be strong, Berdt, someone says. Maybe Idrissa? Things are all mixed around. I don't care anyway. I fight with everything in me, everything left, until someone says, "Berdt, if you struggle, he might miss and kill you." I'm sure that was Allasambe.

The cut is quick, vicious, excruciating, and soundless, except for my scream.

Alaine then holds my bloody foreskin before my eyes. His bloody hands are shaking, and he looks as afraid and sick as he should. He says to me, in his perfect French, "I could have made you a woman, but I decided to make you a man. Go in peace." He drops the thing on my chest, and he rises and walks away.

———

Nov. 4

Dear Rose—

I'm writing you from a hospital bed in Dakar. The people here say that folks only go to hospitals here as a last resort or for a clean, well-lighted place to die. I can see that. There are few private rooms, and I'm not in one. It's clean, but unsanitary in comparison to White World. It smells like puke and ammonia. Depending on how crowded the place is, sickrooms aren't segregated according to gender, age, or affliction. There's a young, attractive woman two beds away from me who seems to be suffering from cancer. The little boy next to me, seven, eight years old, is covered from head to toe with open sores and scabs. My doctor assures me it isn't leprosy, but he never touches the child. No one comes to visit him. He spends every day strapped down and drugged. Nurses come to wash him once a day, and every day he asks for his mama. I can relate.

My folks, by the way, are due here any day now to come and take me home. Neither of them have passports, so it'll take longer than I'd like.

Nov. 6

You remember when I had the kidney stone a couple years ago? I'm sure you do. You were so angry with me when you called and called and called my apartment, my office, my folks' place, my sister's. Couldn't reach me, had no idea where I was. Drove up to my place, read my calendar, etc. You told me you knew I was dead. You told me how you sat on my bed and wept for God knows how long.

As I'm sure you'll recall, I told you that I'd asked an emergency room nurse to call you to tell you where I was and what had happened. The guy never did, even though he'd told me he had. I'd lain there in that ER bed for several hours thinking he'd called you and that you'd soon be at my side. When I didn't hear from you, I felt hurt. I thought you were thinking: "See? See what happens when you live an hour away from your wife? Well, Mr. Live-Alone, you just lie there in your agony for a spell. See if I care." All the while you were terrified that I was dead in some alley.

I got to the hospital by myself and even walked home less than a day after surgery. *Then* I called you. Your reaction was typical of those who worry about loved ones in this manner. First you were relieved; then you were furious. You wouldn't talk to me for four days. I don't blame you now, though at the time I thought you were being unreasonable. After all, I'd tried to contact you. Wasn't my fault the nurse failed to call you, etc., etc. I'm pretty thick when it comes down to it.

But I don't want to give you the impression that I'm writing you about the kidney stone deal to give you one more example of how I've grown and have overcome my thickheadedness. "For I was blind but now I see . . ." It's too late for all that now. No, I bring it up to confess that it wasn't my first trouble with a kidney stone but my second.

The stone the doctor removed had actually bothered me some three weeks before my surgery. It woke me up from a dead sleep. At first I thought it was really, really, really bad constipation, so I tried to go. Nothing happened, and the pain got worse. I began to believe my appendix had burst. I called 911, and in fifteen minutes, a span that felt like 150 minutes, the ambulance arrived. I tried to walk out to meet the medics, but they had to carry me down the stairs; they tossed me in and took me to the hosp.

They threw me into a wheelchair and rolled me to the ER. Suddenly, I felt like vomiting, and before I knew it, I did. They cleaned me up and put me in a bed. I felt better; one upchuck, and that stunning pain shrunk down to the size of a sock in the eye. I thought I'd eaten something bad, and that had caused the pain, and apparently the doctor did, too. He wasn't going to argue. I looked all right. I felt good. He sent me home.

The jagged little monster had apparently just moved to a comfortable spot, then lay in wait for nearly a month before it tore its way through those tiny and tender ducts all over again. And it was twice as bad as before. For weeks after the operation I was horrified thinking that something so painful could lie in the body and take its time to abruptly surface with such mindless violence. I thought about all those movies where people wake up from

benders, surrounded by cops who tell them they're under arrest
for murder, or people who feel in tip-top shape and then suddenly keel over from some terrible disease. I even thought about
this woman in the Midwest, who, while bowling, suddenly
clutched her belly, howled out in pain, and fell where she stood.
Twenty minutes later, she gave birth to a six-pound baby. And
she never knew she was pregnant. Urban folktale? Who gives a
goddamn anymore?

Later

Several days ago, a group of men kidnapped me (more or less)
and accused me of sleeping with another man's wife. They inter-
rogated me for two days, a kind of tribunal (no pun intended). I
told them I had no memory of sleeping with her or even touching her, but they didn't see it that way in the end. Who were
they? I don't know, maybe a secret society. The place is said to be
lousy with them. They included my friend Idi, whom I've told
you about, a man named Doudou (Amadou Gueye), with whom
I had an altercation some weeks back, a bunch of men I don't
need to tell you about. I don't have the energy, either, but I suppose I should tell you that I was found guilty and my punishment
was a very crude, very sloppy circumcision. Don't worry, I'm
healing nicely, and they tell me I'll recover 100%. A couple doc-
tors around here think I did it to myself, since some American
men do circumcise themselves in order to become, I guess you
could say, "palatable" to African women. I don't care what they
think. I wouldn't do something like that.

Anyway, the men (or someone) seem to have given me something that makes me sleep all the time. I sleep all the time now,
though little by little, I'm able to stay awake for longer periods of
time, two, three hours a day, now.

Nov. 9

I'll always love you, of course, but you can have your divorce. I've lost the papers, though, so please remail them to my parents' place when I get back. I'm babbling. What am I trying to say? I sleep all the time. That's the main reason I'm hospitalized. The wound is ugly, but I'm healing nicely. I sleep all the time. That's why I'm writing this letter in pieces.

Nov. 10

I am writing to tell you how sorry I am for loving you so poorly. I'm writing to confess that every time we were together, I couldn't keep my eye squarely on you. It was as though I had one eye on you and the other scanning the corners, looking out for the invective, the evil eye, the shaking, shaming heads. In a way, I got used to it.

As you know all too well, I've been dating white women since I began dating. My folks never complained. Not once, not ever. My friends never rode me about it. No one ever said anything while we were together at the movies, or out shopping, or in restaurants, but I always felt eyes on us, always believed there were people who hated us because we loved each other. I never kept pictures of you in my office. I never mentioned your race to my students. Private, private, I had to be private. Secret as a kidney stone. I let all these stories mess with my mind.

I remember this young couple who were murdered out on Gold Camp Road, back when I was in high school. Black boy, white girl, both sixteen. They were out hitchhiking, not far from where the girl lived, near Cheyenne Mountain. Some guy picked them up, drove them down Gold Camp, shot them dead, and cut off their ears. You remember that? The fucker went to a bar to

have a few and, when he was drunk enough, started bragging
about the murders. When some dude told him he was full of shit,
the guy pulled the ears out of his pocket and tossed them on the
bar. Police picked him up in minutes, and I'm sure he'll finish his
life in Canyon City. I was 16, myself, when I read that story, and it
made me feel that our homeland, our whole fucking country, is
full of people like this. The whole goddamn planet. So I suppose I
learned to believe that people like us need to be quiet and careful. I let other people's nightmares poison my dreams. Uh-oh, I'm
being "poetic," which means I need to go to sleep for a while.

Same day, but later . . .

I knew this older woman when I was in college who had a thing for
black men. She was from Denver, and she told me she put a personal ad in the *Rocky Mountain News,* which read something like:
"Pale Damsel in Distress Looking for Black Knight, etc. Love
sweet soul music and jazz, etc. Very blond, but black on the inside,
etc." She received a response from a guy who called himself White
Knight, and it read something like: "Don't you know that whenever a white man sees one of his own women with a black guy, all
he can think about is his King Kong dick in her white pussy? It's
sick, and wrong, what you do. Don't breed monsters. You should
be ashamed!" She actually showed this letter to me. I didn't really
know what to say. Don't ask me to explain that, Rose, exactly what
the guy meant. I don't think that he was merely saying that all we
are interested in is sex. I think he was saying that people like you
and me are no more than the ganglia that lead from the reptile
brain to the soft buttons and knobs down below.

I don't think he was as complex as some of my black friends in
academe who're reminded of Emmett Till, the Afrocentrists who
can see no easy rapprochement between those who may have

enslaved and those who had been enslaved. And he certainly wasn't as "generous" as the dewy-eyed liberals who disapprove of our "kind" because our progeny would be bereft and friendless. The White Knight saw only walking cunts and cocks, adrenaline-driven obsessions, bestial lusts, dirty misbegotten boys and girls, the undeveloped core of animal life.

I didn't live with you, Baby, because I thought they'd track us down, chuck rocks through our windows, burn crosses on our yards, cruise our street all night long, plotting, planning—they'd lie in wait like kidney stones or nightmares. They'd slither in, slice our ears cleanly away from our heads, and whisper into them all their lubricious desires. And I'm afraid that there must have been part of me that thought and felt that what the White Knight said was true, for though I was afraid sometimes, there were other times I was also ashamed. You can't be aware of a thing without in some small, subtle, deeply subconscious way believing it, no matter how it may contradict truth or mother wit.

My dreams are a lot less nasty than all those horrid things some men dream. They are doozies, Rose, and if you find the time, and have the desire, and if you are still willing to be the soul mate you have always been, I'll sit with you and tell you about them now and then.

All My Love—
Bird

ACKNOWLEDGMENTS

The author would like to thank the following individuals for their support, prayers, encouragement, criticism, advice, friendship, and love, without which this novel could not have been written: Julie S. McKnight, Moriah Rose McKnight, Rachael Elana McKnight, Regina McKnight, Celeste McKnight, Bryan K. McKnight, Frank and Pearl McKnight, Walter and Lucille Anderson, Ludie P. Wooley, Maryruth and Fred Buchness, Nora J. Bellows, Dr. E. G. Rosenthal, R. H. Haapamaki, M. L. Davis, Laura J. Bellows, Merce Levine, Kevin and Jan Casey and son, Steve Farrington, Harry Olofunwa, Don Kinney, Annie Dawid, Mark A. Terry, Keith A. Owens, Gerry Lafemina, Charles Baxter, David Lynn, Renee Olander, Tim Siebles, Alex Marks, Nick Delbanco, Michael Collier, V. Thalley, Michael A. Honch, Jennifer Barth, Christina L. Ward, and J. I. Miss. I thank you all with my whole heart.